Death of a Fairy Tale

Book 1 of the Mari Fable Mysteries

Emily Fluke

Also by Emily Fluke

*"To my daughter, who asked me to write a story about Guinea pigs.
But I wrote this instead."*

Chapter 1

Birth of a Fairy Tale

It could have been the epidural, or the fact that the pain ripped through even the strongest of spinal drugs, but I swore on Wendy's peach fuzz my OBGYN had fangs. Could a mom get postpartum anxiety if it wasn't even post the partum?

The nurse in Mickey Mouse scrubs shoved an oxygen mask over my mouth, and I sucked in as much air as my little lungs would allow. They felt little compared with the voice of my mini-me. Wendy was born screaming like a bat driving a Harley out of hell… or something like that. They said labor made a woman's brain fuzzy so that she'd endure it again.

Screw the human race.

I would never. Do this. Again.

"You're doing great, Mari." My husband offered a thumbs up, but he swayed and had to catch himself on the railing of my hospital bed.

After one more push, Wendy was out, and my woozy husband went down.

A tiny body appeared on my chest as if she had teleported there. Instead, I had Mr. Mickey Mouse to thank for nearly dropping her on me as her slimy body slipped from his blue nitrile gloves. There was too much blood. Not on her, thank *goodness*.

Still, the spots of crimson over yellowed linoleum almost made me vomit on my newborn's head. And if that didn't label me Mother of the Year, I didn't know what would.

"Kai!" My husband's name came out in a shriek. It took me a full two minutes to realize what I was staring at. A slight cut on his head bled droplets on the floor of our overpriced labor and delivery suite. "If you try to get out of this by dying, I'm going to kill you!"

Mr. Mickey Mouse swooped into my personal space and shifted Wendy away to a checkup table while scrubs surrounded Kai. If only I had two heads, I'd look both ways at the same time. But it didn't matter, because the OB smiled, her lip catching on a sharp tooth as she told me to push again.

I didn't know why I needed to push again until the OB mumbled something about the afterbirth. Why didn't prenatal classes prepare green moms for the placenta delivery? I couldn't be the first newbie to assume a hidden twin behind the original baby. But I couldn't trust my brain right now, considering I was seeing fangs on my doctor and panicking over my husband fainting.

"Is he dead?" I wailed between breaths while straining to see over the side of the bed. The nurses' red-streaked hands worked their way around Kai's dad-bod and hoisted him up. He dabbed at his split lip with shaky fingers and looked woozy all over again. The nurses led him back to the window seat before he could take them all down in another attention-grabbing faint of the century.

Oh my goodness, I'm a mom now. I need to focus on my child. Guilt struck me harder than the pins stabbing into an area of my body I liked to pretend didn't exist. If it didn't exist, it couldn't tear.

I leaned forward and snatched Wendy back from Disneyland dude and shot him my evilest glare that still couldn't hold a candle to my OBGYN's dead eyes.

"Is she here?" Kai asked from the window seat. I didn't know why I hoped to see a little fairy there, coming to put an ice pack in my underwear since my insides seemed like they'd fall out. Instead, all one hundred and ninety-nine pounds of brand-new daddy lay curled in the fetal position drinking a juice box.

"Keep her close to your bare body," the nurse with the icy hands said. "Skin-to-skin contact helps a child bond with its parent."

I was about to *skin* my husband alive, but my baby's pinched pink face and goopy eyes swept the breath right from my mouth. A momentary wave of calm washed over me. The numbness of my torso, scratchy fabric from the hospital sheets, and shortness of breath didn't worry me anymore. Wendy's soft head rubbed against me, and her strange, sweet smell melted my anger.

I loved my husband but hated that he got to faint while I had to keep pushing. I wasn't angry per se, just envious because I needed another moment of calm and a juice box of my own. But I was expected to bond with my baby and dive into the process of feeding her directly from my own body. No, calm wasn't an option for me. To make matters more chaotic, my mom burst into the room with glassy-eyes and rosy-cheeks.

"Kai! Are you okay?" My mom's heels tapped right past me and knelt by her son-in-law.

Kai nodded and waved for her to look at our baby. Only then did she turn and gush over the pinky squishy human on my chest. She reached her manicured claws toward the bundle.

"Isn't he just precious?" Mom twisted her matte, red lips into a smile.

"*She,* and her name is Wendy." I hugged my new daughter a little tighter.

"Did you decide on a name?" Kai popped up, suddenly bright-eyed and bushy-tailed. I flashed him an 'aren't you proud of me' smile and all the 'why me and not you' anger melted away. He had wanted a kid since the day we adopted a cat.

"Want to hold her?" I lifted Wendy toward her daddy, but Mom interjected with an intrusive swoop. Typical. I snatched Wendy back toward my chest.

"We're going to ask everyone except the immediate parents to leave and give quiet time for the new family to bond," my OBGYN interrupted. The doc slipped an arm around Mom's shoulders and pulled her from the bedside.

Kai scooped Wendy from the crook of my elbow. Though I didn't want to let her go, I didn't object. Where there was quiet, there was sleep, and it called to me. The room emptied of nurses, and that was my muscles' cue to melt into the bed. Finally, the calm I'd been longing for arrived. Or did it? As my mom and doctor chatted, the doc's eyes shifted toward me. She ran her red tongue across her lips and snagged it, for a second, on the pointed tooth.

"What in the ever-loving world?" I mumbled.

"What? Am I holding her wrong?" Kai shifted Wendy to the other side of his chest as carefully as holding a mirror. I'd picked up a few of his superstitions in our six years of marriage, but mirrors never bothered me. "Mari? Are you okay?" he asked. He bravely balanced our baby in one arm to wipe away stray hairs from my face with the other hand.

"I just squeezed a human being out of me. I will never be okay again." I slurred the words as a deep, painful exhaustion slammed me like a bus with motherhood splashed on the side in crayon graffiti.

Doctor Perrault led Mom from the room, but not without a glance back. All good doctors should check on their patients, but her look wasn't one of concern. Her gaze met mine, and her pale eyes narrowed for a moment before she tossed her head back in a barking laugh at some complaint my mother surely shared. Mom was good at whining with a comedic twist.

"I'm just exhausted and a mess," I said. I tugged the gray hospital gown over my exposed skin even though Perrault had already seen all the goods during the past hour of labor and delivery. Something about her slanted side-eye made me feel like a piece of meat.

"Nonsense, you look like a queen to me." Kai lifted Wendy to his face and planted the first kiss on her brand-new forehead.

"Me? Or her?" I muttered, already confused about the relief I felt that he held her. It was nice to rest, but my arms felt empty without her. Plus, I was jealous of the attention she got, even though I had done all the work. Also, if I could shove one more emotion in there, it would be that icky sticky feeling of greed, since I wanted to be the only person to hold Wendy ever again.

"She's the princess, you're the queen," he slipped in with that masterful wording of a journalist, which he had learned from me, of course.

"Nice try. I know I look like ground beef."

"Hey, I happen to like hamburgers," he said with a shrug. An eerie quiet hung in the room, and I realized all the nurses and staff had finally disappeared. Here we were, alone, left with the sole responsibility for another human life.

"Did you give up on the 'queen' description that fast?" I asked and settled back into the pillow, wincing at every movement as the drugs wore off. I could have sworn someone set everything below my belly on fire.

"Queen of the Big Mac realm," he offered, a classic dad-style joke.

"Yep, with a whole crown of grease." I swirled my finger over my head to show the sweat-soaked ponytail. The uncomfortable delivery bed could have been a cloud for all I knew. My former complaints vanished; the bed didn't need to be perfect, just a place to rest. As long as it held my body up, I could relax. I sank into the sheets and the towel beneath me, complete with an IV wire and catheter tube, and whatever else shared my mattress. But I didn't mind sharing as long as I could grab a quick catnap. Of course, hormones wouldn't let me rest that easily. A sudden, powerful longing to hold my baby overwhelmed me.

"Wendy!" I shot up. Pain sliced through my belly and below.

"What! What? She's right here," Kai said. He offered her to me, knowing I needed to hold her. Tears stung my eyes before spilling out and rolling down my cheeks.

"I'm a terrible mother," I said with a sob. "I almost went to sleep right after she was born. I didn't even hold her that long, and she hasn't looked at me yet. She just stared up at the light like she could see something I couldn't." Words came faster than tears, but the flood wasn't far behind. The medical staff had pumped me with so much fluid I might burst into a tsunami of why-do-I-already-suck-at-this.

Kai had the gall to laugh. *Laugh!* I snatched his shirt sleeve and yanked him down to my level.

"If you're judging me right now, you will not live to regret it."

"Mari, relax." He chuckled again. "It's the hormones, and you're exhausted. Let yourself rest for a second."

But I never got a second, and I was pretty sure I never would again. Motherhood had begun, and something else felt *different*. Doctor Perrault materialized in the room. Weird that I didn't catch the light and sounds from the hall when she came in. I blamed the fuzzy birth-giving brain. Her eyes glowed brightly in the dim room since the fluorescent bulbs had been flicked off for our bonding time.

"Smart father," she said in a deep voice that matched the low-key after-birth vibes. "The mother needs rest. And I can help with that." Perrault reached out toward Wendy.

A song blared in the speakers overhead, causing both Kai and I to jump out of our skin.

"Whoa!" Kai cupped one palm over Wendy's tiny, squashed ears.

"It's your lullaby. Every time a baby is born, the hospital plays it," Doctor Perrault explained.

The music droned from the scratchy, sound system in drawn-out notes that resembled the blow of a pipe organ in an old, forgotten church. I shivered.

"It sounds a little ominous for a lullaby." Kai took the words right out of my mind.

"We're traditional here at Golden Heart Medical Center. The lullabies are copied directly from centuries-old tales. They're called cradle songs." Between each word, her pointed tooth revealed itself. She turned, and I glimpsed two identical sharp edges protruding from her mouth, like an ever-loving *vampire*. She took a step toward my husband, and I almost launched out of the bed to pull him back, crippling pain and all.

Kai shot me a look that I affectionately called 'caterpillar eyebrows' where he scrunched his face up in confusion and concern for people's strange behavior. Of course, he never did it to me. Until now.

"Is something wrong, Mari?" Doctor Perrault asked. "Is your catheter bothering you? I'll have a nurse come remove it for you."

"No, no." I sat back. "I mean, yes. Get the pee tube out of me. But

I'm just ready to bond with Wendy more." I held out my arms the way one might balance a bale of hay.

Doctor Perrault smiled. "You'll have plenty of time for that later."

"Doesn't she need to eat?" I pointed at my chest as if I had any clue how or when to nurse a baby.

"Don't we all?" She laughed. "But we're much too busy for that yet. Come now." She beckoned to Kai. But he didn't move to hand Wendy over as he glanced between us.

"Maybe we can catch a few moments of sleep before the sun comes up," Kai joked. Or maybe he was serious. I had no idea what time it was.

"Can't we wait for my regular doctor to do her checkup?" I asked.

"No need to worry. I'm good at what I do." Perrault winked. All awkward arms and bony elbows, Kai transferred the bundle to the doctor's smooth hold. "Relax now. I'll bring her right back."

I straightened up against the hard mattress and watched until I could no longer see Wendy. Maybe I should have listened to my coworker, Elsie, when she'd insisted I employ her wife as my midwife. How was I supposed to know she wasn't just trying to get her spouse more business? I finally understood that being a birth advocate was an important job.

"Close your eyes for a bit," Kai said. "We need to rest before the day gets busy. Today is our first full day as parents." The cut on his lip had darkened into a brown scab.

I laid back and felt anything but relaxed. "I don't think I'll know the difference between day and night for a long time now."

A nurse exploded into the room with icy hands and all the gentleness of a rodeo bull. She yanked the catheter out, and I ranked the pain higher than the birth itself.

Another guy, an intern maybe, watched from a distance as if I were a one-woman horror show. Kai chose that time to hide in the bathroom. Probably smart since the last time *I* was in pain, he had passed out. Mr. Intern stepped from the shadows and pushed a wheelchair into the dim light.

"Time to take you to your room," Cold Hands announced. She offered her frozen fingers and prodded me to stand with a curt wave.

"Wait, what? My baby isn't here. We can't leave yet."

"They'll take him to your room," Cold Hands said. She swung her arm to urge me up. I might have mistaken her for an angry cab driver waving another car through a four-way stop if she wasn't wearing scrubs.

"It's a girl. I mean, she's a girl. I mean, Wendy is my baby." It sounded foreign coming from my mouth. Sure, I had nine months with her already, seven of which I knew about her, but that didn't mean I knew how to 'mom.'

"Right, right," Cold Hands said with a thick, unrecognizable accent. And I should know, Kai and I traveled a good part of the world before planning for parenthood. Mom said we got lucky. Babies usually came way earlier than wanted or much later than planned. "Let's go."

"Okay, but my husband is in the bathroom—"

Cold Hands didn't care. She hoisted me into the wheelchair, her strength much more suited to the transfer rather than the catheter removal. Mr. Intern swiveled the chair. In two huge strides, he pushed me through the door.

"Kai!" I called. I heard the bathroom door squeak open and some shuffling before the general hospital noise drowned out my last connection to someone familiar. I longed for privacy, to simply be left alone with my husband and daughter. It wasn't fair, mothers should be able to get the drugs *and* give birth at home. Next time, I'd hit up Elsie's midwife and distract the pain away with a good cop drama on TV while I popped out a baby on the living room floor. Even if it hurt, it had to be better than this.

The stark white of the hallway walls kept me more alert than the dim room we'd left. I craned my neck to look both ways, hopeful that I'd spot Doctor Perrault with Wendy nearby.

Ding! The elevator ring forced me back to reality. A reality where clueless mothers like me didn't even know where their babies were ten minutes after birth. And here I thought I could give birth by myself, *right*. Mr. Intern spun me around to face outward in the elevator.

Kai appeared with about twenty-seven reusable tote bags slung over every limb that we'd packed and brought from home. He ran for the elevator, limping from the weight of the bags, and squeezed through the doors just in time.

"Whew!" Kai breathed. A few bags dropped to the floor. "I thought I'd lost you there for a second."

"What time is it?" I asked.

"Six forty-five," Mr. Intern and Kai said at the same time. They exchanged silent glares over my head as if in an unspoken competition. I didn't care, they'd both seen the goods.

"Did you say *six* forty-five?" I asked. "Didn't we get to the hospital at six? I know I was in labor longer than forty-five minutes." My voice squeaked and cracked. A couple of innocent bystanders raised their eyebrows at me. Kai crouched by my side and used a tone that said I was a crazy woman.

"Hun, it's, uh, six forty-five in the morning."

It was my turn to raise my eyebrows, except I didn't have enough energy left. The elevator rang its arrival, and we exited into a long hall, darker and slower moving than the rest of the hospital. Except for the sound of Kai grunting and dragging our crap along behind us.

"Will they find us up here?" I asked Mr. Intern. He cocked his head while sweeping me into a room with two empty beds.

"Oh no, Golden Heart is very safe. Did you see our security system? The maternity ward is locked except for approved visitors."

I needed more than a minute to process what he said. Twenty-four hours of back-searing labor and a ripped downstairs did a number on your critical thinking. "Wait, what?"

He helped me into the fresh bed that I welcomed more than I wanted to admit. Kai followed up with a collapse in the visitor's chair. He acted as if he was the one who had just grown and spewed a whole, entire human from his body.

"I need to see my daughter," I said, as I tried to make eye contact.

Mr. Intern shuffled the blankets around, focusing on 'making me more comfortable.'

"If you're feeling a concerning amount of anxiety or sadness, be sure to alert a nurse," he said. "They can refer you to a postpartum therapist."

"I'm not anxious. I just want to know where my child is," I snapped, my energy suddenly surging back. Or was it adrenaline? "Kai!"

"Huh? What?" Kai blinked to life.

"You need to find Wendy," I said.

"Isn't the doc bringing her here?" he asked groggily.

"I need to see her. Can I walk now?" Why was I asking the nurse for permission? I forced my legs over the edge of the bed.

"Careful." Mr. Intern cupped my elbow. "I'll help you to the bathroom. Once you have a bowel movement, you'll be free to leave."

"I don't need to poop, I need my baby," I said slowly, hoping he'd acknowledge my actual needs this time. At first, it seemed everybody cared too much before the birth. Now, nothing mattered to the hospital except avoiding lawsuits, like not letting me fall out of bed. He propped me up and tried to turn me toward the restroom.

"It's common practice for those who have had cesareans to pass their first bowel movement before leaving. That way, we know everything is working as it should," he explained.

"I didn't have a C-section." Though, I had wanted one. Elsie had almost convinced me that a scheduled two-hour surgery was far better than an eternity of labor and the potential for an emergency cesarean at the end. Her wife didn't agree, so I ultimately went with the trained midwife's opinion and opted out of the elective C-section.

Mr. Intern blinked. "You're not Mrs. Andersen?"

"No." I tugged my arm from his grip. "How can the hospital make such a simple mistake? Does that mean they brought Wendy to someone else?" Tears built. "Where the hell is she?" I pushed past him and marched for the open door.

Mr. Intern beat me to it.

He slipped his short body around me and swung the door until it clicked shut. The light from the hall vanished, and it left the room with only a hazy glow from the low morning sun. It tried its best to illuminate the room in streaks while trapped behind heavy hospital curtains.

"Please, don't tell my boss," he begged. "It's my first week—"

"Look, dude," Kai interrupted. "Find our kid. Now."

I never needed my husband to save me, but at that moment, I could have married him all over again.

Mr. Intern straightened up, and his face transformed from desperation to anger. "I don't work for you."

"You're our nurse, though, can't you help—" I started.

"I don't even know why I'm here!" In his declaration, I caught the glint of the hospital fluorescents shining off of a particularly sharp tooth that snagged on his lip. He ripped the lanyard from his neck. My heart rate topped the charts, probably even faster than when I had pushed Wendy out. The intern shook his head and furrowed his brow as he stared at the floor. "I work on a different floor, but I felt like I had to come up here."

"Are you okay, man?" Kai asked, as he stepped toward the intern.

Mr. Intern blinked and glanced up at him. "Sorry, I'm just confused. I don't know why I thought I needed to come up here. My shift wasn't in this department." He paused and looked at me. "But I remember you. You didn't hold the elevator for me. And I was running late for work."

The memory flashed across my mind. I had waddled into the elevator, sweating with contraction pains, and had jammed the button to the labor and delivery floor. Kai had gotten stuck parking the car after dropping me by the hospital doors. Alone and nervous, I had focused on one thing and one thing only: get to my doctor. I could recall a figure hurrying toward the elevator, but another contraction had overwhelmed me, and that was all she wrote.

"I'm sorry," I said. "Do you know where our daughter is? Or the doctor?" Doctor Perrault wasn't my chosen doctor, and she knew it. I may or may not have begged her to bring me to a doctor I 'trusted.' I winced at that memory too. How many hospital staff had I alienated while in labor?

"I have no clue," he said. The intern licked his lips again, and I noticed all of his teeth looked flat. The pointed tooth was gone.

I blinked. A sickening chill washed over me, and I glanced at Kai, who shared my worried expression. "Where is Wendy?" I stepped past the intern and yanked the heavy door open, hoping Doctor Perrault would be standing there with Wendy in her arms.

Instead, an empty hall greeted me. A piercing scream ripped through the quiet ward and echoed off the pale blue walls.

But that wasn't what brought me to my knees, or at least halfway to my knees, while I leaned against the door frame. I expected a scream or two when women gave birth.

I didn't expect the growling.

Chapter 2

When It Rains

As cliche as a character in an action movie, I clung to the wall, white-knuckled and all. I would have peed my pants if I wore any. What was a little pee on the ground when chaos erupted?

Several nurses sprinted down the hall toward the source of the scream, including the intern. I looked down the white corridor colored by blue and pink and a multitude of other shades from the nurses' bright scrubs. It seemed I wasn't the only one feeling frantic. I stepped from the room and marched toward the gaggle of nurses. My child was missing, so despite the desperate rest I needed and my desire to believe that the doctor would bring Wendy to us soon, I refused to wait.

"Mari," Kai shouted. "Where are you going?"

With a glance back, I waved for my husband to follow me. "Let's ask the nurses." Instead of heading to the empty nurses' station across from our room, I started down the hall.

I wrapped my hands around my protruding belly, only a little softer and squishier since Wendy was gone. *Gone.* I had created life, I could end a life. And I knew I would too, if anyone hurt my daughter.

"Did you hear that?" I asked, as I froze, halfway to the group of nurses. Another low vibrating growl cut through the beeping and buzzing conversation in the busy hospital.

"The scream earlier? Everybody heard it," Kai said. A nurse appeared at the station and sat behind a computer. He stormed up to her. "Where's our doctor? Doctor Perrault. I'm going to give her a piece of my mind." My husband was a silly guy, laid back and never angry. I'd never seen him so fired up before.

He stood at the nurse's station, ready to demand answers, since the nurse hadn't looked up from the computer yet. I followed, but a woman stepped between Kai and me. Her bright crimson cloak and curled red hair were a stark contrast to the plain whiteness of a sterile hospital. Freckles dotted her cheeks and pointed nose. She smelled of lavender and oranges, not the typical sting of sanitizer like the rest of the hospital and its staff.

"Mari?" she said.

"Ye-yes?" I shuffled back to create space in my personal bubble again. She moved with me and spoke in a soft but firm voice.

"You need to come with me." The woman's eyes searched mine like she was trying to see inside me and read my mind.

"Why?" I arched an eyebrow, feigning casual confidence. *I'm a mom now, I can do anything, right?*

"Mari Fable, correct?" She confirmed her own question with a nod of her head. The ethereal curls flowed, moving like water rather than bouncing the way hair should. *How'd she know my maiden name?* I'd gotten rid of that awful surname when Kai and I had created our family's own identity by paying the government to give us the last name we chose.

"That's not me anymore," I said, as I glanced at Kai. He held his hands in tight fists and looked to be arguing with the nurse.

"Follow me, Fable," the woman said before she marched toward the group of nurses. Her sensible heels tapped on the linoleum as she headed right at the crowd of nurses, crash cart, and chaos. She didn't look back to check if I had listened to her demand.

The woman in the cloak didn't match the rest of the hospital. If I had to guess, I'd say she was cosplaying Poison Ivy or had just come from a Renaissance Faire. She looked distantly familiar, but I couldn't place her—just another face I'd seen in the city, perhaps.

"Are you a doctor?" I asked. The redhead only glanced back and curled her finger, beckoning me to follow. The crowd of nurses partially blocked the hall as they surrounded the open door of a patient's room. On the other side, several steps past them, were the elevators.

Maybe she has Wendy. I limped along in her wake like a zombie, lost and desperate for more information. The floor felt cold and harsh against my bare feet, but I followed because the investigator in me knew I could get answers faster from my own actions rather than waiting for the hospital employees to tell me.

The nurses moved around us, only pausing to glare at us for getting in their way. A security guard and the half-dozen nurses stood with two women in hospital gowns that matched mine. They donned frazzled hair and tired eyes, also matching me. But their clothes weren't what bothered me. Splotchy red spots covered their faces like they'd just been crying.

One used her hands as she spoke. "Someone took her." Her fingers shook as she pulled them to her chest. "Someone took my baby!" A nurse raised his arms and tried to quiet her.

Why are the nurses denying it? My investigator's brain wouldn't turn off, not even after a day of labor and delivery. I'd seen people try to cover up mistakes before, especially to avoid lawsuits.

The redhead didn't wait for me when I paused to listen to the woman. The Renaissance woman's black skirt swished back and forth about her knees with every tapping step.

"Your child is probably in the nursery," the nurse said to the nervous woman. I caught his quick, worried glance toward the security officer, who gave a slight nod. *They've misplaced our babies. . .*

"Fable!"

I whipped my head back around to see the redheaded woman at the end of the hall in front of the elevators.

"I-I need to stay with my husband," I said. I shook my head and rubbed at my temples. A lump of overwhelm gathered in my throat. The choking sensation spread down into my chest, heavier than guilt. How could I lose Wendy when I had become a mother only hours ago?

"If you want to see your child, you will come with me." Her cherry lips settled in a flat line. The elevator doors dinged. She made eye contact with me and nodded toward the open doors.

"Hey!" the security officer bellowed. He tried to shuffle out of the group, but the crowd of nurses and onlookers and worried mothers blocked his path. "We're locking down this floor, nobody leaves!"

The redheaded woman didn't care. She marched into the elevator and smiled. "You should hurry, Mari." Her eyes flicked to the security officer as he pushed past the women.

"I can't find my daughter," another mother from the group cried and attached herself to the security officer's arm. He tried to shake her off, but the altercation gave me a moment to decide.

"Wendy is waiting," the redhead said, as the elevator dinged again, and the doors slowly slid to a close.

That solidified it for me. I wasn't proud to say I acted on impulse, but the mention of my baby's name stirred something wild and less rational in my normally organized brain. I cursed under my breath and made a break for the elevator. The distraction from the desperate woman allowed me to slip past the security guard and squeeze through the doors at the last second.

Inside the elevator, I pinched my arm. It felt like a Disneyland ride where it would drop out from underneath us at any moment. At least, that was how the rollercoaster of emotions felt from giving birth, to losing my daughter, and finally to following a stranger despite my better judgment. Before I could gather my thoughts and question the woman, the elevator came to an abrupt halt that sent my head spinning.

"This way," she said, as she exited into a dark hall, a stark contrast to the chaos upstairs. I tentatively stepped out, unsure if the floor was really there or if it was all an illusion. A magic trick. A hoax of epidural, and birth brain, and no sleep. But the ground didn't shift underneath me, and the hall looked like an ordinary hospital with regular office doors.

"Where are we?" I asked.

"The offices," she said.

"Your office? Who are you?" I jogged up beside her. *Why didn't I ask that before? What in the wonderland am I doing? I need Kai.*

"I am the Keeper." She offered no further explanation as she stopped in front of a door with no label and jiggled the handle. It did not turn.

"Okay, and your name?" I demanded. Frustration silenced the guilt and fear and surreality for a moment. I found it a welcome relief from worry, though it didn't last long.

Redhead leaned back, skirt and cloak dusting the floor, before launching her heel into the door. I jumped at the slam, but the door didn't budge.

"Whoa! Hey!" I moved out of her range, then remembered she was taking me to my baby. *Supposedly.* She scooted back and readied to kick again, but I moved to block her attack. "Enough with the mysterious tough-chick act. You might have thought you were tricking a dumb, exhausted mother, and I'm not saying I'm not that, but I am done! Where the hell is my daughter?"

Redhead showed no emotion, but the freckles combined with the crimson cloak created an innocent yet professional vibe that I jived with. Besides, I didn't know if I could trust the nurses after the intern and my doctor and those. . . fangs?

"In here." Her blunt black heel shot forward and bashed into the door. I couldn't breathe, or maybe I forgot how for a moment, and I almost wanted the oxygen mask I had handy while in labor. Redhead shoved past me into the room. After I processed her response, I spun around to follow.

The tapping from her heals quieted as she marched from the linoleum onto the scratchy blue carpet of an almost-empty office. Four clear bassinets lined the walls. On the left, several locks lined a door to keep it shut. *The Keeper.* I mulled over her answer.

Redhead peered into each bassinet, her expression never changing. I crept closer. One baby stirred in its swaddle.

"Wendy?" I whispered. Each face looked the same, pinched and squished. One baby donned a cone-shaped head, another dark hair, and the last two were balder than my mom's last boyfriend. *Wendy had hair. Or was it fuzz? Was it a dirty blonde like Kai's or black like mine?*

I ruled out the pale one. Though if she took after Kai, she could be any one of these babies. My breath quickened. The stuffy room felt tighter and smaller, and though I wanted to run, I couldn't grab them all.

I groaned and hunched forward, hands waving at my sweaty pits. The overwhelm and the unsteady feeling from the elevator ride all came crashing at me at once. The hot, light-headedness threatened to waste me. If I didn't sit soon, I'd collapse on the ground, passed-out like Kai during Wendy's delivery.

"Fable? What's wrong?" Redhead almost sounded nice this time. She kept good on her promise. . . *if* one of these babies was Wendy.

"I don't know," I said, but my voice cracked. My head throbbed with each increasingly rapid pulse. I wiped my forehead with the back of my arm. A queen. *I'm Kai's sweaty, frazzled queen. Maybe Wendy sweats too. Who knows? I don't. I don't know my own daughter!*

One baby released a squeak that sent the one next to it into a full-blown wail. I slapped my hand to my chest. *Calm down.* The volume wasn't the problem. The dry sound scratched at my ears while the baby sucked in rapid breaths between cries. That couldn't be her, she wouldn't cry at the sight of my face. Right?

I needed two heads again to look both directions at the same time and see all babies at once. I would know my child. She came out of me, for goodness' sakes. *Where are you, Wendy?* My chin quivered, and the extreme heat shifted to goosebumps across my bare arms until everything turned icy. I gasped. I needed oxygen before I found myself blacked out on the floor beside Redhead's sensible heels.

I took a long breath, but the moment only brought tears. A sob spilled out of me. Snot trickled and joined the rest of the wetness on my face.

"I can't tell," I cried. Redhead merely tilted her head in patient anticipation. My chest rose and fell as I hyperventilated. "I'm a horrible mother." I smashed the heel of my palm against my cheekbones and swiped the floods away. "Doctor Perrault said she'd bring

Wendy right back, and I didn't even think to memorize what my baby looks like. I thought I'd just know. But the doctor took her before I could get a chance." I didn't care if I spilled my guts out to the strange woman or what she thought of me.

"Perrault," Redhead muttered. "It can't be. . . Fable!" She snapped her fingers and pointed at my eyes, then back at hers. "Look at me. Focus!"

I sucked in a wracking breath and tried to straighten.

Redhead held my gaze. "I brought these babies to the nursery. But you said someone named Perrault took yours from you?"

I sniffed and swallowed a whole wad of phlegm while simultaneously trying not to puke it back out. "Yes. The on-call doctor. Wait, you kidnapped them?"

"The wolf is here," Redhead said, more to herself than to me. "I don't know who it is yet, but I sense the story aura so strongly." The woman spoke with an old-fashioned air, serious and articulate, but it didn't match her youthful appearance. I pinned her somewhere in her early twenties. Her look of mixed determination and fear made her look both mature and young at the same time. She flicked her sharp eyes up to me.

"Take your daughter, get out of the hospital, and run far away from here." She edged around me between the bassinets and my newly expanded hips.

"Excuse me?" I tugged at the gown and used it as a tissue.

"I can't have the wolf finding her before I know who she is." Redhead flicked the locks on the door in one smooth movement and paused on the threshold. Darkness flooded in from behind her. I backed away from the chill that swept in and bumped into one bassinet. The child squealed her annoyance. I turned to apologize, but the wide, bright eyes stared up at the fluorescent lights above, and I knew. I knew my daughter's squeal.

"Wendy," I said, as relief flushed through me.

"Promise me you will run," Redhead snapped and demanded my attention again. I only glanced back since I was too distracted by the tiny human I awkwardly tried to scoop into my arms. "The story aura will settle on someone already interested in harming her. It cannot be the doctor."

A chill trickled down my spine. Who was harming who? But Redhead wasn't talking to me, and my brain couldn't wrap around her cryptic messages.

"None of this makes any sense," I said. But it didn't matter what made sense because I held my daughter against my chest, a bundle of warmth and sweet smells. This woman's drama was not my problem.

Footsteps echoed from the open door that led to the hall. Redhead froze, her striking brown eyes staring at the floor while she listened. The curls on her head never strayed out of place. Suddenly, her gaze flicked up to me. "I brought you to your daughter, now you will do this for me. It's too much to explain right now, but a very old story is coming true, and I think the villain wants one of these babies."

"You're insane." But even as I said it, I wondered at my sanity. What did I think I saw? How could I tell Kai I followed a strange woman? She'd called herself the Keeper, which told me nothing. How much of this did I imagine?

"The villain and I are in a race now," she said, stepping one foot into the darkness of the strange door, "and he can't have her yet."

Wendy fidgeted and burped out inconsistent cries that rolled into longer wailing. I shifted her in my arms more carefully than Kai had, sure I would drop her any second. Only the second-worst thing I'd have done as a mother. When I looked up to push Redhead for answers, she had disappeared.

Along with the door.

Oh no, this isn't happening. What in the portal-hallucinating-insanity is this?

Chapter 3

Speak of the Devil

I cursed myself for listening to Redhead and not taking matters into my own hands. After another doctor arrived in the office, finding me and the four babies, he had called for security. The entire ordeal ended happily ever after. Each baby was returned to their parents.

Hospital administration swiftly shushed my attempts to question the situation. They offered a flimsy explanation. Something about separating the babies for hearing tests. I tried to dig deeper, but exhaustion slammed me, and my arms shook, barely able to balance Wendy.

A nurse comforted me and said I needed rest. I didn't disagree, so I let her guide me back to my room, where I collapsed on the bed. The nurse recited the same 'hearing test' explanation to Kai while I struggled to keep my eyes open.

This bed, better than in the delivery room, sank under my weight and folded around the soft parts and aching parts and parts of my body I didn't even recognize anymore. It felt good to collapse, but my brain refused to stop. Since when did I become a follower and not a leader? I let a weird lady who somehow knew my real name lead me to another part of the hospital. It wasn't like me, but nothing about this parenting gig was what I expected.

Advice blogs and pregnancy forums convinced me the hard part was over. Labor, birth, and then *tada*! Like magic, a child would appear in your arms, and you'd already love it and instantly know how to feed it.

Who would have thought babies were born not knowing how to eat? How could you teach that to a being who could barely move? When would I stop feeling relieved that someone else took over surveillance duty? Did my baby even know me?

Redhead's prim hair and long cloak appeared in my mind's eye. The only eye I could keep open after the exhaustion of it all.

Mom took Wendy and fussed over how small she was while back-handedly blaming me for not eating enough in the prenatal timeline. I chose not to care, or at least pretend I didn't, as I rolled to face the wall and Kai's empty chair. In my semi-private corner of the bed, I granted myself permission for tears to come out of hiding. Of course, they wouldn't have waited for my say anyway, it seemed I lost all control of my body, crying included. Nurses had told me I must accept the IV. The doctor had instructed me when to push. Mom had insisted I swaddle Wendy this way and not that.

I tugged at the pillowcase and soaked the evidence of my crying from my face into the fabric. Mom swayed back and forth, pacing in a circle at the foot of my bed. Wendy stayed silent, likely as tired as me. I allowed my eyelids to fall. Sleep should clear it all up. With a rested mind, I'd understand what I saw and experienced. I slipped my hand under the weak pillow to prop it up more and settled my face into the softness. I chalked up Doctor Perrault and the intern's fangs to a combination of bad dental work and that weird thing pain does to your brain (dang failing epidural) before allowing the void to swallow me whole.

When I came to, it took more than a minute to process that the wetness in the sheets wasn't from a leak in the roof. Rain pattered against the window on the other side of the room. Wind blasted it sideways, not letting gravity have its way. I rubbed the sleep away from my eyes and grimaced at the sweat-soaked bed. When I sat forward, I hurt in all the places I didn't expect. My head throbbed as it tried to catch up with time lost, and my chest ached.

"Where's the baby?" My voice broke from disuse. I silently chided myself for not calling her *my baby* or *our baby* or whatever would have been more acceptable for a mother. Something of which I did not *feel* like yet.

Fear struck my chest and I could have sworn a school bus had hit me. Losing sight of Wendy a second time might kill me, but my husband's calm demeanor told me I didn't need to worry.

Kai clicked the screen off on his phone. The only light left came from the flood of yellow cutting in through the cracked door. He scooted to the edge of the chair.

"Your mom has her," he said. "I held her for a while, but your mom insisted I'd fall asleep and drop her."

"Don't let her push you around like that. She sweet talks you with all that babying, and you let her do whatever she wants," I said. "My goodness, if I had been the boy she had wanted, I can't imagine how she would have treated my girlfriends." I edged to the side of the bed and let my feet dangle. "Hey, can you dig out my sweats from the overnight bag and hand them to me?" I pointed past him to the pile of prepared belongings. It was only half-packed since Wendy came two weeks earlier than expected. Unusual, my doctor had said, for a firstborn.

Kai tossed the faded gray pants that used to be black and one of his t-shirts that were five sizes too big for me. It looked like heaven in cotton and cheap polyester.

"Did you bring this for me?" My eyes welled with tears. *Oh for goodness' sakes, here we go again.* Tears dribbled down my face, and I wondered where those little baby towels went that my neighbor Tala had claimed were for spit-up. I deemed them more useful to salvage hormonal attacks like this one.

"I know you like wearing my shirts more than your own," he said with a shrug. "What I can't figure out is why you don't stop buying women's shirts. Then, we might save enough money for you to quit working."

My eyes dried faster than the rise of anxiety when I'm trying to shove change back into my wallet. I wadded up the bottom of the pants and swung the other side at him. His teasing eased my sudden burst of emotion.

"It got you to stop crying, right?" Kai smirked. "Besides, if you quit journalism, then how will you get rich and famous and support me while I stream games online all day, every day?"

I stood and shimmied out of the damp hospital gown, happy to be rid of the heavy fabric and ickiness. Even Kai's retro Gameboy shirt fit snugly. Why didn't anyone warn me that my boobs would go all gargoyle and turn to stone? My body didn't feel like my own. I barely recognized myself.

"Doctor Perrault came by and said Wendy passed some sound test," Kai said.

"What?"

"The room you found her in. I guess they separate the babies to a quiet place to check their hearing." Kai unscrewed a blue Gatorade bottle and offered it to me.

"Oh, right. That's what they said, isn't it?" I took a sip. "Huh. What about the weird nurse?"

"Oh, that intern kid?" Kai said it as if we weren't kids ourselves, barely twenty-nine. Mom would say it's a late start for a family, but Mom's old-fashioned, despite what her Botox would have you believe. "I asked about him, but nobody seemed too alarmed, and apparently, Mrs. Andersen was just a name mix-up."

"Okay, that's weird." I stepped into the pants and tightened the drawstring against the oversized adult diaper that held all my insides where they belonged.

"I know you like to investigate, Ms. Journalism, but you promised you would take full advantage of your maternity leave." Kai pointed his phone at me like a teacher's stick. "I was panicking too, but Wendy is safe now."

I wanted to object, but hormones gave me a pass and let my brain work correctly for a few moments. He was right. All that mattered right now was getting a good start to raising a healthy child. But dang if I didn't love discovering a good secret.

Yellow turned to white as light poured into the room. Mom

emerged, perfectly balanced in ridiculous shoes. She cupped Wendy in one arm while her long fingers propped up a squatty bottle on the other side.

"What are you doing?" I asked as I jumped up. "I'm supposed to be breastfeeding when she's hungry."

"Nonsense," she said, "Wendy was hungry, and you needed sleep."

It was thanks to that rest that I had enough energy to argue. I resisted and almost wanted to thank her. Without sleep, I'd still be hallucinating magical doors and. . . was it growling?

Mom popped the bottle from Wendy's mouth, which seemed to unplug the volume. Wendy burst into a persistent cry, and I thought I would follow. Something soiled my shirt, but it wasn't from tears. I plopped down against the bed, frustrated at the fresh shirt already wet from the two leaky bottles forever strapped to my chest.

"Fine." I gave in. Mom returned the bottle so Wendy could polish off the last couple of drops. "But if she can't learn how to nurse now, I'm going to hunt you down."

"Who's hunting?" A man with a wide, pearly white smile invaded the room. He wore his thick hair greased back with enough gel to shine the fluorescents from the hall off his head and into the room. "I wouldn't know anything about that. I'm vegan. Except for breast milk, of course." He chuckled.

Kai and I exchanged horrified glances. Clueless (or careless), Mom shifted Wendy to my arms and spun around to admire the fresh meat.

"Oh." Mr. Grease furrowed his brow and looked at each of our faces. "Uh, I'm the lactation consultant. Not great with jokes, but good with boobs!" He shot two finger guns in our direction.

Nap or not, I was still so wiped I actually giggled at the awkwardness. Normally, awkwardness wasn't in my vocabulary. I dug into the dirty stuff, the raw stuff. As a journalist, nothing was too 'out there' for me, except maybe a vanishing door. Of course, a story like that could launch me closer to the Pulitzer I'd been dreaming about since I was a little girl.

"Thank you so much for coming," Mom fawned. She patted his forearm, already chummy with the strange, kind of funny man. "You know how it is for first-time moms." She smashed her lips into what I assumed was supposed to be a smile.

"Well, despite the one-man show," Mr. Grease paused and glanced between us again as if waiting for a specific reaction, "I'm not here to entertain. I'm here to help." The finger guns folded into two thumbs up.

Relief rolled through me as if it were a real gun he'd put down. I knew I needed all the help I could get with this motherhood adventure. Someday, I'd write about it, and my readers would appreciate the honesty of parenthood struggles.

But for now, feeding my child would be a good start. The consultant instructed me to unwrap Wendy and hold her skin-to-skin. A thousand thoughts flashed through my head from 'what if my breastmilk is poisonous since I don't know what I'm doing to 'shut up, Mari, you're insane, you thought you heard growling.' It finally settled on 'I love my daughter so much it hurts.'

Or was it my boobs that hurt? Some might consider it child abuse to snuggle my poor innocent child next to these rock-hard babies. They were about as big as her anyway. I was in no hurry for their size to go away. According to Elsie, her wife, and my neighbor Tala (who had kids approximately forty years ago), the milk balloons would deflate like an old beach ball.

Mr. Grease got Mom to laugh while somehow tricking her into leaving the room. She hurried out, a shawl wrapped around her shoulders, and on a quest for something called Three-Butter cookies. Whatever it was, I wanted to eat it. Hunger pangs slowly inched their way into my attention through the rest of the pain competing for number one in my body.

"Will those help with lactation?" I asked while I slipped the shirt off my shoulder and held Wendy somewhere in the right vicinity.

"Who knows?" Mr. Grease said. "But most new moms appreciate a baked good over the presence of a hovering mother-in-law."

"Hey! My mom doesn't hover," Kai said, "and she's not even here."

"See?" I held my hand up, indicating toward the consultant. "Even he can see that my mother loves you more than me. Her own daughter!"

"Thanks a lot," Kai said, as he folded his arms, putting on his best pissed-off look. But he winked at Mr. Grease.

"My apologies," Mr. Grease said. "It was an honest mistake. It is most often the mother-in-law who causes the new mom to stress. I sensed some tension, and in order to help your baby eat, it's time to relax."

As if on cue, another piercing scream ripped through the static noise of hospital bustle. Kai jumped from his reclined position in the visitor's chair. Mr. Grease raised two thick brows that could very well have been the culprit for the scream itself, considering they were liable to crawl off his face at any moment.

What in the red-hot hell is wrong with this hospital? I should have listened to Elsie. Home birth next time. It was nice to pretend at least. If I were honest, I'd never make it through labor without even the half-way-useful dose of an epidural.

"What was that?" Kai looked at me. This time, the scream didn't produce any chaos, and our interest dissipated as fast as it came.

"Apparently, not a distraction." Mr. Grease pointed at Wendy.

She latched! For all of three seconds. . . My baby smashed her face into the most unpleasant of squishy wrinkles and turned her nose away from me.

"I knew it. My milk is poison," I said it as a joke, but tears still stung my eyes. Kai reached out and gave my hand a squeeze.

"Not unlike your cooking," he said. He smirked because he knew I needed a laugh almost as much as I hated cooking. I laughed until it turned into crying somewhere in the middle and I forgot what I was doing and didn't know who I was anymore and. . .

"I'm sorry! I'm sorry! You usually like that joke, babe," Kai said. He scooted the chair closer and rubbed his thumb against my chin to catch the tears.

"It's not that." I sucked in sobbing breaths. "I just can't stop crying. I don't even know why?"

"Is that a question?" He cocked his head, more confused than me.

Mr. Grease stepped out from the shadows by the protruding 'closet' on my side of the room. *What was his actual name?* I likely had heard it and already forgotten because my brain didn't seem capable of holding more than about three and a quarter things right now.

I should have appreciated the space he gave a wallowing mother, but a chill distracted me. Goosebumps pricked my shoulder. I tugged the shirt up as if the paper-thin fabric would warm me.

"Crying is normal for you," the consultant said. I didn't notice how deep his voice was until now.

"No, it's not." I swiped at the snot dangling from my nose and glared at him. He laughed and shook his head.

"I mean for new mothers, of course. You're flushing out hormones." He stepped closer. The light from the hall seemed dimmer now, no longer shining off his hair gel. "Now, give me your baby, and I'll demonstrate the correct nursing holds."

I swear, if this dude whips a fake boob out from his shirt, I'm leaving this hospital right now. Numb rear-end and all. I tightened my hold around Wendy, already defensive of another person taking her, but he wasn't the one exposing himself to half the hospital.

Brightness flooded the room. Our dark little corner of the maternity ward switched to a packed sell-out crowd in less than a minute. Two nurses pushed another mother into the room. A man and three gray-heads followed. Mom returned with seven different bags of baked goods. And finally, the parade ended with a familiar face that I actually wanted to see. Tala, my declared adopted grandmother and actual next-door neighbor, lit up the room with her beaming smile.

The new mom rivaled Tala with a massive grin of her own. She rolled in with coiffed blonde hair (brighter than the dang hospital lights) and a perfectly latched baby tucked under a thin nursing sheet that matched her handmade birthing gown.

It wouldn't be the first time I almost threw up on Wendy's head—and she wasn't even a day old yet. The woman waved and welcomed me to motherhood as if this were Disneyland and we'd both just gotten on It's a Small World where everyone knew your name. *Wait, I don't think those go together.*

"I don't know about three kinds, but these cookies have butter in them," Mom said. She shoved her way through the crowd of onlookers, staring at my worthless boob. "Except this one." Mom nibbled the edge of a particularly crumbly cookie. "But this one's mine. I think it's Bay Area Diet approved." She scrutinized the cookie and took another rabbit-sized bite. "Would you like one?" Leave it to my mother to offer what she believed to be lactation-boosting treats to the potentially single man in the room instead of her own daughter.

Mr. Grease patted his stomach. "No, thank you. I'm vegan."

You said that already. Hey! Maybe my brain remembers more than I give it credit for.

"It's a cookie, not a steak." Mom licked her lips, either to flirt or to check if the nibbling didn't undo the shining gloss. Mr. Grease fed right into it. He laughed, a hearty sound that melted my previous shivers.

"Still," he said, "I only indulge in meat for the most special occasions." He mirrored Mom's open mouth, and I thought they might kiss right there. I pictured him tossing her onto the end of my bed and devouring her with overacted lust like a soap opera star. Third time almost puking on the tiny human? *Check!*

"Oh." The new mom's squeaky voice jutted in. "Are you a lactation consultant?"

Mr. Grease nodded and shot finger guns again. "That's me."

"Wonderful!" she beamed. "I just think it is so important for new mothers to have access to all the help they can get."

"How many others do you have?" I asked. I didn't mean to sound rude, but I half-expected her to answer somewhere in the hundreds.

"Stanley is my first," she said, as she patted the diapered butt sticking out from under the nursing sheet.

I nodded and bit my lip before I raged out on the innocent woman. "Congrats," I said through gritted teeth. If jealousy could show, I'd be doomed with a face greener than Mom's weird diet cookie. *Please, just eat.* I silently begged my daughter to have a snack of breastmilk. *I want to do this for you.*

Wendy yanked her fist around like a tiny cheerleader in the audience that was my hospital room. *Next up, Mari's amazing ability to down six cookies in two bites.* If only my daughter wanted to eat as much as I did. Her tiny mouth burst into an earth-shattering yawn. My earth anyway. One that achieved world peace through one itty-bitty, perfect human. Not even Blondie could ruin this moment.

Kai's coffee breath sweetened the mood. His green eyes went all googly, and he sank into the place between my neck and shoulder, snuggling close to his place in the bedside chair.

Instead of dinner, Wendy chose a nap. She gave in to her heavy eyes and breathed in rhythmic contentedness with her cheek resting on my chest. I did one thing right. Mr. Grease could correct my breast-feeding hold all he wanted, but Wendy knew she was at home in my arms, and that was enough for now.

"I'll be back for another round in a couple of hours," Mr. Grease said in a soothing, deep voice that reminded me of *The Witcher*, or Mr. Darcy, or even Mr. Big. Mom visibly swooned. "We can try again, then. For now, rest is best, and breast is next!" He chuckled at his own joke, and Mom fell prey to the whole 'overacting' thing with a raucous laugh. "But I'm quite serious." His face darkened, and his thick eyebrows pulled forward. "You have many exhausting days ahead of you, Mari, plus a lot of unknowns—"

"And long nights," Blondie cut in. *I thought this was your first.*

"Enjoy the downtime." Mr. Grease tipped his head and pinched an imaginary hat between his thumb and forefinger. The noir mystery vibes dissipated with Blondie's family flashing lightning bolts from oversized cameras while she posed all Marilyn Monroe with her white bedsheets.

"Sure thing," Kai said. He shot Mr. Grease's favorite finger guns back at him as the consultant left the room. Mom trailed behind, already rambling about how he looked like her favorite late-night comedy host. All the while, he humbly denied any resemblance.

Several of Blondie's family members followed not far behind, nearly emptying the room. *Except for no disappearing doors. Right?*

Tala finally emerged from the back of the group. A small red balloon floated above her hand that held a stuffed gift bag. As always, she drew a deep breath in from her nose before speaking. She talked in a low, soothing tone, followed by a closed mouth laugh that sounded like several hmms in a row.

"She is lovely," Tala said. The older woman leaned into the edge of the bed to rest. After standing for so long, her aging knees needed it. Her wide hips sank into the mattress as she leaned forward to wrap warm arms around my neck in a hug. "I didn't know whether to go blue or pink since you waited until birth to find out the sex." She held up the red bag and balloon after our hug ended. "The gift shop guy said it would be dated to choose one color anyway."

"You didn't have to bring anything, Tala. A friend is all I needed." I accepted the bag and found it almost too heavy to hold in one hand. I picked through the gift paper and pulled out a pile of books."

"You know me," she said. Her golden eyes glowed with motherly warmth as she gazed at the baby. Wendy's chest rose and fell in no particular pattern while her lungs grew used to air. "I can't resist books."

I shuffled through the hard board books and glanced at the titles. *The Ugly Duckling* donned fuzzy, touchable pages of yellow fluff. I turned the pages, and the picture of the tiny bird in tears struck me harder than it should. I sniffled and willed my welling tears away, then flipped to the next book. I didn't want to think about work right now. A horrific case about a young woman who committed suicide had been titled *The Ugly Duckling*, and it still haunted me. I had written the article on that case and tried to forget it since. Her death was borne from a feeling I hoped my daughter would never experience. Even my tough and crude coworker, Jameson, struggled with that case. He'd agreed that something about it unsettled him.

I picked up the next book from Tala's gift pile. The illustrations in *Little Red Riding Hood* were a *little* darker. The wolf bared its teeth. A small girl in a crimson cloak twisted her face into a silent scream. Saliva dripped from the wolf's mouth, and its tongue looked sunken back inside, a mouth that shaded from red to black. I didn't breathe until slapping the cardboard pages shut. *I'm just tired. That's all. This is like when I dream about Thor and wake up the next day thinking about him. Not real.*

I tossed the book aside and took a much-needed breath. It ended in a big, forced smile. I was happy to see Tala, but emotional exhaustion took its toll.

"Does this remind you of when you had your kids?" I asked. Tala's face twitched. The wrinkles settled back into familiar lines as her lips curled back into a small smile.

"Not quite."

We chatted about our crazy neighbor's Halloween decorations and how the police had to come to investigate the fake bodies. I almost felt like myself again. Me, myself, and a tiny bundle. And Kai, of course. He offered to get Tala dinner while he stood and readied to head to the restaurants across the street. I shamelessly ordered nine tacos and still wondered if it would be enough.

Before I knew it, Mr. Grease returned, Mom in tow. Kai tried to squeeze around them, but a shout in the halls stopped him in place.

"Stop him!"

Growling. Real-life growling transformed into ear-splitting barks. A black Labrador skidded into the room with his canines showing. Blondie shrieked. The dog lunged forward toward my bed. Mom fell back, landing against Mr. Grease's unmoving body. Foam flew from the dog's mouth. He barked and jumped at us again, but Kai intercepted at the same time as the dog's owner, two nurses, and a security guard made it to the room.

I scooted back up the bed and squeezed Wendy tightly to my chest. The owner gripped the dog's vest and yanked him down, but not before the dog's tooth snagged on Kai's wrist.

"He's never done this before," the owner spewed while dragging the dog backward. "He's a trained professional. A seizure dog for my son." The words spilled from his mouth, but the attempted apology didn't stop Kai from bleeding all over my white sheets.

The security guard prodded them from the room and demanded the dog be removed. My arms shook so hard I worried Wendy would fall.

I tried to slow my pounding heart. Dogs always sensed I was afraid of them, but that usually resulted in them attempting to lick me rather than attack me. It was like they were trying to convince me that they weren't to be feared. This dog, however, solidified my fears.

Wendy wailed in my ears, but my eyes trailed to the pile of books that had fallen from my mattress.

I rocked side-to-side while shushing her and averting my gaze. *Little Red Riding Hood* had landed on the linoleum, halfway underneath the bed. The book laid open, showing brightly colored pages. Little Red wasn't on the last page.

But the wolf was. *The villain of a very old story.*

Chapter 4

Home is Where the Nightmare is

Someday, I would decide which was scarier: an attack from a dog gone wild or driving with a newborn in the car for the first time. But today was not that day.

I wasn't even the one driving. My poor husband's hands shook worse than mine after my third shot of espresso. Did coffee seep into breast milk? I filed that question away in my brain to research later.

I leaned against the backward car seat and yawned. "Thanks for being our chauffeur," I said. "But can you try not to crash? I'm worried you'll dent a headlight at these speeds."

"Look, you try driving with your baby in the car. It's terrifying!" Kai gripped the steering wheel tighter and sped up from ten miles per hour to eleven. I smiled. The bandage around his wrist reminded me of his bravery. It was always the jokes between us when life got scary that kept us going. From the humiliating talent show during our high school sweetheart days to parenthood, we thrived in the face of danger. Our car inched along while a semi-truck passed us with a blaring honk.

"At this point, I'm more worried that the longer we take to get home, the more chance there is to crash." I peered out the window with half-lidded eyes.

Clouds moved overhead, carrying their looming threat of rain. I watched the fading fog shift against its cloudy backdrop. Wendy still breathed in stutters. The doctors had insisted she wasn't broken, so I believed them, even though I birthed her and always attracted trouble. I let the in and outs lull me. As long as I could hear her breathing, my brain gave me permission to rest.

The hard plastic edges of Wendy's car seat shouldn't have been so comfortable. I sighed. Mist swirled outside the window, though we drew closer to the center of the city. The blinker clicked to signal our exit from the freeway. Tall buildings cast shadows over the car, and I knew we were almost home. Raindrops splattered against the window in a scattered pattern.

Go, go, go, I silently cheered the droplets racing down the glass and tried not to think about Kai operating heavy machinery under the new daddy drug: Exhaustionium. What if we didn't strap her in right? When did we last get the brakes checked? Why do we even own a car in San Francisco? *That's it, I'm going to walk with a stroller everywhere.*

Finally, the rain fell in a rhythm. Among the clear drops, a dark red spot dripped down the window. I sat up. The spot trickled and left a stain behind. More joined it, water turning into wine. No, *blood.*

I moved toward the glass to get a closer look. *Kai?* I couldn't hear my own words. Our car came to a stop and massive claws slammed into the side. Glass shattered and exploded into millions of deadly shards all around me. A hairy snout and jaws jutted through the spiking glass, chomping at me. I scrambled back, my limbs heavy, and rammed into the car seat. *Wendy!* I whipped around to see the other door open into blackness and my baby gone.

This is your story.

I shook. A body pressed against me. Was it the beast in the window? I clawed back, fighting with pathetic energy.

"Mari, relax."

I gasped and lunged forward, instinctively shooting my fist out in front of me. It connected with my husband's throat. He fell into the space between the back and front passenger seats.

"Kai!" I yelled. "Red-hot hell."

He rubbed at his Adam's apple and choked for breath between coughs. "Are you insane?"

Yes. "No. I'm sorry! It was—uh, a bad dream."

This is your story. Let it be.

The words echoed in my head. Where did that last part come from? Rain soaked the inside of the car through the open door. Footsteps passed on the cement sidewalk and splashed more water on Kai's back.

The city dwellers remained unphased by my domestic attack. Hundreds of pedestrians passed by our condo building every day. Today was no different. But *I* was different. I wasn't just Mari the journalist, Mari the note-taker, Mari the wife of Kai anymore. And I couldn't blame motherhood entirely. The fangs, the redheaded woman and her disappearing door all piqued my interest in a way no story or case ever had before.

"Are you okay?" I brushed Kai's dusty brown hair from his face.

"I guess those martial arts classes paid off, huh?" He shook his head. "I will officially stop worrying about you when you're out hunting stories. If you can clock me like that when half-asleep and wearing an adult diaper, I think you're good to go."

I smirked. We'd be fine. We'd be just fine keeping Wendy safe. But Kai's choice of word nagged at me—*story*. I tracked down the news, the dirty parts of the city, and all those swept under the rug. I exposed what needed to be known. And I needed to know what story that redheaded woman was talking about.

* * *

DIRTY DIAPERS, constipation drugs, and round-the-clock detective TV shows dominated my life for the next two weeks. I had lost all control of whatever the strange woman's *story* was. At least, for now. The comfort of our little condo kept me sane.

With Kai and I always so busy, we hadn't needed much in our house before the baby. But a bassinet, Moses basket, diaper pail, changing table, and mounds of laundry had taken over our simple living room that before only donned a couch, sitting chair, and our TV on a bookshelf. Though the kitchen was only a few steps away, and the counter split the room into two, I didn't have the energy to get up and raid the fridge for food.

Wendy's cries, burping smiles, and poop dictated my every move. I would personally rip anyone to shreds who called my maternity leave a vacation. I didn't know what day it was, or the time, and though I spent a lot of time on the couch, I never rested.

Another storm had rolled in since the heavy rain on the day we brought Wendy home, and raindrops pattered the large windows behind me that gave us a view of Main Street.

I splayed out on the black suede couch, a horrible choice, really, for someone with kids. *X-Files* whistled its familiar opening song, but the violent start to the episode made me click out. Even though I'd seen the monster kill the unnamed character a thousand times, I couldn't handle the violence after only forty minutes of sleep and two slices of leftover pizza. I bounced Wendy in one arm, a pro at the whole breast-feeding bit (if pro meant *I suck at it,* and breastfeeding meant sticking my boob in my baby's face until she cried for a bottle).

Tala had left not twenty minutes ago, but I'd already exhausted her cooking kindness. This time, she brought only her company and some juicy gossip about Mr. Geppetto, the other neighbor that shared the condominium's third floor with us. And my work's 'mama meal train' had ended a week ago, at the same time Kai's paternity leave at the high school came to a close (AKA his accrued vacation time while a substitute took over and played Band of Brothers instead of lecturing on January's World War II unit).

I scrolled the newsfeed on my phone while *The Office* theme song blared in the background. Elsie posted a picture with her wife at our work's annual New Year's Day Do Nothing party. They clinked bubbly in thin glasses, and I ached for that familiarity. It was the first work function I'd missed in years.

Wendy squeaked in her sleep and twitched. I eased forward and descended the precious package into a Moses basket on the floor. The moment the baby touched the bed, her eyes popped open.

Oh no.

She wailed in protest.

"I was warm, Mommy!" I spoke in a pitchy baby voice and lifted her back up. She settled into the crook of my arm. She liked all my pits, armpit, elbow pit. They were where she curled up best, like a little tick. *A squishy and adorable bug sucking my lifeblood.* But a bug I would gladly die for. I sighed and started another round of zombie zoning on social media.

One of my old high school friends reposted some pictures from a photography page with dozens of babies dressed as different Disney princesses. I clicked and flicked through the images of squishy fat rolls in tiny Tiana and Aurora frills. Princesses bled into fairytales, and a little blonde baby wore a crocheted red hood while gnawing at a stuffed wolf's ear.

I quickly swiped away and clicked out of the thread. *Forget it. Forget it. Forget it.* But the thought of the service dog that had bitten Kai triggered more memories. The growling, the dream, Doctor Perrault's pointed teeth, and the gross way the lactation consultant talked about meat rolled through my head.

This is your story.

I grimaced and tried to focus on a post in one of the local mom groups I'd joined. My thumb flicked up to send the newsfeed scrolling down the comments section. A mother had asked for nanny recommendations. I selected 'read more' and scanned the list of names, curious about what I would decide for when I returned to work. Kai suggested daycare, but my hours weren't consistent enough. I couldn't follow a missing persons investigator by clocking in at 9 am or make it to cover a political rally and then home by 5 pm.

My thumb bumped the news button, and the first article caught my eye.

Runner's Body Found Half-Eaten in Pioneer Park.

I immediately tapped on the title. It was the 'eaten' part for me. This already sounded much more interesting than the last incident I had covered before Wendy made her debut diva entrance two weeks before schedule.

My eyes scanned quickly, suddenly more awake now. At only eight o'clock in the evening, I already wanted to go to bed.

Jeanne Price was out for a jog before weekly visits of caring for her grandmother on hospice. Price was found mutilated, with most of her limbs missing. Police have yet to determine the source of her injuries. Pioneer Park is partially closed to the public during an ongoing investigation. She is survived by her parents—

A howl erupted, splitting through the city's white noise. I lurched forward, but Wendy didn't wake. My phone fell from my hand and clattered against the wood floor. I slapped my palm against my chest.

"It's the TV," I said to no one. But the show depicted two characters discussing pranks in an office setting. Not exactly the setting for the howl of a beast. But neither was San Francisco unless that beast was a parking enforcement officer.

The deep sound bellowed again, causing my arms to prickle and feel sensitive, even against Wendy's plush blanket. I hugged her close and stood. After pacing the floor, I finally forced myself to the window. Would I hallucinate a wolf? The view faced out over a street full of traffic. Cars honked at one another, and someone blasted booming music.

"It's just angry drivers," I assured Wendy. She responded by peeking her eyes open for a second.

The howl burst out, closer this time. I covered my ear with one hand. *I'm the only one hearing this. Like the growling at the hospital.*

I padded to our front door and waited, listening for another call. It didn't come. I exhaled half a breath before it haunted me for the fourth time. I yanked the door open and tiptoed across the hall to Tala's door.

Another howl echoed. I banged on her door. The tighter I squeezed my fist, the easier I could convince myself it wasn't shaking. *Tell me I'm not crazy.* I rapped again, but she didn't answer.

"Tala? Are you home? Tala!" I ran back into the condo and scooped up my phone. I tapped the screen while balancing Wendy with my other arm. I flipped to recent calls and clicked the last on the list. The phone trilled while we waited for an answer, but the howling, louder now, drowned the sound. Then, a voice cut through, crisp and clear, and the howl ceased.

"Doctor Perrault. This is my work line. Is this an emergency?"

I had forgotten I called the OBGYN to ask about Wendy's 'hearing test,' but she never returned my voicemail.

My mouth didn't catch up with the situation as fast as my brain. "Kai?"

"This is Doctor Perrault."

Footsteps boomed from the hall louder than they should. I spun to see I'd left our door wide open.

Click. The line went dead. I expected to hear another howl as I hurried toward the door. If only I had as many locks as the disappearing door. *Forget about that stupid dream, Mari. There's a real story out there that needs your attention and a baby right here that needs your milk.*

The footsteps stomped closer, but I didn't peek to see who was out there. I pushed the door. Instead of latching, it smashed into something.

"Whoa! Hey, don't lock me out."

I pulled it back at the familiar voice. "Oh my goodness, Kai." I palmed my chest again.

"What'd I ever do to warrant such total rejection?" He shuffled through the doorway. Tied white plastic bags full of Styrofoam takeout weighed down both of his hands. "I brought you your favorite food, and here you are, trying to lock me out of our house."

The spicy scent of hot and sour soup helped slow my heart rate. My stomach groaned at me, angry that I'd neglected it. I recalled a children's book where a dragon ran away from the growling of his own hunger and felt positively idiotic. I'd read the book only a month or two ago to Wendy in the womb. Of course, children's books bored me quickly, and I'd slipped into reading news articles and research aloud to my protruding belly. She never seemed to mind. Any stories would quiet her kicking and rolling, which helped me sleep. Sleep was a precious luxury I'd never be able to indulge in again.

"Excuse me?" a deep voice said.

Kai and I both turned to the door. A man in a worn leather jacket, muddy work boots, and a receding hairline jogged up the hall. He waved his hand as if our apartment was an elevator and he requested us to hold the doors open for him.

"Excuse me," he said again. When he arrived at our threshold, he brought the choking scent of cigarette smoke. "Does Mari Fable live here?"

Not again. But Smokey here didn't match Redhead at all, what with his dirty clothes and stinky breath. Not a single hair split from its place on Redhead's. . . well, head.

"Hey, that's Mari Rowan to you buster." Kai thought he was funny.

"Sorry," the man said, as he shook his head, and I swore I watched dust fly out like he was the grown-up version of Charlie Brown's friend Pig-Pen. If this were a story I was reporting on, I'd pinpoint him as the nearby construction worker who had witnessed a murder. "I forgot she got married. Are you Mari?"

I angled Wendy away in case Smokey had a hidden knife in the cracked leather somewhere. Reporting didn't come without its fair share of angry people. I wouldn't call them enemies, but they might consider me one if the story had been particularly ruinous to their reputation.

"Who's asking?" I asked. I narrowed my eyes, half because of the sting of nicotine and half because I knew it was my best defensive expression.

He wiped his hand on his pants, which probably made them dirtier, then jutted one forward. "The name's Johnson. I'm a friend of your old man's."

"Is he okay?" I jumped at his words before he could finish. Mom didn't let Dad come around. I hadn't seen him since the age of six, and Mom wouldn't have it any other way.

"He's as good as can be, under the circumstances." Johnson coughed and cleared his throat. I grimaced at the low, crunchy sound of phlegm rattling around in his chest.

"Is everything all right over here?" Tala's kind eyes peered between Smokey and me, and our group of three in the doorway quickly became a crowd. Why did it always happen that way? One minute, I was alone, banging on Tala's door, and the next, everyone packed into my personal bubble.

"We're fine," Kai said. He liked our neighbor until she became too nosy for his taste. I couldn't speak to nosiness. *I'm a journalist, for goodness' sake.*

"This is my dad's friend, uh—" I paused and waited for him to fill the silence with his name.

"Johnson."

"Johnson, that's right," I said. Whether it was his first or last name, I couldn't tell.

"Is that right?" Tala echoed. She trailed her big brown eyes up and down with apparent interest. Though I knew she had a crush on our neighbor, Mr. Geppetto, Tala always enjoyed admiring rugged young men. Kai and I exchanged glances as she gave Johnson the same hungry look Mom prowled my lactation consultant with. Typical for Mom, though. "I have only known Mari for a couple of months, but we already feel like family. It is nice to meet someone from her past."

Johnson didn't share her interest. He sucked in a breath through his teeth and shoved his hands in his coat pockets. "Well, I'm just here to get in contact with Schwanna."

Mom never went by that name. Never. Not since she had gathered the strength to leave Dad. I was seven the last time I heard it.

"She wouldn't appreciate that," I said, but I didn't want to believe it. Back then, I didn't understand why she left him. Dad loved her and me so much that he quit his full-time job to spend more time with us. I believed Mom hated having less—less money and fewer clothes. But I'd grown to understand he'd suffocated her and their marriage had been a codependent, unhealthy lifestyle.

Johnson chewed on my response. His jaw shifted back and forth, either from impatience or mouth cancer.

"I wouldn't feel right giving you her number." I itched to pull Mom's contact info up on my phone and show it to him. But that was my dang journalist curiosity and not in Mom's best interest.

"All right, break!" Kai mocked the split of a football huddle. When nobody moved, he whispered to me, "I'm starving."

"Maybe come back another time," I suggested. "We're a little busy right now." I lifted Wendy to indicate our new parenthood distraction, but Johnson showed no sign of recognition.

"I expect you'll let your mother know that your pop is looking for her," he grumbled. "I'll be on my way."

"Storm is rolling in," Tala said quickly before Johnson could split. "Did you hear that thunder, Mari?"

Thunder. Of course! And here, I'd blamed the growling on my stomach.

Kai lifted a bowl of hot and sour soup to my face. He wafted the steam toward my nose with a dramatic wave of his hand.

Mom's younger self, seventeen years ago, the day we left dad, forced its way into my mind. She wore her thick wavy hair in a now-outdated side braid. The streak of white from a peculiarly placed birthmark weaved in and out through the darker strands.

He's an untrustworthy man. She had said it more to herself than me, probably assuming I didn't pay attention or couldn't hear her. Not only did I hear it, *I never forgot it.*

"Why don't you let me get you a cup of tea before going out in the rain?" Tala asked. Our neighbor cocked her head up at the man. She was too nice. She didn't even know him.

Johnson pulled a bag from his pocket, picked out a piece of dark red meat, and ripped it in half with his teeth before chewing and staring down at Tala. My overly sensitive postpartum nose (along with everything else) tickled at the scent of too much salt.

"I'll take something to wash down this jerky," he said.

"Mari. . . " Kai whispered. He poked me and pointed down at Wendy. She squirmed and stretched, breaking her tiny arms out from under the blanket. "I'm guessing we have approximately two and a half minutes to scarf down dinner before Miss Princess is going to demand hers."

I sighed. Curiosity melted into exhaustion, and hunger took over. Still, would Tala be safe with this strange man?

"We're just a knock away," I said to my neighbor, but it was Johnson who nodded. "If you need anything, Tala."

She smiled. Her sweet wrinkles curled into a reminder of her vast experience with life beyond mine. It assured me long enough to turn my attention to the Styrofoam cups of sugar and spice. But I kept my ears pricked and eyes peeled, as a good journalist should, when we closed the door.

We locked the door and settled into our spots on the couch before an array of Chinese food.

"Do you think your dad will try to get your mom back?" Kai asked between bites of shrimp chow mein.

I didn't make it past the soup and half an egg roll before my heart set fire. I'd thought heartburn was a pregnancy thing. Another good excuse to call Doctor Perrault. I only wanted to squeeze in another quick question. Maybe a woman with red hair worked as a medical professional to test babies' hearing? *Always get the full story.* It was in my blood.

"He's never stopped trying," I answered. I stretched back onto the couch after scooping Wendy from the basket at our feet. "He lost contact with us for a few years. Then, Mom dated that cop for a while, and I think it deterred him. You know you're stuck with me, right?" Dang postpartum insecurity. I planned to name this a new and official diagnosis.

He laughed, and dimples sunk into the middle of his cheeks. "Oh yeah? I thought it was 'till diapers do us part?'" He tried to smirk, but the puke-inducing stench of green newborn poop twisted his face. I swatted him with one of those burping cloths I didn't find useful but carried around anyway.

"You're only saying that because it's your turn to change her," I said.

He mocked vomiting and took Wendy from my half-dead arms. *Half-eaten. . .* I shook it off.

I needed a full night of sleep before diving into that investigation. Of course, 'full night' right now meant two hours scattered here and there between twilight feedings, squeaky cries, and leaky boobs.

Plus, I promised Kai I'd relax. But relaxation was no longer in my vocabulary. I listened to him sing his made-up diaper song from the other room and closed my eyes. The moment eyelid hit eyelid goose-bumps rolled through me. *Someone's watching me.*

I shot my eyes open and looked around. Nobody was there. Of course. But I couldn't settle back down. A shiver stole through me, and I snatched Wendy's tiny blanket to wrap it around my shoulders like a cape as I stood. The rain started but was not heavy enough to hear from inside.

The window behind the couch overlooked the street, where droplets splashed against the cement and washed the city's usual dirt and grime away. The streetlamp was dim and in desperate need of a replacement bulb.

I tiptoed to the front door to check on Tala through the peephole. Empty. My shoulders slumped in a forced effort of relief. I didn't have the time or energy to be creeped out. I secured the door's lock and couldn't resist peeking one more time through the peephole.

My heart jumped into my throat, but I forced myself to brush it off and get some sleep. Still, *I know what I saw.* Two yellow crescents stared from the other side of the glass. Again, the redheaded woman's words struck me. Could this be the villain she spoke of, or was that simply the rambling of an insane person?

Chapter 5

Between a Stalker and a Hard Case

It took me a month to forget those eyes. But after many sleepless nights with a fussy baby, I focused on life as a mom since nothing else strange occurred.

Wendy kicked and batted her arms about like a little boxer ready to take out Rocky in the big ring. I perched over her, one foot on the coffee table and the other on the arm of the couch because, apparently, five hours of sleep turned me into a parkour genius. I angled my phone to catch just the right section of daylight streaming in from the window and beaming across Wendy's little onesie.

A smile! Her tiny face burst into a toothless grin, and I went to tap the circle on my screen, but nothing flashed.

"What the heck?" I kept tapping while twisting my face and crossing my eyes, hoping her smile would return. Though, I knew it had more to do with a string of baby farts rather than actual joy or entertainment. "Come on, she probably made a poopsplosion for that smile, and I missed it!" Stupid phone.

"Mari?" the phone said.

I dropped it, just missing poor Wendy's leg, and hopped down from my perch where I landed in what Kai and I called the 'superhero pose' with one knee down and my hand balancing me.

"Do I need to call an ambulance? It sounds like a car just crashed," the phone spoke again.

"Elsie?" I said, as I grabbed my phone and realized I'd answered an incoming call rather than taking the picture I spent all afternoon trying to get. "What's up? I'm not supposed to be back at work for another two weeks. Please tell me you're arranging another meal train. I'm sick of takeout and Uncrustables."

"Nothing like that, I'm afraid," Elsie said with a squeal that I knew meant she had gossip. But it was her drama that had guilted everyone at the office into cooking homemade meals for me, so I appreciated her intensity. Plus, I didn't need anything more serious than Wendy's cries right now, so I welcomed Elsie's call and hoped for some juicy gossip. "It's bad."

"You're scaring me. Am I losing my job to Jameson?" I scooped Wendy into one arm and pinched my phone between my ear and my shoulder while I bounced her around. She screamed louder, and I couldn't blame her. I wasn't a fan of being a kangaroo when I was hungry, either. But I kept on bouncing, hoping it would somehow soothe her.

"Quite the opposite," Elsie said. "Pam wants you down here ASAP to cover these crazy zombie stories. She's already asked me three times today how many weeks it is until you return."

"Zombie stories?" I asked, as I carried Wendy to the window where I watched a car attempt to parallel park. The young guy in the driver's seat pulled forward and back, forward and back, forward and—*oof!* Up he went on the curb and smacked his bumper right into the meter.

"Yeah, haven't you been following the local events? Baby or not, I know you can't stay away from the truth for too long."

I snorted in agreement. She wasn't wrong. The blasting bright light on my phone helped keep me awake most nights to make sure I didn't drop Wendy. Each night, I'd scroll through news articles while attempting to breastfeed. Eventually, I'd give up and wander into the kitchen like *I* was the zombie where I'd mix formula into a bottle. I had read all the stories, except for last night, since Wendy slept for five hours in a row.

"Two young women have been found dead and torn to shreds, right over in your neck of the woods."

"Gross," I said, but I secretly wanted to know all the gory details. This was why Pam assigned me to those cases. I had a stomach of steel and wasn't afraid of the nitty-gritty to get the truth of a story. Last year, when a woman had been accused of poisoning her own daughter-in-law, Pam had pulled all the strings to send me up north and get the scoop on a girl whose dead body was hidden in plain sight. The victim had been found in a glass case at a museum where her mother-in-law worked as a curator. I never even flinched when I interviewed the crazy woman and she straight-up admitted she wanted to murder the young woman for being prettier than her.

"Here's the thing," Elsie lowered her voice, and I wondered if Jameson was milling around outside her cubicle. He'd do that when he hoped to grab some info that he did zero research on himself but planned to claim as his own. "At both murder sights, someone has left the same message. They're not publishing this in any of the public accounts because the investigators don't know what it means."

"What's the message?" I asked. Wendy finally soothed when I popped a boob out. I jumped back from the window when I realized I was flashing someone on the street. The guy who'd crashed his car offered me a thumbs up on the boob front, and I groaned.

"Fable's story," Elsie said.

"Wait, what?"

"The message says 'Fable's story,'" Elsie repeated.

My jaw dropped, and I tightened my hold on Wendy so she didn't follow suit. *This is your story.* It had to be a coincidence. My name wasn't even Fable anymore. And what did I have to do with a bunch of random killings?

"It's written over and over. With the first murder, someone scribbled the victim's blood all across the concrete in the park. And in the second, there were pieces of torn paper with the same words everywhere like doggone confetti." Our boss didn't enjoy cursing, so Elsie and I had come up with a few fun decoy words for the office.

"You know this has nothing to do with me, right?" I dropped to the couch where I could switch the phone to my other ear and prop Wendy on a nursing pillow. "It's all crazy happenstance." *I hope.*

"Tell that to Pam. You know she's superstitious as all hell—" Elsie coughed. "Heck, I said heck. Jameson shut up!" Her voice was muffled, as the phone must have moved away from her mouth, and I was grateful she didn't shout that in my ear. She sighed and spoke into the phone again. "Jameson is especially rude to me with you gone. He despises the fact that Pam wants you to return soon and doesn't trust him to cover things on his own."

I sighed. "He's always like that when she assigns me to something."

"Well, this is exactly the type of story you usually cover," she said. "None of us want to get close to interviewing people who might be involved in *eating* other people."

I frowned. My stomach garbled and whined like I had gas to match Wendy's. Of course, all the fried foods didn't help. What else was a mom to do with a child sucking the life right out of her and the only places open in the middle of the night being Taco Bell and Carl's Jr.?

"It's like they're targeting you, Mar."

Wendy's angelic face made this threat that much worse. I needed to return to work, right now, and solve this. But I was pretty sure my heart would crack open and a little alien would burst out screaming, 'Your baby misses you, your baby misses you.'

"Oh my goodness!" I said, as Wendy snuggled into me.

"I know, it's scary, just take it all in—"

"No." I laughed and bit my lip before bursting into an old high school cheer chant and disturbing the perfection that lay in my lap. "Wendy latched! I did it. She's actually nursing." Tears sprang to my eyes, and I felt like a teen watching *Gilmore Girls* for the first time with the most embarrassing expression of joy—happy crying.

"I don't mean to downplay your boob's success over there, but did you already forget that there's a murderer on the loose in your neighborhood who's leaving messages with your maiden name on them?"

"Ebenezer Scrooge." I used my favorite curse. "Can't you let a girl celebrate for a second?"

"I'm at the office, you're not. You don't have to censor yourself."

"I'm holding six pounds of pure angel, maybe I *want* to censor myself." I didn't, but bantering with Elsie kept me on my toes. We were technically competitors, always vying for the best stories and wanting the good juice that could win us a Pulitzer someday.

Beep. The line ticked between us, and I peeled my phone off my cheek to see Kai's name flashing on the screen.

"I've got to go, Kai's calling. But I'll look into returning early to dive into those murders."

"I'm not voting for you to end your special bonding time early. Olivia would have my head if I encouraged you to do anything like that. I honestly believe you're the best journalist here, Mar, and this is something you might need to get to the bottom of."

"Thanks, Elsie. Say hi to Olivia for me."

"Will do," she said.

I clicked over to Kai, who popped up with an unexpected video call. I missed his scruffy beard since he'd returned to teaching and he shaved his skin baby-smooth again.

"There's my queen," he said.

"What bad news do you have for me?" I smirked, knowing Kai better than he knew himself. The queen line only came out when I wore thigh-high tights or he needed to tell me something I wouldn't like. And I definitely wasn't trading my mom sweats for thigh-high tights any time soon.

Kai sighed and scrubbed his hand over his face. "I totally forgot about the parent-teacher meetings tonight. I'm sorry. I know I promised to go grocery shopping and that I'd cook up some of my famous garlic bread."

"I've been craving it." I pouted.

"You'll have to order from the Cheesecake Factory and enjoy life without me. I'll be drowning in parent complaints about how it is entirely my fault that their hormonal teens are more into each other than reading the unit on the judicial system."

I nodded and pursed my lips. "I've got some weird work junk

going on too. I'll tell you all about it when you inevitably wake me when you come in tonight."

"Love you," Kai said with a chuckle.

"Yeah, I know." I responded with our usual nerd quote, as per our wedding vows. After we hung up, I threw my head back to rest against the sofa cushions and stared at the ceiling.

I needed to make sense of the story. Whenever I didn't have all the answers to write a clear report, I'd gather whatever information I had and write it on sticky notes. Then, I'd arrange and rearrange the notes like a puzzle until the story came together and an idea sparked.

Fable's story.

Dead girls in my neighborhood.

The feeling of someone watching me.

Yellow eyes?

The weird lady at the hospital.

Doctor Perrault's fangs.

And the growling. . .

My imaginary sticky notes on the ceiling didn't help this time. I needed a real pen and paper, but I didn't dare move Wendy during our first successful breastfeeding sesh. Doctor Greasy Lactation Guy would be so proud.

Before I knew it, dreamland took both Wendy and me on Mr. Toad's Wild Ride where I was suddenly too cold, then too hot, and then the doorbell was ringing. I sat up with a start, but not because of an epiphany, or even because of Wendy's sudden bite on my most sensitive body part.

Wendy stirred when I woke, and I shifted her to the Moses basket. My legs almost buckled underneath me, and I swore to get into mommy yoga before *all* my muscles atrophied and the psychopath who might be coming after me wouldn't even have a fun chase.

I swung the door open to see a dude with a cheesy grin and white plastic bags that said *Cheesecake Factory* in colorful letters.

"Order for Mari," he said.

"I didn't. . ." *Did I?* Nope, I definitely fell asleep with my chest out and. . . *Yup, it's still out.* I cringed and yanked my shirt back up, after inadvertently flashing a stranger for the second time in one day.

"I prefer banana cheesecake, personally," the guy said, as he snickered and his pale face colored the same as my strawberry dessert. I'd thought eggplant was the universal signal for inappropriateness, but apparently, this dude wanted his joke to be cheesecake-correct. "Of course, I'm lactose intolerant, so I can't eat cheesecake in real life."

Growling drowned out the guy's rambling, and my eyes nearly popped out of my head. The delivery dude didn't even seem to notice. Did he keep talking about food and. . . robots? I tuned back in.

"So yeah, I know this job isn't exactly like working at the Pentagon, but it might surprise you how many smart people are delivery drivers with side projects—"

"Shh!" I snapped. His head sunk back into his neck until it looked like he didn't have a chin. "Do you hear that?"

Delivery Dude glanced around, then leaned in. "Do you mean your baby crying?"

"Crap!" I spun around and rushed to crouch over Wendy's basket. I scooped her up and started swaying side-to-side.

"I'll, uh, just set this right here," he said. He'd stepped into my living room and placed the cheesecake bag on our coffee table. "Hey, you're a journalist?" He picked up a magazine off the table where it showed a small portrait of me beside an article I'd written about staying safe in the city as a woman. "I've got a story for you. Can I tell you about it?"

It wasn't the first time someone had asked me to shine a spotlight on their life story, and it wouldn't be the last. But the request rarely came from a stranger standing in my living room. Could he be the person writing my maiden name near the murder victims in my neighborhood? A stalker of some sort? I glanced around for something sharp, some object to impale the psycho with in case he planned to rip me to shreds and eat me. I owned a gun, but I kept it locked in a safe. Thankfully, Delivery Dude only assaulted me with his words and body odor.

"So yeah, I'm building the first conscientious mechanical person.

It's technically a robot, but I prefer the term 'mechanical person' because the real story is how many similarities I've found in my MP to me. It's wild, like, man, I'm wondering if they programmed me somehow. Big Brother maybe—"

"Thank you for bringing my food in," I interrupted before his conspiracy theories sounded interesting to me. There wasn't a story I didn't want to tell, but my time was limited, and I had to pick the most important ones. Right now, targeted murders took precedence over robot boy. "I don't have any cash for a tip, but if you want to take my business card, I'll think about writing your story." I snatched a card from my jacket pocket hanging on the coat rack as I ushered him out the door.

"I already got your tip on the app," he said, as he made his way to the door, still rambling. Outside, he turned to me with an enormous smile. "You could call the article *The Pinocchio Project*." He splayed his arms out as if presenting a banner.

"Perfect, call me," I said. I went to shut the door before he could convince me, but my arm froze.

"Carlo!" A woman with hair so red I could have sworn she was cosplaying Poison Ivy walked up the condo steps. The hood of a familiar crimson cloak peeked out from under her button-up peacoat, and I knew it was Redhead—the same woman from the hospital. When she saw me, she froze for a moment. "Carlo, let's go," she demanded, as she spun around and nearly ran back down the steps.

Delivery Dude Carlo followed obediently. When I closed the door, my back fell against it as I took it all in. I latched the lock and shoved off the door. Balancing Wendy in one hand, I tore out a pad of sticky notes from the drawer on the coffee table and started scribbling the imagined notes from earlier.

I stuck them against the Cherrywood tabletop, arranging them in a circle around the most important one.

Redhead could be my stalker. But was that synonymous with murder? And was 'Fable's story' enough to link me to the killer? The redheaded woman's mention of a villain still nagged at me. Had she been trying to draw attention away from herself after kidnapping four babies in the hospital?

The look of determination and fear in her eyes that day stuck with me. She didn't look like the other killers I'd interviewed. But I couldn't deny the facts. I dropped my head in my hands and peered through my fingers at the notes on the sticky papers.

Redhead called me Fable.

The murderer's message used the same name.

But if she was the villain she'd mentioned, why'd she bring me to Wendy and tell me to run?

Chapter 6

A Dime a Dozen in the Living Room

The first time I changed out of sweats and into yoga pants, I cried. The second time, I went to mommy-and-me yoga where I planked over Wendy with plastic keys in my mouth while the other women did push-ups with their older babies sitting on their backs. The third time I pulled on the tight pants, I planned to solve a murder. Well, three murders actually, two involving poor young women and one regarding whatever I'd done to my nipples with the breast pump.

Tala didn't appreciate the comparison when I told her my boobs were about as bloody as the crime scenes, but it didn't stop her from listening to the juicy details I'd learned after hours of research. What else was I going to do at three in the morning when Wendy took her sweet time enjoying a late-night meal?

After Tala agreed to hold Wendy for me, I headed for the bedroom to get a sweater. I spun around in front of the mirror that hung on the door in our bedroom, checking to see if my granny panties were obvious under the thin black fabric of my yoga pants. They were, but I decided I didn't care. I'd thrown on one of my maternity tops that doubled as a button-down so I looked at least halfway professional. If people only saw me from the waist-up, that is. Satisfied, I pulled on the sweater and returned to the living room.

"Is it safe for you to be out running around when someone is stalking you?" Tala asked. She bounced Wendy in her lap. Foamy spit bubbled around Wendy's mouth as she looked up at the older woman's face.

"It wouldn't be the first time my job wasn't safe."

"Yes, but you're a mama now. You can't risk leaving this little one without a parent." Tala gave me her best 'listen to me because I'm more experienced than you' face. If she were under sixty, I'd consider her a mean girl, but I knew she only wanted to help.

"And being a sitting duck would be safer?" I shook my head and sat on the sofa with an armful of cups and tubes and other pumping paraphernalia. "Now, unless you're prepared to watch me cry while my body fails to do its job and fill up these bottles, I recommend you hand over the baby and get out while you still can."

Tala obliged, setting Wendy in my lap, then shuffling for the door. She moved slowly and with a slight limp because of bad hips and less-than-sharp eyesight. Though we looked nothing alike, with her all pale, once a blushing blonde, and me the exact opposite, I forgot she wasn't my real grandmother. But I'd never met my real grandmother since Mom's parents died when she was young, and Dad wasn't in our lives. So, Tala filled the role easily.

After a month and a half of momming, I'd learned how to balance a baby in one arm, attach the breast pump, and scroll on my phone all at the same time. I flicked through my calendar and a list of 'to dos.'

Meet with the lactation consultant.

Learn how to use the baby sling.

Interview the victims' families.

Visit the crime scene.

A knock on the door indicated the lactation consultant had arrived right on time.

"Come in," I shouted since I left it unlocked after Tala went home.

"Hello there," Mr. Grease, or Edward Banks, M.D., to use his official name, said. "Ah, yes, pumping. That is an excellent way to stimulate milk production." He stepped inside and set a briefcase down on the coffee table.

"Thank you so much for meeting me," I said. "Do you usually do home calls in business suits?" I couldn't help it with the questions. It was in my nature as a journalist.

Edward smoothed down his coat jacket and blushed. "I felt the need to look my best today." He wouldn't meet my gaze. I raised my eyebrows.

"So, I just need to make sure I'm able to pump enough to provide her with breakfast, lunch, and dinner while I'm at work," I explained, as I eyed the briefcase. He unclipped the latches and pulled it open to reveal an array of pumping supplies, lactation supplements, milk bags, and basically nothing you'd ever expect to see inside a business suitcase.

"First things first, have you been hand-expressing?" Edward asked, as he pulled a foam breast from the briefcase and started showing me how to milk myself like a cow.

The door swung open and interrupted the uncomfortable one-man show. Kai tossed his jacket over the top of the coat rack and kicked off the newly acquired dad sneakers that had earned him endless teasing from his high school students.

"Whoa! If I'd heard there were fake boobs here, I'd have expected your mother." He laughed as he came around the coffee table and lifted Wendy from my full hands.

Edward perked up, adjusting his slouched posture with a pin-straight spine. He glanced around the apartment as if looking for someone. "Oh heavens, is Mrs. Fable present?" His prominent cheekbones flushed a shade of pink I'd have killed to find in lipstick. If I ever got around to wearing makeup again, that is.

"I hope not," Kai said, as he knelt in front of the couch and rolled Wendy in a red blanket. The little bundle of baby reminded me of a burrito. My stomach groaned. It seemed an easier feat to track and hunt my murderous stalker than eat enough while breastfeeding. I was ravenous.

"Curious, but are you not a fan of Mrs. Fable?" Edward asked, blinking too rapidly at Kai. I glanced between them and furrowed my brow. He was here to talk about my milk supply, not my mother.

"Who, me?" Kai pointed to himself, as he flipped the free edge of the blanket on top of Wendy's head like a tiny red hood. "Sure, I'm a fan, but that's not what I meant." He shifted his eyes to me and spoke out of the side of his mouth. "I passed your father's friend on the way up. I think he's stalking you."

"He can join the club," I said, as I popped the suction of the pump off my skin. Distant growling filled the silence between us. The hair on my arm raised, and I widened my eyes at Edward, trying to find fur or fangs or who knew what. *Okay, so I'm still crazy. Clearly, nobody else heard that.*

My stomach twinged, and I shot a look at my husband that caused him to scoot away from me on the couch.

"Hungry, hun?" He laughed nervously.

It was my starvation the whole time. My stomach groaned again. I hopped to my feet and pointed between the men and Wendy. "Does anyone want a sandwich? I'm going to make a sandwich or four. Let me know if I should add a fifth to that list."

"Since you're offering, I'll take a PB&J." Edward smiled as he picked up one of the half-empty pumping bottles and swirled the milk around. His eyes nearly crossed as he examined it like a science experiment, or maybe a magic potion. It *was* magical that the milk came from me. Well, it would be if I could nail this whole breastfeeding thing.

"Okay, four turkeys on rye it is." I smiled. "I'll add jelly to the grocery list."

Edward didn't indicate that he heard me. He flicked on the breast pump and put it up to his ear as if it could whisper the secrets of success to him. And I hoped it would because then he'd translate those secrets to me and I'd achieve my lifelong dream of being in two places at once—my milk at home with Wendy, and me on the streets hunting a story before the story hunted me.

I slapped a mustard-lined knife against the spongy bread and dragged it around in swirls. The spicy smell only made me hungrier. I munched a slice of turkey, too impatient to complete the sandwich before devouring the pieces. The doorbell chimed, and I called for Kai to answer it. Hopefully, my new planner and notebooks had arrived and my stationary-loving little heart could revel in all the organization. Though I had my back turned to the living room, I heard the conversation picking up. Either Wendy had suddenly and miraculously learned to talk, or a woman had joined our little living room meeting.

I plopped the sandwiches on plates and spun around. My old restaurant serving skills came in handy as I balanced three paper plates and shuffled into the living room. Our intimate gathering of family plus lactation consultant had quickly turned into a crowd in the span of my sandwich-making time.

Johnson, Tala, Edward, Kai, and Wendy all spoke at once in the middle of my living room. Wendy's conversation was more grunting than words, and likely came with a dirty diaper, but I listened most carefully to her. After plopping the paper plates down, I hurried to the front door where Kai still held the door open. I scooped her out of his arms and started comfort-bouncing more for myself than for her.

"I didn't know we were hosting lunch," I mumbled to Wendy to calm my nerves. They say that visitors often inundate new mothers. Usually, these visitors included extended family and overbearing friends. My visitors, however, were a random mishmash of people with half the group in search of my mother (Edward didn't hide his interest in *Mrs. Fable* as well as he might have thought).

Kai shot me a desperate look of pinched-up eyebrows and a healthy dose of fear in his green irises. I shrugged, trying to stay as calm as possible before my introverted brain exploded.

"Your father wants to meet his granddaughter," Johnson said.

"Mari needs rest and recovery right now, not unwelcome arrivals," Tala scolded him.

"Father?" Edward turned around and joined the conversation. "Is this Mrs. Fable's previous—" he cleared his throat and looked between each of us "—husband?"

"Now I wish I didn't have that minimum day at the school today," Kai muttered, as he dropped his forehead against the open door. Tala started to speak again, scolding Johnson for worrying a busy mother, though her voice was soft and I suspected she wanted to invite the gruff man over for tea again.

"Let's leave them be," our neighbor said.

But Johnson did the opposite. He stepped up to me and brought the smell of smoke with him.

"May I have a word?" he asked.

"Are you Mr. Fable?" Edward interjected, nosier even than Tala.

Johnson only shot the lactation consultant an irritated look.

In his momentary distraction, I whirled Wendy and I back to the coffee table where I snatched a sandwich and stuffed my mouth full before I could release a string of curses upon the room.

It was all too much. With only one item checked off on my to-do list, it almost broke my organizer's brain to skip ahead. But the front door called to me. I could slip out behind everybody, learn how to use the baby sling on the go, and find solace in a meeting with the victims' families where I'd ask about motives and study bloody crime scene photos. That sounded like heaven. I sighed, squirreling away in my mind's eye to the soothing picture of myself on the job.

Johnson stepped up to me. His dirty boots left footprints on our beige shag rug. "You're going to want to meet with your father. He has something he needs to give to—" he tilted his chin toward Wendy. "It is of dire importance."

"Is it?" I nodded and pursed my lips. What could my deadbeat dad possibly have for our baby? I shook my head. My dad's wishes didn't take precedence over returning to work, solving this stalker fiasco, and getting Wendy the best food possible, whether that meant milk from mama cow herself or Target's most expensive formula (AKA whatever they had in stock).

Tala pointed an accusatory finger at Johnson, taking a personal interest in his presence, Edward raised one finger and stuttered something about which sandwich was his, and I bounced Wendy more and more until I realized it was soothing neither of us and resorted to tapping my foot aggressively.

And in all the chaos, another skinny little body squeezed in through our open door.

"Mom?" My jaw dropped. "I thought you were in Mexico finding your inner peace."

Mom's half-frozen face revealed another round of Botox. She managed a sideways smile and flicked her newly bleached hair behind her shoulder. "Still haven't found it, but I couldn't stay away from my granddaughter for too long." Her dark eyes sparkled as she cooed at Wendy.

"Mrs. Fable?" Edward turned around in his prim, stiff-necked fashion.

Johnson inserted his body into our personal family bubble and glared down at her. "You have abandoned your duty to your people," he growled.

Say what?

Mom crossed her arms, arched an eyebrow, and didn't even flinch at the smell coming from her ex-husband's creepy friend. I needed to know what his comment meant and why his presence didn't even phase my mother when she spent years running from Dad. But that was a story I'd have to research another time. My chest tightened, and no matter how quickly I breathed, I couldn't get enough oxygen in my lungs.

"I've got to get out of here," I whispered to Kai, and he nodded. My perfect opposite, extrovert to my introversion, and silly guy to my bitter sarcasm.

"Thank you, love you."

"I know." He beamed, proud of himself for saving a damsel in distress. Two, if you count the fussy child in my arms. "Let me take Wendy so you can have some me time."

"You're sweet, but no." I shook my head and pecked him on the cheek. "I'm trying to nail this whole nursing thing, and if she gets hungry, I don't want my mom to give her a bottle. Wendy needs to stay with me."

Kai nodded and gave Wendy a kiss on the head before he turned to the crowd in our living room and clapped his hands. "Okay, who wants a soda?"

I snatched the baby sling from the coat rack and slipped out the door behind an arguing Johnson and Mom, while Edward watched with a fake boob in his hand and Kai offered Tala one of my sandwiches.

After a quick walk to clear my head, I'd return ready to face the drama. Maybe Mom would care to explain a few things, and I'd be able to convince Tala to cook another lasagna casserole for my insatiable breastfeeding hunger.

My slip-on shoes slapped against the concrete steps. Wendy liked the rhythmic bounce of walking down the condo staircase and fussed again when we reached the boring, flat sidewalk. I flipped the dangling corner of the blanket over her forehead to keep the chill of the breeze off her face as we headed to Pioneer Park.

A glimpse at the crime scene would help during the interview I'd scheduled with the last victim's boyfriend that evening. I'd known the exact location inside the park and planned to question if the route was a routine for the girl.

After two blocks and a lot of gymnastics, I secured Wendy into the sling. Her face smashed against my chest, but she quickly quieted and looked up at me with big, dark eyes. *Okay, half-check on the to-do list's second item.*

I rounded the corner into the park. A playground greeted me, but the mid-afternoon left it empty since most children were still in school. To the right, running trails broke off in three different directions. I chose the middle, knowing it was the longest and most secluded, where it made sense for a murder to occur.

I huffed and puffed but found no yellow crime scene tape. Another twenty minutes of walking sent me turning around to head to the second running trail. The cool afternoon wind knocked the blanket off Wendy's head as we walked down the trail. A little bridge connected the two trails. I peered down at the babbling brook as I crossed over, and red caught my eye.

My eyes trailed from the stain on the rock below to the shadow. A shadow in the shape of a woman.

I swallowed and floated my palm over Wendy's eyes as if she could even see or understand the twisted scene before us. A scene yet investigated or even discovered, except by us.

A body lay sprawled in the bushes by the stream. Water flowed over her legs, carrying dark blood with it. Her knees looked backward and bite marks covered her bare arms. And right there across her forehead was an array of illegible scribbles written in blood.

Chapter 7

The Fable is in the Details

What if the murderer didn't want to attack me? What if the mess of words didn't say my maiden name? I could make out an *F* and half the word 'story,' but that proved nothing. And maybe if the murderer was sending me a message, it was because they liked my style of journalism and sought to entice me to write about *their* style of killing. As a reporter, I looked at the story from every angle, and the angle where I didn't get murdered in the park was my favorite.

Kai arrived first, bringing with him a fresh bottle of mixed formula (AKA my nemesis and ultimate sign of failure). He seethed when he saw the dead woman, and I only nodded in agreement.

"I can't believe you have to look at this stuff all the time." He glanced away, eyes wide.

"I can't believe you have to talk to teenagers every day." I laughed. "Besides, I cover more than murders."

Kai raised an eyebrow that spoke for itself, saying, *you make me watch true crime documentaries every night*. He wasn't wrong.

"Okay, they're mostly murders," I said. I handed Wendy to him while I readjusted the baby sling, tightening it around my back so that it didn't dig into my neck. Then, I tucked her back inside the wrap of fabric and wielded the bottle with one hand while balancing the other on the corner of the bridge.

"You could at least let me take her," Kai said, as he took my hand and helped me climb down the rocks beside the bridge. I double-checked the stability of each one since Wendy was along for the ride. Once I confirmed the rock wouldn't tip, I shifted my full body weight down to it and repeated the process until I'd almost reached the stream.

I shook my head. "I have to learn how to multitask someday. I'm a mom now, but that won't stop me from going after that Pulitzer."

"It's exciting to see you in action." Kai peered over the edge of the bridge, eyeing the body with obvious trepidation.

Scratches covered the woman's face and mutilated whoever she once was with a mask of blood. Something had chomped half of her left hand clean off. I reflexively stretched my fingers to ensure they still existed.

"So, what are you looking for?" Kai asked.

I glanced up to see my husband resting his elbows on the bridge, chin in hands like a little girl gossiping at a sleepover. Pure pride beamed in his eyes as he watched me at work. I felt the same way when I'd pop over to the high school to drop off a book or a stack of graded tests he'd forgotten at home. Listening to his lecture about the Cold War may as well have been boudoir photography. It was his passion that did it for me, and I suspected the same for him as he observed my interest in the crime scene.

"I'm finding the story," I said. It was my usual answer, but something about it didn't feel right this time, not with that same word, *story*, tattooed on the victim's face in her own blood. "The families get to know the details from the police. But the rest of us have to live in darkness, wondering what led to this woman's demise."

"And as a woman in a big city yourself, you need to know the nitty-gritty in order to stay safe," Kai finished my famous line for me. He'd heard it a hundred times over, but he still quoted it with admiration. I'd told him the same explanation on our first date years ago. After that, he'd said, it was history. *It* being our love life, and *history* being the love of his life.

"That's right," I said, as I smiled and took a long step over the stream. But my other foot didn't want to follow. I stood stuck over the flowing water, legs bridging the gap and one hand still propping Wendy's bottle up at a particular angle that reduced the risk of air bubbles, and later, gas cries. I yanked, but my foot wouldn't budge from the muck. "Crap."

After another forceful pull, I freed myself with too much force and went tumbling forward toward the body. I twisted Wendy away from it and bashed my elbow against a rock as I landed on my side.

Kai had already scrambled halfway down the bank when I waved him off. "I'm fine. Just a few bruises."

"Do you really have to do this right now?" he asked.

I pushed off the rock and wiped the leaves and dirt from my legs and arm. Except the brown on my sleeve didn't clean off so easily. I grimaced as I realized the stain came from the victim's body. I'd bumped into the place where her fingers should have been.

"It's a rare opportunity that I get to see the scene before the police get here and move everything around. Their job is to find the murderer, effectively ending *these* murders. But my job is to get answers that will inform the public how to best keep themselves safe from the inevitable threat of future attacks."

"Right, you're the keeper of the stories." Kai waved his hand in a big arc over his head.

Sirens finally rang in the distance. If it took this long for the cops to respond to a reported dead body, how much had changed in the other crime scenes before they arrived? What did they miss?

Wendy emptied the bottle, and I tucked it into my back pocket. With one hand now free, I used it to cup her and support the weight of the awkwardly placed sling. Maybe I'd learn how to use that someday too.

"Tell me again what's so important about this Pulitzer?"

"It's not." I shrugged, and the sling dug deeper into my neck. I ignored it and crouched beside the victim. A small, triangular object protruded from her eyebrow. At first glance, it appeared to be a killer bone piercing. "I don't care about the prize itself, it's just knowing that my work has helped someone."

"Uh-huh, and the gold medal and fame, and—" Kai exhaled extra loud, mocking the sound of a large crowd cheering in the distance, "has nothing to do with it?"

My mother's face flashed in my mind. *Never walk alone, Mari. And if you see something, tell everyone.* Her words stuck with me all these years. Mom never claimed to be brave, but something about that phrase, and the way she had rubbed the space between her neck and shoulders with both hands, told me she'd survived something. And whatever she survived didn't have to happen in the first place, if only someone had warned her. At least that's the story I put together. It was my first story and my worst, considering I didn't secure any facts, details, or statements.

"I wouldn't hate having a gold medal hanging over our fireplace," I said, as I shrugged off the memory and pulled my phone out of my jeans. Footsteps approached, and I heard Kai greet the officers' arrivals. I quickly snapped a picture of the strange object, the scribbles on the victim's forehead, and the bite on her hand.

"Well, if it isn't Mari Rowan."

I spun around, my feet sinking deeper into the mud. Detective Wilhelm clucked his tongue at me and crossed his arms, which he only did to draw attention to his unnecessarily large forearms that didn't fit in his too-small leather jacket. He didn't bother getting close to the victim, or even looking at her at all. His lackeys would do that work. He didn't care about what led to the crime, how it happened, or even why, he only cared about getting the killer off the street as fast as possible. And his track record was nothing to sneeze at. I appreciated his work, but hated the way he approached it.

"Mucking up my crime scene?" he asked.

I frowned and resisted the urge to glance at the mud covering my shoes and the bottom of my pants. He might have been right this time. *This time.* Plus, something about this attack prickled me more than any other murder had. And I'd interviewed deranged serial killers. Still, this unsettled me the same way *The Ugly Duckling* case had with a sick twisting in my stomach and butterflies in my chest.

The redheaded woman's statement came to mind. *A very old story is coming true. The Ugly Duckling* was an old story. All of the little board books Tala had given Wendy were old stories. And here, the word *story* haunted me again, right on the victim's body. But could these murders really be related to that strange woman's words?

"Just gathering info," I said. The medical examiner and a couple of uniformed officers climbed down the rocks and surrounded the body, effectively pushing me out of the circle.

"Look here, Rowan," Wilhelm said. He gnawed on an indiscriminate object, then spit it on the bridge, narrowly missing Kai's feet. Kai jumped away from it. He arched his eyebrow and tossed his thumb at the detective while mouthing 'what's with him.' "I've got a murderer to catch, and you've got a baby to feed. So, how about you watch us work from a distance while you gather some quotes for your little stories?"

"I have every right to be here." I stood my ground.

My phone buzzed, and I pulled it out to peek at the message from Kai.

I like long romantic walks away from dead bodies and jerk-hole detectives. Wanna join? Blink if your answer is yes.

I smirked and glanced up at my husband. I shook my head, and he shrugged. He knew better than to interfere with Wilhelm's drama. I'd spent hours after many investigations complaining about the misogynistic detective. If Kai jumped to my defense, it'd only confirm Wilhelm's attitude toward female investigators.

After giving my statement to a uniformed officer, I traded Wendy for Kai's jacket. I tugged the too-big coat over my sweater to block the breeze as the investigation took us into the evening.

I missed my pen and notebooks, but secured a good pile of notes on my phone. Kai took Wendy home with a promise to dish on all the details about the little party with Johnson, my mom, my lactation consultant, and our neighbor when I got home. I'd normally never cancel or reschedule an interview, but the last victim's boyfriend was going to have to wait since I had a warm body right in front of me.

Rubberneckers gathered on the edge of the crime scene. People took their city dogs out for evening walks around the park and found themselves entranced by the crowd of cops and a body bag. Some looked on with horror like Kai did, while others watched in curiosity. Their innocent faces motivated me to push for the story. Who would be next? The old woman with the kind face clutching her poodle to her chest? The young woman out for a nightly jog?

Or me?

"Mari." Wilhelm coughed. "Isn't this your old name? From when you wrote articles under a pen name or whatever you creative types like to hide behind?"

I swallowed and finally forced myself to acknowledge what I didn't want to see. The illegible words weren't as poorly written as I wanted to believe. But why in the ever-loving world would a murderer target me?

"Right there." Wilhelm pointed his stubby finger at the victim's forehead before the medical examiner pulled the zipper over her face.

I sucked in a sharp breath and nodded. "Yeah, that's my maiden name."

"Well, if that ain't an odd coincidence." The detective shook his head and spat something on the ground again.

I sighed, not wanting to talk with him about it any longer. I needed information; I needed interviews and motives and details about these victims. But I'd never seen this woman before, and none of the other victims had any connection to me.

Still, a shiver trickled up my neck. Despite my layers, the cold wind cut through the fabric and chilled my arms and chest. By the time the sun went down, they'd cleaned the crime scene, and the crew wrapped up. My stomach screamed at me. It protested its empty state while my boobs did the opposite, aching and overfilled with the milk I should be pumping.

"You watch yourself," Wilhelm said. He nodded to me as he walked away, following the rest of his crew. I half-smiled in acknowledgment, but his warning set me on edge. Wilhelm was the last person I ever expected to suggest I stay safe. And since he did, it meant he entertained the idea that the killer could have a connection to me.

Pioneer Park fell silent, and I quickly found myself in a place as empty as my angry stomach.

I pulled Kai's jacket tighter across my chest and headed for the entrance. I didn't look back at the crime scene, not even when I heard the growling. My feet went from shuffling to speed-walking to a full-on sprint at the low, grumbling sound. I emerged, heart pounding, onto the well-lit sidewalk. I should have had a moment to breathe, but the busy street didn't ease my fears because I heard what nobody else did.

Howling echoed down the sidewalk and bounced off of the tall buildings. But none of the passersby indicated they noticed. I pushed past a laughing couple taking a Friday night stroll and ran for my building at full speed. The howling grew louder.

I'd lost my mind, and the worst part was, it isolated me in this werewolf-induced nightmare.

Never walk alone, Mari.

Chapter 8

A Method to Mom's Madness

There were only two things I wanted in life: to breastfeed my baby successfully and to find a conclusion to the *Howl Murders*, as I'd nicknamed them in my brain. Preferably, the end of this story would be a happy one where I didn't get ripped apart by a cannibalistic serial killer whose motive I never identified.

Wendy wailed from her bassinet beside our bed. I rolled to my side and scooped her onto my mattress while simultaneously elbowing Kai in the ribs to get up and get a bottle ready. Who said I couldn't multitask?

Kai grunted in agreement and zombie-walked out of the room, narrowly missing the wall. My phone pinged again, and I rolled my eyes. How many times would Edward the Lactation Consultant contact me about my breastfeeding? The answer was five. He'd emailed me four times and called once to check-in. It was getting a little creepy, though it was his tone in the voice message that came across as nervous and stuttering.

Wendy angrily cried at me when my milk quickly ran out.

"I know, I know." I sighed. "It's not exactly a Thanksgiving meal."

Or was I? I pawed at my nightstand until my hand found my phone and flipped it open to the crime scene pictures. I tapped the close-up of the victim's hand.

"See those bite marks?" I angled the screen toward Wendy. She squinted and squeaked at the bright light. "Oh, sorry, sorry, I'm really losing points on the mom scale, aren't I?"

I snuggled her closer and kissed her peach fuzz. The woman's missing fingers indicated a clean bite. Nothing was mangled or mauled, just ripped clean off. Could a human jaw even bite that powerfully? The writing on the body didn't leave room to ponder if the attacks came from an animal. But I wanted to believe Sharknado had come true and an ocean beast had bitten off the victim's fingers before acknowledging that we could have a cannibal on our hands. A tornado of sharks was less disturbing.

I grimaced at the picture and wondered what the victim's life was like. Like mine? Why did the bodies have to have Fable written on them?

Wendy grunted and cried.

"I agree," I said to her.

So, Elsie *didn't* concoct a juicy hook just to get me to return to work. Detective Wilhelm's acknowledgment of my name on the victim's body was proof that my coworker didn't pull drama out of thin air to drag me back from my maternity leave early.

Where Elsie leaned into sensationalism, I dug for facts. Her gossip columns drew hundreds of thousands of readers, but since I knew she stretched the truth, I didn't want to believe the whole 'fable's story' drama until I saw it with my own eyes. And then San Francisco's most efficient detective confirmed it despite my serious attempt to blame my paranoia.

Kai returned with a warm bottle and flopped back on the bed.

"We locked the front door, right?" I whispered, as I took the formula from him and popped it in Wendy's mouth. Her eyes instantly closed, like I'd pressed a magic sleep button.

"Mmhm," he mumbled and yanked the comforter up to his ears.

"Kai, I'm serious. Someone is stalking me, remember?" I swiped through the photos until I landed on the one with the victim's forehead and flashed the bright screen in his general direction. He threw up his hands to protect his eyes from blue light bullets. After a moment, he squinted and nodded.

"You're sure that's what it says?"

"Detective Wilhelm even confirmed it. I'm not looking for things that aren't there, and I can't just blame this on my tired mom-brain anymore. It's right there!" I shook the phone for emphasis.

"It is pretty spooky," Kai frowned and threw off the blanket again. "I'm going to check that we locked all the windows too." He shuffled off, my knight in wrinkled Stormtrooper with Santa hat PJs.

I tipped the bottle up higher to avoid air bubbles and opened the notes app on my phone. If the clock didn't read two in the morning, I'd have busted out a pen and sticky notes to arrange the new pieces of information. Who was I kidding? I wouldn't sleep until I'd color-coded this out.

With my phone in my mouth, I slipped an arm under Wendy and scooted myself off the bed. I tiptoed out of the bedroom and grabbed a block of rainbow sticky notes and a clear plastic jug of pretzels, all while still feeding her. Breastfeeding was a flop, but my bottle-feeding skills could compete in the mom Olympics.

Kai gave me a lazy smile as we passed one another. I plopped on the couch, perched Wendy on the Boppy pillow, and leaned over the coffee table. Each color sticky note showed a specific type of information.

Names in orange were my potential stalkers. *Redhead from the hospital. Johnson. Edward the Lactation Consultant. Weird Intern from Wendy's birth. Jameson from work* (he has a motive after I got the promotion over him). *Detective Wilhelm?*

The blue notes included all the facts. *A dead young woman close to my neighborhood. The words 'Fable's Story.' Is the story possibly referring to my journalism? Stalking started after Wendy's birth.*

Finally, I pulled out the block of pink sticky notes for all the strange, unexplainable pieces of information. *Howling. Wolf attack? WEREWOLVES? Redhead's disappearance into the strange door.*

Redhead's reappearance with my DoorDash delivery driver. And where in the wonderland did I recognize her from?

I leaned across the coffee table and added another orange note with robot boy. He was weird, but Redhead looked the guiltiest at the moment. Her nickname covered more notes than anyone else's. Now I needed to make a note of the biggest question. I peeled a red sticky from the block and slapped it in the middle of the rest.

What is the stalker's motive?

Wendy polished off the bottle and dozed in my lap. I caressed her tiny cheek with my thumb and hummed a Disney song. Her little lips twitched into a sleepy smile while her eyes stayed shut. Whatever she dreamed about, I hoped it wasn't the creepy nursery rhymes where kids got eaten by witches in the woods.

I glanced at the pile of baby board books on the shelf under the TV. Did I already mess up my child by bringing her to a crime scene? I shook my head and peeled off several more red notes to line up under the question. But I couldn't focus. My gaze trailed back to the bookshelf, and my brow pinched.

Tala's gift sparked a thought. The spine of *Little Red Riding Hood* showed a girl by herself.

All the victims were young women, walking alone. Mom had warned me about this so long ago, almost like she'd predicted this. Or perhaps she was being an overprotective mother and simply trying to keep me safe.

Kai poked his head out of the bedroom. "Are you coming back? It's lonely in here."

"I can't sleep," I mumbled.

"Me neither." He sighed and pulled the door all the way open. He dragged himself out into the living room, raised his eyebrows at my homemade evidence board, and then posted up by the front door with the jug of pretzels in his lap.

"What're you doing?" I cocked my head at him.

"Keeping watch," he said. "All your stalker talk got me paranoid."

"And the snack jug is your weapon?"

"Nah, this is." Kai balled up his fist and shook it at an imaginary intruder.

I laughed and leaned back, letting myself sink into the couch cushions while I traded my arm for the Boppy pillow. I needed to keep Wendy's nose and mouth free from potential suffocation dangers. "In that case," I said, "let me riff my theories off you so I can organize my brain."

He waved a pretzel around as if to say *be my guest*. Before I knew it, evidence talk turned into a dreamless sleep and I was waking to the smell of baby poop. In my fog, I mistook the wetness in my lap to be my water breaking, then I thought it was blood and the murderer had caught up with me. I'd almost take either over the diaper explosion. The stench made me gag, but Wendy beamed with pride at her yellow and green masterpiece. She'd busted her arms free from the swaddle, hands curled into tiny fists. They jerked around and waved at nothing.

"Are you going to beat the crap out of the bad guy? Huh? Yes, you will." My baby voice encouraged Wendy to kick her legs and pull the swaddle all the way off. "I bet you could do a better job than Daddy over there." I nodded toward the pile of husband and pretzels snoring on the floor in front of the door. He held the jug wrapped in one arm. "He doesn't wake up from anything, but you're awake all the time, aren't you?"

I stood and waddled to the changing table in our bedroom where I could peel the soiled diaper off her. Once I cleaned her, sanitized the changing cover, changed and burned my clothes, I needed a nap. But first, coffee. Because young women were dying, and it could be my fault. Plus, I had an almost two-month-old with no sleep schedule on my hands. Caffeine was more than necessary to keep me alive.

Even if the murders didn't connect to me, the people of San Francisco, especially those of us who enjoyed Pioneer Park, needed to know when, and if, it was safe to go for a jog and move freely about the area.

I secured Wendy in the crook of one arm and carried her to the kitchen. Several bags of coffee lined the countertop, and I considered dumping the grounds directly into my mouth and chewing my way to caffeine. A click caught my attention, and I snapped my head up from the aromatic description on the back of one bag.

The handle on our front door dipped slowly, then yanked back up. It dipped again in several quick motions. Someone was trying to get inside.

I yanked our largest kitchen knife from the block on the counter. "Kai," I whisper-shouted, but the door woke him first.

Our front door swung open and smacked him in the side. He yelped, then rolled and jumped to his feet, ready to karate chop the intruder's head off with one hand and swing the snack jug at him with the other.

A woman with drawn brows, frozen skin around her eyes, and lips so large she looked disfigured, pushed into the room—my mom. I still almost screamed. Did she get more work done since I saw her only yesterday?

Mom threw up her hands in surrender to Kai and squealed something about it being just her. I slightly regretted giving her a key to our condo. After her marriage to a codependent man, she had some skewed ideas about boundaries and enjoyed getting into our business a little too much.

"Mom?" I asked.

"Kai, what are you doing?" She slapped her palm over her chest and heaved in big breaths.

"I-I thought you were a serial killer." He dropped the jug, and the tension in his shoulders followed. Mine didn't. Mom always set me on edge. She lived her life in constant caution, regarding everyone she met with fierce vetting before even considering that they might not have ill intentions. I loved her, but I didn't want to live like that. And that's exactly what first drew me to journalism, real, true journalism that got to the facts and offered knowledge to help people make informed decisions to stay safe, but not live in fear.

"Did you get more lip fillers?" I asked. Though I'd never judge her plastic surgery pursuit, I still wished she found satisfaction at some point and didn't give in to the addiction. Our several interventions never helped. Mom kept going under the knife.

"Yesterday morning," she answered. "Doctor Dom works Saturdays if I request it."

She had her own personal surgeon now? The addiction was getting worse.

"You scared the crap out of us," I breathed and finally set the knife on the counter. It clattered and fell into the sink, but I gave it no notice.

She wrinkled her nose and sniffed like a bomb-searching dog, then raised her brows. "Smells to me that your vulgar language is factually correct this time."

I shrugged and tilted my head toward the poop factory in the crook of my arm. "Wendy had an explosion." I shuffled from the kitchen and plopped onto the couch. Mom mirrored me, but she never plopped anywhere. With all the poise and grace in the world, she perched herself on the chair, kiddy corner to the couch. Kai shut the door and stuffed his hand inside the snack jug for a pretzel breakfast.

Mom's eyes raked over the color-coded evidence board, and she might have pursed her lips—or maybe they deflated, I couldn't tell. "Already back to work, I see. I'd have hoped you would focus more on your role as a mother now."

"You know I love my job," I said, as I tossed the fresh blanket I'd grabbed for Wendy onto the coffee table. It blocked Mom's view of my theories.

"I'll never agree that chasing after danger is a smart choice." She pinched the edge of the blanket between her forefinger and thumb and lifted it delicately to peer underneath.

"I do it so people like me can know the facts and be safe—"

"What does this mean?" Mom nodded at the orange sticky notes. "What is wrong with Edward?"

"Edward? You're on a first-name basis with my lactation consultant now?" I exchanged glances with Kai, who only shrugged and shoved more pretzels into his mouth to avoid getting involved in mother-daughter drama. She was a strong, confident woman that raised me to be the same, and I'd forever be grateful for it. But Mom hunted men harder than I did evidence. She acted like each new Tall Dark in a suit would save her. And from what? I never knew.

"We had a pleasant conversation when I ran into him here on Friday," she answered. "Edward is quite the gentleman," Mom spoke while picking up the blanket, still pinched between two fingers. She held it out for me to take, but didn't take her eyes off the coffee table of theories.

Now that's a killer article title: Coffee Table of Theories. I'd have to remember to gift that one to Elsie when I return to the office tomorrow. Coffee tables didn't exactly match my journalism style with all the blood and murders.

Despite all the Botox, Mom's eyebrows moved as fluidly as ever. The thin lines of shapely hair pushed together as her eyes darted from one note to another. Her lips parted, and she looked up at me with all the fear of a bird bursting out of a tree.

She stood suddenly. "You have a stalker?"

"It's not for sure—"

"We need to go," she interrupted, her voice shaking. Kai tuned in now as he stopped chewing and secured the top of the snack jug. "Mari, you need to get away from here."

"It's really not a big deal." I shook my head, half at her intensity and half at my botched swaddling job. Wendy kicked right out of the blanket.

"You're not listening to me. Kai," she spun around to face my husband, "tell your wife to make the right decision and keep her family safe."

"Look, I might agree with you if I didn't know my wife," he said. "But Mari hunts killers for a living. Well, their stories anyway. You should have seen her in action yesterday at the crime scene—"

Mom's head snapped back to me. Her lip twitched with an emotion I couldn't place. Fear? Frustration? "I don't like this."

"You don't have to, Mom." I finally secured Wendy's arms inside the blanket and tucked the edge back into the burrito of fabric. I looked up and met my mother's gaze. "It's my life. Not yours."

She folded her arms across her chest, which always made her shoulder blades jut out from her back. They poked up underneath her thin cardigan.

Kai snuck past us and slipped into the kitchen to warm a bottle of formula, a good excuse to get away from the rising heat between the Fable women.

Mom's jaw shifted back and forth as she chewed on my words. I didn't intend to be harsh, but the lack of control over her own choices always led to her overstepping into my life. Sometimes she listened and calmed down. Others, she'd give me the silent treatment and disappear for weeks at a time.

After several tense minutes, she bent at the waist and perched again on the edge of the seat cushion. She folded her hands together, and her manicured nails crossed one another like claws. Mom was beautiful, fierce, flighty, and far too plastic, but graceful in her mannerisms. When not afraid of something, every move she made dripped with elegance while I was all awkward elbows and clumsiness. My finesse came in organizational skills that helped me track the facts, not in the swing of my hips or the curve of my neck.

"Okay." She nodded. "If I can't convince you to leave, then I want to help."

It was my turn to raise my brows. The expression quickly reminded me of the two hours of sleep I ran on. My eyelids barely propped up the bags that hung on either side of my nose.

"Tell me how to help," she repeated, a tactic of hers when my listening skills didn't keep up with her demands.

"Well, I typically interview suspects at this point," I said. I rubbed my eyes with the heel of my palm and held Wendy close as I scooted my butt to the edge of the couch. I glanced over at my chicken-scratch, late-night handwriting. "But I don't really have a solid suspect or any solid proof that someone is targeting me."

"I see plenty of names here." She waved her shiny fingernail over the orange notes. "Edward is one of them. Why is that?"

Kai returned with a giant yawn. He shook his head and handed me the bottle with the formula still floating in chunks. I couldn't blame him. The poor guy slept on the floor and listened to me talk in circles last night until we both passed out.

"He's taken an odd interest in me," I answered. "Well, not in me specifically, but he is overly helpful. He's called and emailed me multiple times to check up on the success of my breastfeeding since my appointment here with him on Friday."

I shook the bottle gently to mix the powder. In my sleep-induced state, I'd forgotten to cover the tiny hole in the nipple and the milk sprayed a stream of liquid around the room. It soiled my paper notes, but my brain didn't catch up with what was happening in time to stop. When it splashed in my eyeball, I flinched and pretended to be at least halfway put together for Mom's sake.

I didn't need her worrying more since I'd go into the investigation with only a half night's sleep from now on. "It means nothing, but I have to consider all the angles when I'm uncovering a story. Hunting the details of my story is no different."

Mom only nodded, taking in my explanation. "Interviews, you say?"

"Yeah, I have one today with the second victim's boyfriend. I had to reschedule it after the murder on Friday night."

"I can do that," she muttered, not listening to me.

"Hey, what did you come over here for anyway?" I asked.

"Right, yes." She flicked her eyes around the room as if trying to remember something. "I wanted to tell you not to worry about Johnson. He's harmless, but a nuisance, so don't give him the time of day. You have enough on your plate." She waved her hand at Wendy. "Just let me deal with your father."

"Sure," I agreed, as I tilted the bottle so Wendy could get the last drops. I didn't have the time or energy to think about my father, much less his lackey, Johnson. I glanced at the sticky note with his name and made a mental note to remove it once my hands were free.

Mom stood and plucked her phone out of her handbag. If I didn't know better, I'd have thought she was attending an evening ball based on her attire rather than a visit to her daughter's at dawn on a Sunday morning.

She excused herself to our condo's porch and made a phone call while Kai plopped down beside me and took Wendy. I chose to clean the bottle over burping, since rinsing out the formula didn't come with the risk of sour milk smell on my shoulder. He patted her back in the rhythm of the happy birthday song.

Once I changed into real clothes and twisted my hair into the best bun I could pull off, Mom had finished her phone call. She offered to walk with me out of the condo. I kissed Kai goodbye and followed Mom out the door with Wendy in my arms.

"You're off to your interview, and I'm off to mine," Mom said with a smirk.

I cocked my head.

"I'll be on a date with Edward." Her quirked lips expanded to a full smile.

"What?" My head snapped up from my endless deep dive into the recesses of the purse for my keys.

"Seems he's been a bother to you because he wanted to take me out," she said with a sparkle in her eye. "I called him. He gave me his number on Friday, and you said he's been pestering you since then. I figured the two could be connected. Five o'clock this evening, he invited me over for a home-cooked meal."

I should have known. It wasn't the first time a guy pretended to befriend me just to get to my mother. At least it was another sticky note I could pull off the Coffee Table of Evidence.

"Have fun." I smiled as we went our separate ways.

My interview was not only *not* fun, but an enormous waste of time. I asked the victim's boyfriend if he knew anything about the writing on his girlfriend's crime scene. *Does fable mean anything to you? Did your girlfriend have a story she wanted to tell?*

Nada. Zip. Zilch. The poor guy cried most of the interview, and I recruited Wendy to help with that. She smiled at his sniffles (of course, I didn't tell him they were gas bubble grins). It worked, and I even let him hold her.

I took my baby back and gave the guy a hug before dismissing him from the interview. He definitely didn't have the cold-blooded attitude of a killer, and he didn't know about the other victims, nor did he have a clue about me. I sighed and tried to parkour Wendy into the baby sling while my brain worked overtime.

Does fable mean anything to you? I repeated the question I'd asked him. Multitasking had me pulling out my phone and typing into YouTube about how to adjust the sling. You'd think the creators of parenting products would make this crap easier to use. As if motherhood wasn't already hard enough.

"Your mommy is a mess," I told Wendy, as I finally secured her in the wrap. She grunted back to me as her face turned red. Her noises seemed in response to my voice, so I kept talking. "I'm a mess and an investigator and a multitasker. Well, I have to be a multitasker because I'm a mom and a Fable, which apparently means I'm a target—"

Mom. Fable. I cursed silently. *My mom is a Fable too.* Why didn't I think of it before? I scrambled for my phone and tapped the screen. 5:39.

Maybe Edward's pursuits had nothing to do with my mother's beauty and everything to do with his murderous intentions. And she was on a date with him.

Chapter 9

Can't Have a Case and Wendy Eating Too

Mom's line rang and rang until her voicemail answered for the fourth time.

"Pick up!" I screamed at the phone. First, Wendy had disappeared at the hospital, and now Mom. Who wanted to hurt me? My journalism was honest, sure, but I'd never created enemies that I knew of.

I hung up and re-dialed as I drove just over the speed limit. Wendy's presence kept me from speeding, but Mom's situation pushed me to drive a pinch faster than the law allowed.

I followed the route to the hospital where I planned to demand Edward's address from the HR department. None of it made sense. He didn't have a motive that I knew of, and my mother, while paranoid and flighty most of the time, usually charmed men rather than angered them. Well, most men. My father didn't count. He'd lost his marbles along the way, according to Mom, and we left him before my third-grade daddy-daughter dance.

I flicked on my blinker and tapped my thumb along with its rhythmic click. "Hang on, lovey," I told Wendy, as we pulled into the hospital lot and swerved into a parking spot.

Was Edward involved in my father's pursuit to find Mom again? No. I refused to believe my dad could be related to the murders. Us

Fables were a little odd, but not American Psycho odd. Still, the thought turned my stomach. He desperately had wanted a romantic, picture-perfect marriage with Mom, and Mom had denied him that with the claim that he suffocated her. She had once explained that his extravagant displays of courtship were merely devices by which to control her.

I tapped my phone again and selected 'Lactation Consultant' from my contacts. His line rang several times before a cheery voice answered with a lame joke about boobs. *Sicko.*

Wendy watched the rattle hanging from her car-seat handle as I pulled her seat from its latch and did the sideways mom limp into the hospital. I carried her in one hand and tapped Mom's number in my phone again with the other.

"Goodness, Mari, what is it?" Mom answered without her usual formal greeting.

I stopped halfway inside the hospital. One sliding door separated the outside from the inside with a second sliding door, so I was both inside and outside the hospital at the same time.

My head rolled back, and I took a huge breath. "Finally!"

"I didn't see your calls. Are you trapped?" Mom spoke between breaths.

"No, what?" Why did she always jump to that first? "I think you need to leave the date. You could be the Fable that the messages on the victims are referencing."

Silence. Only the continuing open and close of the hospital doors responded.

"Mom?"

"I don't feel trapped—"

"What is your obsession with that?" I interrupted, desperate to get her to safety. "You know there are worse fates than being trapped? Like death."

"Okay, okay," she said. "I'll tell Edward it is a family emergency. But he's a great guy. He has classic manners and can hold a conversation. Plus, he's handsome."

"Ted Bundy handsome?" I scoffed. For an intelligent and

cautious woman, she sure was being stupid. A woman exited the hospital and side-eyed me for standing right in the middle of the walkway.

"I'll call you when I'm on my way over, and you can explain when I arrive."

"Stay on the phone—" A click followed her words, and my phone blinked. "Mom? Ugh!" I shouted, and the woman frowned at me.

"Sorry, it's this murderer." The journalist in me wanted to inform the woman of the world's dangers. *Don't go out into that parking lot alone.* But she curled up her lip, then hurried away.

A hoard of EMTs barreled through the doors and swarmed past me. Their radios buzzed, and a dispatcher called out for their next job.

"Young woman attacked. Found still alive at Charleston Condominiums."

No.

"Did they say Charleston Condominiums?" I asked a passing EMT, but he didn't seem to hear. "On Main?" I set Wendy's car seat down before my arm ripped off and reached to stop one of the medical technicians before she could run out the door.

"Please, that's where I live."

I grabbed the woman's forearm and her long-sleeve navy shirt felt lumpy and stuffed with layers. I glanced up to meet her gaze, and chocolate brown eyes stared back at me. She wore her hair tucked up inside a baseball cap, but a strand of fiery ruby escaped out the back behind her ear.

The EMT arched her eyebrow, then yanked her arm from me. She rushed off without a word to follow the others and climb into an ambulance. I turned and watched them pile into the vehicle. Outside of Redhead's shirt was a misplaced garment that didn't match her dark blue button-up or the professional style of the EMT uniform. A velvet crimson hood poked out from the collar of the shirt and hung down her back.

"Who are you?" I whispered to myself. *And why do I recognize you?* Redhead acted as if she heard me. Our eyes connected before she pulled the double doors at the back of the ambulance shut. The siren blared and lights flashed as it sped out of the drop-off loop and away from the hospital.

The hum of the sliding doors snapped my attention to the present as they closed off, separating Wendy and me into a weird purgatory between the hospital and the outside. I stooped to grab the car seat and huff it back into the sedan.

One minute, I was in the hospital parking lot, and the next, I was pulling into my covered spot at the condo complex. Wendy slept on the way back, and I did too, in that day-zoning way where your brain wanders while you drive and you don't remember how you ended up at the correct destination.

Red and blue lights flashed in my face as I made my way around the complex and out to the main street. Wendy snuggled in my arms, eyes wide and curious at the bright colors. In all the chaos of murder and Mom's date and another Redhead sighting, my baby's perfect, giant gaze calmed me. She already took after me, inquisitive and observant—not that she could do much else other than poop and eat and cry.

I gathered a long breath before rounding the corner. My inhalation stopped short when I saw the scene, like I was on another planet and someone had cut off my oxygen supply.

Paramedics lifted a woman onto a stretcher. The victim's eyes darted around, frantic and unseeing. Or seeing something I couldn't. Blood covered the street in a long trail that showed the attacker had dragged her and dropped her right in front of my complex. A cold, nearly dead gift. But it wasn't a giant cat that brought her here. Or was it?

"He had fangs and gray fur all over," the woman spewed words about as fast as the blood gushed from the bite that covered her jaw and neck.

An EMT used gauze to apply pressure while another, one with a familiar baseball cap and red hood, bent over the stretcher. Redhead gently pushed the woman against the stretcher to keep her from moving and losing more blood, but she fought back, trying to get them to listen.

"They're still out there. Do something!" she wailed, shaking her head and flailing her arms. "They're going to attack and eat another woman. They said they would!" Redhead's freckles melded together over the bridge of her nose as she took this in, eyes pinned on the victim and absorbing her every word.

The woman coughed and started gurgling, choking on her own blood. I grimaced and instinctively turned Wendy away as if she could understand what was happening. Still, I refused to scar my poor child in the same way my mother's paranoia sent me to expensive therapy that wrecked my credit score. Though it might have maxed my credit cards, I didn't regret it for a second.

I angled Wendy into me as I stepped closer. Where did they write the message this time? And who was he? My eyes raked over the blood on the concrete and the shredded bits of the woman's Lululemon-contoured workout sweater and leggings. Even a chunk of her blonde hair stuck to the sidewalk, glued down by sticky blood. And right next to it, another small triangular object that resembled a bone.

I crouched and squinted at what looked like a tooth. I wanted to pick it up. Any other time, I wouldn't have hesitated. But with Wendy in my arms, I insisted on only sanitized hands around her and vowed not to break that. If I couldn't nurse her or swaddle her or do anything right as a mother, at least I kept her clean.

"A tooth?" I whispered. *A fang.*

"Fable's story," the woman screeched. My head whipped around at the words, and my shoulder-length hair swatted Wendy in the eyes. She bubbled up into a dry baby wail.

"Fable's story, fable's story, fable's story," the victim repeated over and over, staring up at the sky as they loaded her into the back of the ambulance.

"Wait!" I couldn't help it. The journalist in me, the *investigator* in me, needed answers now. I stood and took two giant steps toward the emergency vehicle before a police officer stepped in front of me. I arched my feet and balanced on my tiptoes. "Did they say why?"

The woman looked at me as the cloud of confusion burst around her. She ignored the gaping wound on her face and neck, likely in shock and not yet suffering from the pain.

"The person who attacked you—"

"Miss—" the officer tried to interrupt.

"Did they say what they wanted from you or the other women they've hurt?" My throat dried as the woman met my gaze. The bite and scratch marks cut so deep I could see the bone of her jaw and shoulder.

"Hunting for her. F-f-fable," the woman stuttered, as her face twitched. Her body followed as a seizure overtook her.

Fable's story. Ebenezer Scrooge. A gasp caught at the back of my tongue like my throat had closed, swollen, and refused to let any more air in. I was pretty sure my eyes would pop out of my head and roll across the sidewalk like a pair of bouncy balls.

Though people surrounded me, paramedics, cops, rubbernecking bystanders, I was alone, isolated in another world where only I understood what fable meant. All I knew was that Redhead wasn't involved, at least not in the attack. The timing of it was impossible.

As if she heard my thoughts, Redhead stared at me from inside the ambulance.

The woman's body suddenly stilled, and the medical technicians shouted orders. Redhead tore her eyes from me and dove into action, compressing her hands over the victim's heart and starting CPR. The doors shut, and sirens sounded.

I turned back to the scene. A rush of feet, conversation, and movement spun around me, but I dodged the chaos and stared at the spot where the fang had been. Though Wendy was still small, my arm ached from the frozen position I held her in. I shifted her to the other side, but she wailed again in the pitch that told me she'd grown hangry with me. She needed a bottle or a boob, and she needed it fast.

But I needed answers. What in the loyal Twilight fandom happened to result in two fangs left in or around the victim's bodies? And why always young women? I'd seen some disturbing fifty shades of a serial killer in my investigations before, but nothing close to this *weird*.

I crouched and plucked the tooth from the cement before the medical examiner could barrel his way in and kick me so far out of there I'd need binoculars to get details for my report.

"Mari. . . Back to work so soon?" Jameson stomped toward me in his ridiculous black boots, skin-tight pants, and a shirt that I couldn't tell if he'd bought ripped or just didn't care that he looked entirely unprofessional as a reporter. "I thought you'd be off at a mommy-daughter dance or whatever parents are so busy doing all the time." His grin spread from ear to ear, and I could have sworn the Grinch stood before me in hideous shoes. I frowned and glanced up at him as he approached. His sly smile wiped when he saw Wendy in my arms, and he stepped back in shock as if she might bite him.

I mean, she bit *me*, but those were the perks of motherhood.

"My baby is two months old, Jameson. Do you honestly think I'd be at a dance with her?" I stood but stumbled forward, thrown from the balance of holding a baby. Heck, I'd only been a mother for seven weeks. With an awkward step out, I caught myself and straightened, though Wendy's blanket was all awry.

"You're at a crime scene with her." He folded his arms and posed in what I'd call the 'mean girl' stance.

"Yes, *my* crime scene," I said.

"Oh yeah? So, you're the one attacking all these poor young women?" Venom dripped from his voice, and the harmless green Christmas character in him quickly turned to the snake he truly was.

Our boss encouraged us to be competitive. It drove us to dig deeper and produce the best, most honest stories, which were as good for our organization as it was for the public. But pure *animals* like Jameson straight-up stole research from other journalists and claimed it as their own, then trampled all over another's reports in front of Pam.

"Wait, were you the one reporting on the first murder?" I asked. Mom-brain kept me from clarity when I read that first article, but I never saw him at the second scene.

"Both," he said.

"Everyone at the office knows I'm the one who investigates violent crimes," I said.

"Yeah." Jameson clucked his tongue. "You sure have a penchant for the disturbing and bloody, don't you?" He angled his palm out toward the stained sidewalk beneath my feet.

Ugh. If my arm didn't ache from carrying Wendy everywhere, I'd have socked him right in the long, thin nose. Of course, that wouldn't help against his argument regarding violence.

Wendy's face pinched as she opened her mouth and let out a wail.

Jameson twitched at the sound and narrowed his eyes toward her. "Looks like you can't return to work right now anyway." He grinned. "Don't worry, while you're making bottles, I'll keep this city safe and informed."

I curled my lip. "Right, Joker. Do us all a favor and just admit you're in this line of business because you like to watch the world burn." My attempt at humor fell flat, but I needed to lighten the mood. An angry baby, disgruntled coworker, and murder in front of my condo felt a little too heavy for one day.

"You have me confused with Elsie," he said. "I'm not the one who stirs up drama and stretches the truth for rumor reads." He crouched and eyed the trail of blood down the sidewalk.

I couldn't argue with him there. As much as I loved Elsie, she'd always believed in the supernatural, the unknown, the Fox Mulder-sized conspiracy theories. I didn't always agree with how she approached her stories, but after the redheaded woman's mention of stories and villains, maybe I should.

Speaking of agreeing, Wendy didn't agree with restaurant-Mom's slow service. Her wail pierced my ears, and two uniformed officers turned to glare at me. I shushed her and nuzzled my chin against her peach fuzz.

Okay, I can do this. I needed to stay here, and my baby also needed food. The moment of truth had arrived.

I sucked in a tight breath and coughed out the city's signature scent of bus diesel mixed with a faint trace of nicotine. I tugged my sweater up and pulled my shirt down, positioning Wendy to nurse.

I'd once vowed only to take Wendy out in Pioneer Park where the birds tweeted and the air smelled of pine like we lived in Cinderella's kingdom. But I had a job to do. And if I didn't catch this stalker, this *murderer*, inching closer to my home with his attacks, I'd end up dead, just like Cinderella's mom. Of course, if Kai married an evil stepmother type, I'd come back and haunt him.

Wendy quieted as she latched, and I almost jumped up and down in glee. Instead, I used my free arm to whip my phone out and take my own notes, better notes than Jameson's. Not because I was better than him, but because I had to be. Women *had to* notice the minute details in their surroundings to stay safe. It wasn't fair, but it was life.

I noted the woman's size, how far the attacker had dragged her, and the fang. I secured the woman's name from an officer who looked genuinely impressed by my multitasking skills, then added the victim, Paige Brown, to my list of interviewees. Most of the looks I'd gotten when attempting to breastfeed in public made me want to detach my boobs and leave them at home. But for now, I stood a little taller.

I scribbled some notes and moved down my usual list. Next, I needed to scour for any witnesses at the time of the attack, either at the park from where she was dragged or here.

Something between a yelp and a muffled scream escaped my lips. Wendy nearly ripped my nipple clean off as her head yanked away from me. My skin burned at the sight. She finished the scream I started with an angry wail that earned me an evil eye from Jameson.

"Go home, Rowan," he snapped, narrowing his gaze at my baby. "Get yourself together." His expression curled into disgust, and he glanced away from my baggy, tugged-down shirt.

I opened my mouth to argue, to fight and tell him this was where I belonged. But nothing came out. Which was true? Did I belong in the investigation? Or did I belong at home with my child? Tears burned my eyes as I turned away from the scene, my life's work, and possibly my death's work if I didn't solve this. As a mom, new expectations demanded my attention.

But this is what I'm good at. I want *to be at work.*

I twisted my face into an apology as if Wendy could hear my thoughts. Was it so wrong to miss my job? I didn't love her any less. In fact, if I managed to breastfeed her, it might overshadow my longing for a Pulitzer. I dragged myself back around the corner to the alley where I could reach the staircase and climb my way home.

Wendy wailed, and my heart cracked in two. If *only* it'd crack in two, then I'd send one piece of me to work and keep the other snuggling her at all times.

"It's okay, my little lovey," I cooed, taking one concrete step at a time with heavy thumps. Wendy didn't agree, and her face turned purple with screams, her way of saying 'more food, Mommy! The tap went dry.'

The long outdoor hall greeted me with a dimming bulb. The buzz of it mirrored my thoughts. Should I let Jameson take my role? Was this Pam pushing us to be competitive and hoping I'll come back to work sooner than expected? Why didn't my body want to produce milk? Was I less of a mother because I loved my job?

Don't cry. Don't cry. Don't cry.

I wasn't normally emotional, but I'd just created, pushed out, and now tried to keep another human being alive, so the tears came anyway.

I scrubbed them away with my free hand as I paused outside the front door. I dug into my pocket for my keys but found something else. My fingers curled around the fang and just like that, I knew I wouldn't give up on this investigation. Or give in to Jameson's rude words.

My breath shuddered, and the sound piqued Wendy's curiosity. She stopped wailing and gazed up at me.

"I don't have any good leads and couldn't stay long enough to get details, but I have the fang," I explained to her while I fumbled with the keys from my other pocket. She squealed in delight at the sound of my calm voice. Or maybe it was the doggone blinking bulb behind me. "Yeah, that's right. Mommy's not a quitter. I don't have a lot, but I've got this, and I know just who to ask about supernaturally weird stuff."

My investigation continued. I smiled at my plan to visit Elsie and her wife tomorrow to have her look at the tooth. The lock clicked, and I pushed into the door.

A shadowed figure greeted me.

"He's innocent," the figure said.

"Mom?" I'd forgotten about her rush here to meet me. Scrappy ol'

Mom took care of herself, and I half-expected she would go straight home from Edward's. But I was wrong.

"You're right." I nodded.

Edward wasn't the murderer. Neither was Redhead. Much like myself, they couldn't exist in two places at the same time. I'd gathered more answers than I realized.

But one major question still nagged at me, and simultaneously belittled all the clues I'd found.

If Redhead was my stalker, but not the murderer, how were the two connected? *The villain.*

Chapter 10

There's No Such Thing as Free Lunch

Mom left with a smile on her face once I agreed on Edward's innocence. I guessed she liked him more than most of the men she'd use for attention. Her one date max broke a lot of hearts and told me she never planned to get serious with anyone. I couldn't blame her after Dad's obsession. I'd never survive in a marriage where my husband wanted to be with me twenty-four-seven, either.

If she pursued my lactation consultant further, I'd both find it weird, *and* be happy for her. My butt sunk further into the couch as I nestled in, not daring to move with Wendy asleep on my chest. I didn't so much as carry her to the sink to wash out the three-hour-old formula leftovers from the bottle.

Kai tiptoed over my outstretched legs and handed me a cup of soup.

"Ramen was a terrible idea," I complained, as I tried to balance the noodle-y liquid away from my baby's head.

"Soup is your brain food, though," he said. A wry smile curled onto his face, and I ached to cuddle into his shoulder and watch true crime documentaries. But his mound of papers to grade on the lazy chair and my coffee table of evidence demanded we focus rather than snuggle.

"You got coffee at eight-thirty in the evening, and it's not even midterm time of year?" I asked, raising my brows at the giant Starbucks in his hand. He shrugged and offered the cup to me.

"Want some? It has two extra shots of espresso."

I shook my head. "I have a hard time sleeping already, what with the feedings, anxiety that Wendy will accidentally punch herself in her sleep, and you know, the whole murder thing."

Kai finished his slurp, then held the cup like a trophy. "That's why I've got this. My midnight fuel for standing guard."

Tears sprang up again. *Seriously? I never cry, and now twice in one day?* The hormone struggle was real. What did I do to deserve this man? "You're the best husband any exhausted mom slash investigative journalist with a serial killer stalker could ask for."

He brushed his fingers through the longer section of his hair the way he knew I liked. With the sides shorter and the middle overgrown, I called him my own personal Viking, and sometimes, he even let me live my wildest dreams and twist his hair into a man bun.

"That's enough of that." I let out a breath and waved for him to stop playing with his hair. "That's what got us into this beautiful mess in the first place." My head tilted toward the snoozing babe, but the movement caused me to splash a bit of hot soup down my cleavage. I seethed and licked the Styrofoam before another drip escaped.

"She is beautiful, isn't she?" His emerald eyes turned starry as he came in for a kiss. To my disappointment, the smooch landed on peach fuzz rather than my lips. Why did people always focus on the new baby instead of the new mom? Wendy was perfect and all, but I'd created a human. Of course, I paid more attention to her than to myself these days too.

I gasped, as a thought struck me like a frisbee to the head. "What if the stalker wants Wendy, not me?"

Kai's brows furrowed. Normally, his thinking expression got me all hot and bothered, but my brain scattered to the far reaches of What-If-Land. What if some crazy person wanted to steal my child because she was so darned perfect? What if someone wanted to kidnap her for ransom? Except teaching and journalism paid pennies. What if an old article I'd published created an enemy? I reported on more than a few murderers, and I wasn't one to skimp on the dark details.

"Who would stalk a two-month-old baby?" Kai asked. "Don't kill me, but that might be your mom-brain talking. I love our little poop factory and all, but she's a poop factory who screams all night long."

"I know it sounds crazy, but listen." I dared to sit up, shifting Wendy from my chest to my lap. She pursed her lips and suckled on air, possibly dreaming of useful boobs, AKA not mine. "The stalking didn't start until she was born. The first murder happened the day I gave birth."

He tilted his head, considering this while munching an egg roll. He scooted forward and surveyed the sticky notes spread on the coffee table, then nodded. "So, to play devil's advocate, couldn't it all be a coincidence?"

"Kai, the murders are getting closer and closer to our house," I explained while twirling a ramen noodle around my chopstick. "Every victim was marked with the words 'Fable's story' or has said them. And—" I paused. Should I tell him about the howling? He never doubted me. Never. But having a child changed our marriage. We were both bone tired, brand new at this, and painfully overprotective to the point of sickness just so we could watch her sleep and ensure she didn't break free from the swaddle and somehow hurt herself. Would he call the howling a sleep-deprived delusion?

"And?" he prodded, as he stacked the sticky notes that said, Redhead and Edward. I took that as my cue that he'd believe me no matter what. He didn't question my crazy story about the woman in the cloak or that I said I'd seen her as an EMT. At least both related back to the hospital. Did I tell him about the DoorDash sighting? Redhead lady had become somewhat of a celebrity in my mind.

I sighed. "I think the stalker and the murderer are two different people."

Noodles fell out of Kai's mouth and splashed back into the giant Styrofoam cup. He slow-turned his head toward me like we lived inside a horror movie, his eyes wide.

"Are you suggesting one person wants to kill you and the other person is stalking our perfect, wonderful poop factory?" He tried to lighten the mood, and I loved him for it, but it fell flat against the reality of the situation.

"Actually, I wasn't. But now that you say it. . . " I palmed my face, leaning forward and creating a human body shelter over Wendy with my hands on my knees. I wondered if I could breastfeed in this position. My bouncing thoughts returned to the issue at hand.

"If that's the case, it sounds like our suspect is out to get me, since they're targeting my whole family," he suggested. He set his dinner on the floor and grimaced, the possibility of what he said sinking in.

Wendy stirred and grunted in her sleep. Her head jerked back and forth as if she disagreed with her daddy's statement. Out to get Kai? No, it didn't connect with the repeat of 'Fable's story.' I tilted the cup of soup to my lips and sipped the broth. The warmth of it comforted me in the most temporary and superficial way. But I needed that right now. Not only did my newborn baby toss my life upside down (in a good way), but her birth sparked targeted attacks that flipped me around like a burger patty on the grill (in a bad way). And I was about to get burned. Maybe even charred and discarded when ketchup and onions couldn't salvage the wreckage.

Wow, I'm hungry. Hungry while eating, this was evidence of breast-feeding. If only the evidence for my case was this obvious.

Kai leaned forward and plucked the fang from the pile of sticky notes. He squinted and surveyed it while he turned the tooth over and over. "So, if we're living in *Twilight*, which character does that make me?"

I shot him a scrunched glare. Someday, we'd need to learn how to handle our fears and anxieties without humor. What would we do when Wendy came crying to us after her first breakup or failed test? Joke about it? Not cool.

Except I understood him completely. "Considering I don't love the werewolf, also known as our resident murderer, nor do I care much for the vampire slash creeper stalking me, you're none of them."

"I love you too," he said. His grim smile told me he knew we needed to stop joking, as well.

I slurped the last of the broth down, fueling myself for a long night of Wendy's wails and unsuccessful breastfeeding before my first day at work tomorrow. I dreaded leaving her almost as much as I dreaded the screech of my alarm.

And screech it did. My arms flailed around, knocking over a glass of water and sending my phone flying. I groaned and rolled halfway off the bed to feel around for my phone and tap the snooze button.

If I breathed wrong, it woke Wendy. But a screaming alarm clock and the chaos that followed didn't so much as alert her. Her tiny chest rose and fell under the fuzzy footie pajamas that read *Chewbacca Baby.*

I rolled off the mattress and hurried to start the day. I snuck out, but not without a crack-of-dawn kiss on Kai's and Wendy's foreheads.

Everything on the walk to my office sounded, felt, and looked different. Even my coffee tasted bitter. My flats rubbed the back of my heels raw, and the usual honking, engine, and buzzing sounds of the city didn't boost my mood, blaring loud and painful in my ears. The buildings stood tall, too tall like they'd lose their balance and collapse with my baby inside.

Anxiety buzzed in my chest, which thumped along with my hurried footsteps. I needed to make it to the office before Jameson so I could discuss the fang with Elsie in private. But after an hour spent pumping, then packing the milk, then cleaning the pumping equipment, then crying over Wendy's crib and whispering apologies about leaving, then —yeah, I was late.

I threw my head back and downed the last of the coffee despite its awful flavor. I shoved the empty cup into the secondary-diaper-bag-turned-purse (how did I live without wipes before?) and looked up to a figure holding the door open for me.

"Jameson." I slapped my palm to my collarbone. "You startled me."

His flat expression stayed stagnant. I started to walk through the door when he pushed past as if I didn't exist. I stumbled back and groaned. *Great start to my first day back.*

The first hour didn't get any better. The first victim's grandmother canceled our interview since her schnauzer needed a vet visit. Then, I discovered the woman that had been attacked in front of my building had slipped into a coma overnight after her injuries led to what the doctor considered an unexpected heart attack. That sent me spiraling into a cry fest and hiding in a bathroom stall. By the fourth hour of my first day, I decided to quit. Pam talked me down by using my own words against me.

"Why did you get into this line of business?" she asked, as she always did when I wanted to give up because the investigation got too dangerous or disturbing. At least her office chairs were more comfortable than a toilet, and the stink of her egg salad sandwich didn't smell as bad as the bathroom.

I sighed and flopped my face into my hands. My elbows rested on her desk, and I bit back a sob. "Because I want to help people protect themselves," I muttered through my fingers.

"And will you be able to do that if you abandon your post?" She said it like I was a soldier and this job was a war.

"Yes."

My answer startled her, as evident by her raised, drawn-on brows. Stress killed Pam's hair years ago and shocked what was left with white and gray. "People," she repeated louder. My head throbbed like it did after a night of parties in college. Baby Hangover was worse than a beer hangover. "Plural. As in multiple people. Not just your daughter."

I shook my head. "Wendy, me, and my husband. That is more than one."

"Rowan," Pam said, as she crisscrossed her fingers and leaned farther over the desk. She dipped her head, forcing me to meet her fierce gaze. "No offense, but this has nothing to do with you becoming a mother."

"Excuse me?" I straightened and folded my arms.

"Okay." She threw up her hands in surrender. "Maybe a little of that mom-guilt stuff is to blame. But you've always been on top. You solve investigations faster than the actual detectives and get the story out to the public. Every journalist comes to a point where they want to give up because the surrounding reporters are flying high while you're slogging through the fruitless interview trenches." Another war comparison. Pam took the job seriously, too seriously.

"So, you're saying I can't handle it when things get hard?" I clarified.

"I'm saying, the investigations that don't unravel easily are the most rewarding, and it's good for you to be pushed by a little friendly competition." Her gaze wandered past my head, through the windowed walls of her office. I suspected she was looking toward Jameson's cubicle where he no doubt sat with his flip-flops resting on the desk beside a reusable coffee mug from an obscure shop and a beanie pulled over his scruffy head. He was never one for professionalism.

"Friendly is when the competition comes from another organization," I said.

"Oh, there's plenty of that too." Pam sucked in her cheeks and released a popping sound. "These attacks are sparking statewide attention. I suspect if another occurs, it will spread across the nation." Her eyes sparkled, and I remembered why Elsie and I joked about Pam's lack of a soul.

Speaking of Elsie, I patted the zipped pocket in the diaper bag to triple-check that I'd remembered the fang. At least I had a lead.

Pam shook her head and seemed to wrangle it down from the clouds and back onto her shoulders as she focused on me again. "Think about it, Rowan." *Use of last name.* Another clue she didn't have a soul because she barely saw us as humans. Except for rare moments like these. She reached across the desk and took my hands into her icy fingers. "It's impossible to know how many lives you've saved with your reports. All the young women in San Francisco have you to thank for putting the call out of the glass coffin girl from Portland and finding her killer had come here to hide. That's just one example."

I nodded and pulled away from her frozen grasp. As much as I appreciated her inspirational speech, I planned to meet Elsie in the break room to discuss teeth over deli sandwiches.

"You're right." I stood and thanked her before heading for the door.

"Mari," Pam called. *Use of first name.* Interesting. I paused on the threshold between windowed walls, feeling like the glass coffin girl myself. My boss smiled, baring her teeth. Straight, small, square teeth. She definitely wasn't the murderer, but I wouldn't put it past her to stalk me, especially if she sensed another media outlet trying to poach me. "Your daughter will be one of those young women someday."

I sucked in a breath. Her statement landed exactly how she wanted, striking me in my tender mom-heart. *Do it for Wendy.* Of course, I knew Pam wanted me to keep investigating because this story could catapult our magazine onto the nation's stage. Still, her words stuck with me as I hurried to the break room and unwrapped the layers of Subway paper.

I joined Elsie at the corner table that sat partially behind a vending machine. We liked to hide from Jameson, who'd come in with his all-meat sandwiches and stink up the entire room.

"I heard he had another sexual harassment complaint from a lady in that accounting office next door," Elsie said. She thrived on gossip, but I knew this wasn't stretched truth. Jameson's aggression was infamous, and that was exactly why Pam kept him around. His investigations got results because he intimidated answers out of people. Plus, he'd use his boldness to push people around.

My stomach groaned at the smell of the meatball sub that wafted out from between the swaddle of wrapping. *Swaddle.* Tears stung my eyes as an image of Wendy staring up at the stuffed fox that dangled from the handle of her car seat flashed in my mind.

"I cried after my first maternity leave too." Elsie plopped down in the seat across from me, her dark hair shining against the awful fluorescent lights. I wiped the tears away with the heel of my palm and sniffled.

"Yeah, right." I forced a laugh to lighten my mood. "You're Ms. Kickbutt Elsie, mom, writer, superhero." I'd nicknamed her that after she gave birth to her and her wife's fourth child at home, on her living room floor, while literally researching a rehab facility that had allegedly lost a pop singer during her rise to stardom.

"You only think that because I hid in my car every time I felt the tears coming on." Elsie laughed, but her laugh wasn't forced like mine.

"Really?" I bit into the sandwich, and a meatball popped out the back, along with some red sauce. The reminder of birth suddenly stole my appetite. I set the sub down. "You're not just saying that to make me feel better?"

Her hearty laugh eased my anxiety. "I love you, Mari, but I don't have enough lies in me to spare one for your feelings. Trust me, all moms struggle with going back to work. That's why Jane became a midwife. Her weird hours usually mean she never has to miss our kiddos' first words or the first day of school."

Tears came flooding back, and I nearly choked on my Mountain Dew. "Do you think I'm going to miss Wendy's first word?"

Elsie shrugged and popped the sealed top off her Tupperware. The delicious scent of stir-fry filled the break room. "You can't be in two places at once."

"Oh!" Yesterday's memories knocked me upside the back of the head, and for a second, my headache eased. I dug into the diaper bag on the floor beside my chair and produced the fang.

Elsie dropped her fork and immediately snatched it from me, her eyes wide. "This was at the crime scene?"

"Stuck right in the blood," I said. "I wasn't thinking straight yesterday. I need to get it to the detectives on this case."

"Not without some of your own research first, I hope." She marveled at it. "This thing is huge!"

"That's what she said," I mumbled the joke in reflex. Elsie rolled her eyes. "I was hoping you might tell me if it resembled any of the conspiracy theory creatures you follow."

"This could be from many things. I mean, it's large enough to be Big Foot's baby tooth if you ask me." She wasn't kidding. "But I'm not the one to ask about creatures. If you want me to use it to contact the spirit it came from, then I can try that, but only if that creature is dead now."

"That's it?" My shoulders dropped. Now I'd lost my appetite and my only lead.

"I'd ask Reese," she said and handed it back to me. "He used to be an archeologist."

"As in Medical Examiner Reese?" I asked, scrunching my nose.

Dead things fascinated Reese a little too much. His obsession gave me the creeps, but he'd definitely be able to identify if this tooth came from a human or. . . something else. He knew bones like the back of his hand.

"That's the one." Elsie took a huge bite of teriyaki rice and nodded. My stomach growled as my appetite returned. I had a plan. And, creepy or not, at least Reese could get me some answers. I dug my hand beneath the sub and scooped it toward my mouth.

"Anything else unusual about the murders? Are they happening only at night?" Elsie asked.

I shook my head. "Yesterday's happened in broad daylight right on Main. No vampires here, if that's what you're thinking."

She scoffed and slammed her water bottle down on the table. A little liquid splashed out. "I take offense to your simplistic assumption. Vampires were not on the top of my list."

"Hey, you're the one who said you're not the creature genius." I shrugged.

"I'm not up to an archeologist's status where I can identify their bones and teeth, but my knowledge extends far beyond the basics." She used her fingers to imitate fangs in front of her mouth.

"Okay, so if not Dracula, then what were you getting at?" I wasn't interested in fantasies. I came to work to catch a killer and release their details to the public before another creep could succeed with the same M.O. But I couldn't deny the weird things that kept happening around me. I'd need to make another list.

"Maybe a type of changeling," she interrupted my thoughts. "The Tooth Fairy is nocturnal *and* from Elfame." She pointed to the fang on the table. "It could be related."

"I don't know if Bone Collector explains the scratch marks across the victims," I said, as I blindly reached into the diaper bag for my notepad and my soft case of color-coded pens. My fingers felt something smooth, so I pulled it out. The diaper I produced was proof I hadn't packed correctly that morning. I sighed and shoved the diaper back into one pocket and dug for the pen case. What else did I forget while floating around in this sleepless fog?

I needed an orange pen to list similarities of the victims to me, blue for the time and location of attacks, and red for. . . *the supernatural?* Alas, my pen case was MIA, and I resorted to my phone once again, where notes could get erased or inaccessible in the event of a broken screen—which happens a little too much to my clumsy self. Mom thought putting me in ballet as a child might help me catch up to her grace and poise. It only ended as another disappointment when she arrived at class and saw me in the corner organizing the costumes on the rolling rack instead of doing my stretches at the barre with the rest of the girls.

"I'm still not ruling out the Fae," Elsie said. "The Tooth Fairy might sound silly, but if anyone tries to trick you into some kind of trade or a deal, don't agree."

Her voice faded from my attention. My jaw dropped at the twenty-nine missed calls on the screen. I quickly tapped on my passcode, my heart pounding. Did Kai need help with Wendy? Did she get hurt at daycare? Did I miss her first words?

Detective W appeared on the call list twenty-eight times. Not the list I was particularly excited for, but still better than seeing Kai's name, or Mom's, or Ruby Slipper's Daycare considering those could indicate bad news coming from family.

"What the heck?" What could be so important that Detective Wilhelm would call that many times? My throat dried, and a knot formed as the possibilities flooded in. Another victim with my name on her? Closer to my home, even, than the front of the building?

My phone lit up with his contact info again, and I swiped right to answer. Elsie knitted her brows together as she munched on a home-made cranberry cookie and watched my face twist with concern.

What is it? she mouthed.

I shook my head as Detective Wilhelm explained, and my lagging brain tried to catch up.

"Paige Brown, the victim from the last attack, is requesting to see the woman with the baby," he said while releasing a sigh. "She won't talk unless it's to you. We need you at the hospital immediately."

Yes! Normally, I had to dig and call and wait for interviews to get information from the victims or families and friends. Then, I'd piece together bits of the story's puzzle.

This request from the victim was a gift. The answers begged me to gather them. My first day back at work might not be a total failure.

"On my way." I tapped the red dot, shoved my phone and the fang back in my bag, and hurried out the door.

"I'm getting major FOMO here, Mari!" Elsie shouted after me.

"Sorry and thank you!" I yelled over my shoulder, as the door swung shut. "The Tooth Fairy is going to have to wait."

Chapter 11

Slow and Superstitious Wins the Race

I skipped the wait for an Uber. With excitement pumping adrenaline through my steps, I'd walk to the hospital faster. On the way, I spoke to Siri, asking her to research Paige Brown and read the finding pages to me.

Siri informed me that Paige Brown was a college student interning at UCSF and an avid track competitor in high school. Other than that, the search proved useless.

When the elevator dinged, I power-walked to Ms. Brown's room, where brooding and overdramatic Detective Wilhelm stood in the doorway. Even under the warm fluorescent lights, he kept his heavy trench coat on and arms crossed.

"I'll be making a note of everything she says to you," he said, without so much as a greeting.

I nodded and pushed past him, ready to take plenty of notes of my own even if I didn't have my color-coded pens.

"And, Mari." He grabbed my elbow. "You are not, in any way, to coax her what to say."

I yanked my arm from his grip and rubbed it.

"I know how you storyteller types are, but this is not an article. It is life and death." His breath came with the stink of bitter black coffee into my face.

My lip twitched. It was no use arguing with a man who still believed women couldn't be investigators. He considered my reports nothing more than gossip columns. I hated that he always assigned himself as my guardian whenever we crossed paths on a dangerous case—the weaker sex and all.

I resisted the urge to roll my eyes for fear it'd only solidify his view of female emotion, so I turned to the woman in the bed instead.

Thick bandages wrapped around her neck, and stitches lined her face. Yellow and purple bruises mottled her jaw, collarbone, and both of her arms. I winced at the thought of the pain she'd endured while I was over here complaining about bites from a baby.

Her eyes slit open at the sound of my footsteps.

"I'm Mari Rowan," I said while offering an apologetic smile as if this was my fault. More motivation for me to solve this as soon as possible since I did feel some guilt.

Paige's eyes widened. "You're the woman from the attack."

I recoiled at the statement. Didn't she mean after the attack? I was at the hospital when it happened.

Her face twisted in pain as she struggled to turn her neck toward me. "I've seen you before." Detective Wilhelm made a huffing sound, but I didn't glance back.

I dragged the visitor's chair toward me and took a seat, keeping my gaze fixed on the victim. "Ms. Brown, are you comfortable telling me a little about the attack?"

"I-I felt someone watching me," she explained, as her eyes rolled to stare at the ceiling. "I run through Pioneer Park every evening. It's always been safe."

"Yeah." I nodded and frowned. "Not so much anymore."

"I'm fast too, so I didn't really worry when I noticed someone following me." Her voice came out weak, likely because of the exhaustion of recovery. "I figured I could lose them by switching trails quickly. I thought maybe they wanted to steal my phone or earbuds."

"Did you get a good look at the person who followed you?" I

asked, digging for facts through the pile of emotions. She had every right to her emotions, but facts would help identify the suspect and keep her safe. And normally, I'd keep a straight face, but the tears burned at the back of my eyes. What if this happened to Wendy someday?

"I saw you," she said.

My heart skipped a beat, and Detective Wilhelm cleared his throat. "What?"

"In the park, you were walking with a baby in your arms." She tore her eyes from the checkered tiles above us and stared at me.

"I showed up after it had attacked you. Ms. Brown—" I leaned forward and spoke softer. "Did you see the person who did this to you? Is there any way you can give a description and help us track them down?"

Paige's lashes fluttered until her eyelids closed, and a tear slipped out from between them. I waited, feeling the detective's gaze on my back. He knew I wasn't at the scene, right? Something told me this case would continue to get weirder. And if supernatural beings were real and involved, how would I ever get the truth? Even if I did, I'd never write about it because I'd lose my credibility. But the public needed the truth. Young women like Paige needed answers, whether or not those answers sounded crazy.

"It wasn't a person," she finally whispered.

Detective Wilhelm's boots stomped forward, and I caught the sight of his dark figure hovering over me from the corner of my eye.

"Was it an animal, then? It's rare, but I've heard of wild animals who travel into big cities when food or water is scarce," I reasoned. "At the time of the attack, you mentioned someone spoke to you. Did the. . ." *Ebenezer Scrooge, how can I ask this with Wilhelm listening over my shoulder? Screw it.* "Did the animal talk?"

"It wasn't a person," she repeated, as if she didn't hear me at all. Paige didn't open her eyes as she spoke. "Not at first anyway. It had gray fur and massive hands." She curled her fingers and held up her hands. "Like eagle talons, that's what it used to attack."

"Ms. Brown, are you saying an animal attacked you?" I tried to clarify before her story descended into a type of madness I didn't want to confront.

"And it's mouth. What a big mouth it had!" Her eyes flew open, and her blank stare caused me to straighten and put distance between us. Paige mashed the heels of her palms into her eyes and groaned. "The howling hurt my ears."

I turned to Detective Wilhelm with a sad expression. Did the injuries mess with poor Paige's brain?

But the detective wasn't looking at Ms. Brown. He crossed his arms and his nostrils flared as he glared down at me. I stood, immediately wanting to regain a sense of power.

"Come with me." He kept his gruff voice low, saying the demand under his breath.

I pinched my brow and didn't follow as he marched toward the door and yanked it open. Rhythmic beeping and the bustle of the ICU drifted in. His grimace deepened when he realized I wasn't behind him.

"Now, Rowan."

"I'd like to stay with Ms. Brown and make sure she is okay," I said.

Detective Wilhelm turned and let the door fall against his back. He crossed his arms again and looked like a model for noir-style clothing with his coat and fedora and heavy boots. "Then, I'll wait."

Paige didn't say another word. I held her hand until she fell asleep. When a nurse edged her way in to check the IV bag, I let go of the victim. With the workday almost over, I needed to make it to Reese's morgue before he closed up shop.

I stood and gave Paige's fingers a gentle squeeze before marching past Detective Wilhelm.

"What a waste of my time," he grunted, as he stomped beside me, narrowly missing a crash with a woman in a wheelchair.

I kept my path toward the elevator. I wanted to avoid a waste of my own time, AKA, another lecture from Detective Wilhelm about how I somehow disturbed his investigation. Of course, he never acknowledged my help when I got him answers or solved a tricky situation before he did.

"You're hiding something," he accused.

That stopped me. For a moment, I pretended to ruffle in my bag for my phone. *How does he know about the fang?*

"A-hah!" He stomped in front of me before I could reach the elevator. The chime dinged, and the doors slid shut behind him. "You admit it."

"I said nothing." I shrugged. *Just let me figure out this supernatural stuff and then I'll come clean.*

"You tricked that woman into saying those things."

My jaw dropped. "You're on some kind of witch hunt, Wilhelm. Not cool."

"You know what's not cool?" he said, as he stepped closer, towering over me in what I assumed was an attempt to intimidate me. "It's not cool that you used pointed questions to guide the victim's answers. She was hurt and confused—" Spittle flew from his mouth, and I resisted the urge to step back from the splash zone. He pointed over my head and back down the hall. "Ms. Brown and the other young females deserve justice. But you come here with your flowery purse and a woman's touch and charm her into talking nonsense."

He was joking, right? "You're joking, right?"

This only angered him more. I'd seen the detective this way before. When he didn't have a lead and the case felt particularly dangerous, he'd start screaming at rubberneckers or fighting with the medical examiner. I didn't blame him, though. When a mystery stumped me, I wanted to punch a few walls too.

"This isn't a story for your readers, Rowan," he said. His fuzzy upper lip twitched. "This is real life."

"My stories are to protect—"

"Ms. Brown told me she saw a woman following her," he said.

My eyes shifted away from him as I tried to piece together what that meant. A nurse gave us a weird look as he pushed some kind of equipment around us.

"Do you want to tell me about that? Huh?" Detective Wilhelm demanded.

"What?" I shook my head.

"You heard her," he said. "She saw you at the park. And she told me a woman was following her."

"Why didn't she tell me that?" I asked it more to myself than to Detective Wilhelm. He ignored me and continued blowing his bitter breath in my face.

"Because you didn't ask about anything outside of the day of the attack." He smirked, pleased with himself for one-upping me, which never made sense considering he already believed himself superior because of his male anatomy. "And Paige described the mysterious woman in a red cloak a lot like someone we both know." He sniffed, and his eyes flicked to my red jacket. "Who else would appear in odd places, stalking a young woman and asking strange questions other than a thirsty journalist?"

Red cloak? Appearing everywhere? It had to be Redhead. When I didn't answer, Detective Wilhelm straightened.

"You stay out of my way." He swiveled at the sound of the elevator's signal and stomped inside. "I better not see you anywhere near my crime scenes."

Did he forget I lived right next to one? I shook my head after the doors slid shut and headed for the stairs. Unlucky for him, I already had a date with the medical examiner.

I waited for my Uber outside the hospital, silently cursing myself that I'd need to make a stop at the office first. I never wanted Reese to have my direct line, but I needed to call and secure the appointment before he left. Plus, my aching chest wouldn't allow me to go another second without pumping.

Unless. . . I hopped in the Uber and pulled out my phone. Kai answered my video call with Wendy's pudgy cheeks on the screen. As much as I wanted to ooh and awe at her perfect face, I needed to discuss a plan. He picked her up from daycare after school an hour earlier, so I asked him to meet me at the morgue.

"Oh, and bring my color-coded pens!"

It didn't occur to me that Reese's 'office' was a disturbing place to bring a baby until I'd arrived and the chill of the room seeped through my thin sweater sleeves.

"What can I do for you, Ms. Rowan?" Reese grinned as he inspected a pale body on the table between us. The icy, stale smell of the room sent my nose wrinkling. I cradled Wendy after two unsuccessful attempts at breastfeeding in the hall. Kai ran to order takeout before he would meet us here after I got an answer.

I shifted Wendy around until I felt her safely snuggled in one arm and offered him the fang with my free hand.

Reese's gray eyes brightened, and he snatched it from my fingers like Gollum finding the One Ring. His translucent skin revealed blue and purple veins in his neck and hands as he bent down and moved into the light angled over the dead body. In this position, he could kiss the deceased with only the turn of his head.

I grimaced as the willies skittered over my arms in goosebumps. "Does anything about it look unusual to you? Elsie said you used to make anatomical models of mythical creatures, so I thought—" *What in the wonderland did I think? That he'd take one look at a random tooth and tell me it came from Loch Ness, then I could run off and slay the beast?* I snorted at the thought of Detective Wilhelm yelling at me for messing up his investigation as I stood over the body of a dead monster.

Wendy squirmed.

"M-hm, m-hm," Reese hummed and bobbed his head. He held the fang perched at the tips of his fingers. And then he licked it.

I gagged and made eyes at Wendy. *Creepy, right?* But my baby didn't find it as amusing as me. Her face tinged pink and pinched.

Reese stayed hunchbacked as he shuffled to another counter where he rubbed the tooth with a towel, then slipped it under a microscope.

"Mythical creatures, hm? Yes, yes," he muttered to himself. I'd been too harsh. Maybe Reese didn't give me the willies—I only interacted with him over a dead body in a freezing room, after all. Guilt struck my stomach and twisted it into knots, and it seemed Wendy struggled with her own tummy issues. Her mouth opened, and a long wail escaped.

Reese didn't so much as glance at us. Wendy sucked in a shuddering breath as I bounced and swayed her. But another wail followed, and another.

"Once upon a time," Reese said, long and drawn-out, "a man met a lovely lady with a crimson cloak."

Wendy's screams bounced off the metal cabinets that held who knows how many bodies. I needed a bottle, stat. But Reese's voice lifted louder and louder with each word. Rather than shouting, it followed a rhythm and lilted.

"And when she spoke, he knew all she said was true," he continued, and Wendy's wailing sputtered for a moment. "She was lovely, sure, but not *her*, and the man thought, yes, he thought a lot until he accepted his spot. But never hers."

Reese's voice, smooth and powerful, commanded the space, and the metal tables and drawers around us felt warmer. My jaw dropped as Wendy's cries receded, and the only sound was the little medical examiner's song that chimed in a constant, clear pitch. The rhythmic tune reminded me of a bell, and I filed a mental note in purple to pull the bells off of the Christmas wreath in storage. Maybe they'd help next time Wendy woke at the crack of dawn. The next note I pictured in orange, my alert color. *Reese mentioned a woman in a cloak. Redhead?*

"And so he dedicated his life to the work of death and worked without rest to ensure the best chance at living and giving her hope." Reese concluded the song with a low-pitched hum that left Wendy's eyelids heavy and her little mouth stretching into a yawn.

I stroked her forehead with my thumb. How'd he do that? "Dark lullaby," I said. "But you have an enchanting voice."

"Like a bell." He nodded as he handed the fang back to me. "I've been told before."

"Did you learn anything?" I asked, hopeful to leave with some kind of answer. Especially after the victim's interview only left me with more questions. And an angry detective.

Reese spun to one side, holding onto the metal table until a series of cracks rippled up his spine. He repeated the process on the other side, but still didn't straighten fully. After hours of leaning over dead bodies, I imagined his back must ache something fierce.

"This tooth does not belong to a human," he said, as he pulled on new gloves and gently turned the deceased's person's head.

"An animal, then?" I asked, trying to line up the evidence with the victim's story.

Reese shook his head, and his pin-straight nutmeg hair fell into his eyes. I wondered how he saw what he was working on. "No, no, not animal, not human, and not alien, either, just to clarify."

That clarified nothing. At least, not for me. Reese spoke in riddles. His eyes rolled up and gazed at me through his greasy hair.

"You'll dislike the answer, I assure you," he said. "I don't feel approved to share the underbelly of the unnatural with you."

"Reese, please," I begged for something to make sense. "Is it a vampire?" I laughed, but the joke didn't land. He flinched and lifted his head, banging it on the bent-over light.

With one hand, he rubbed his forehead, and the other pointed to the tooth in my hand. "This is no joke."

"Not animal, not human, not a joke. Got it." I nodded. "What does that leave us with?"

"Not one." He stared at my hand. "Both. Don't laugh."

I shook my head and furrowed my brow. "I promise I won't. I'm new to all this unexplainable stuff, but I'm starting to see it."

"The supernatural isn't unexplainable if you know what you're looking for," he said. Goosebumps pricked my arms at the excitement and strangeness of it all.

A knock at the door echoed through the chamber of metal, and I jumped. Reese shouted for them to come inside. I expected Kai and the scent of fried cheese sticks and ranch to fill the room.

Jameson strode in without so much as a glance in my direction until he came up beside me and did a double-take at Wendy. He grimaced and his teeth, so white, blinding white, flashed for a moment.

"So, what did you get for me, nerd?" Jameson nodded his chin toward Reese.

Reese raised one eyebrow and started humming again rather than respond to the jerk in the designer jeans.

Jameson folded his arms, impatient. "Come on, I don't have all day for your games. I know you're lonely down here, but I've got a job to do."

What. A. Jerk.

Reese stiffened and blinked rapidly. After shaking his head, he refocused on the dead woman's face and turned her chin to the other side.

"Wait, is this her?" I asked. "The second victim?"

Jameson scoffed. "Go home, Rowan." He turned to me and eyed my stomach and how tightly my sweater fit over it. "Motherhood suits you."

"The first," Reese said. Finally, a straightforward answer. "Return with another piece of the puzzle, Mari. I'll identify what it is. But you should leave now." He looked up again, eyes shifting between Jameson and Wendy. "The morgue is no place for a baby. This is far more dangerous than anything you've seen before, I assure you."

My heart skipped a beat at his words, and the hair at the back of my neck prickled. I didn't want to acknowledge the risk. I've interviewed serial killers and confronted murderers for the truth before. But this felt different, more reckless and out of control, not unlike raising a child. Wendy stirred, and her eyelids blinked as she woke from the brief nap.

Jameson snorted and nodded in agreement with the medical examiner, the same medical examiner he'd just called a nerd. When he held out his fist for Reese to bump in agreement, Reese recoiled and waved Jameson's hand away from his work area.

"And, Mari," Reese called, as I made my way to the door. "The Index of Animal-Human Hybrids."

I quirked my head, and he clarified. "At the library."

Both human and *animal?* I slipped the tooth into my pocket and left. Before the heavy door shut, I heard Jameson take another subtle jab at Reese's geekiness.

In red, I visualized the word *unnatural,* then a line through it and beneath, *supernatural.* I exited the building onto the street and dodged a passing couple with a stroller. My mind's eye switched to blue, *return to the crime scenes in Pioneer Park and find another piece.* It wasn't something I'd normally waste time doing. Detectives would have combed the area clean. But this case was different, and only I knew to look for something different. Something supernatural.

I squeezed my eyes shut for a second to file the thought away. When I opened them again, Kai's cold red nose and cheeks beamed in front of me. He held up a tied plastic bag with Styrofoam boxes full of artery-clogging goodness.

I'd get to Pioneer Park tonight after Wendy had a bottle, bath, snuggles, more snuggles, and. . . I really didn't want to leave her again in one day, but murderers didn't wait. Neither could I.

Still, the desire to quit nagged at me. Pam's inspirational speech only lasted so long to boost me. Digging into this proved dangerous, as evident by my maiden name splashed all over the crime scenes. Should I risk it with a baby at home who needed me? In pink, I imagined another note.

Do I give up and let someone else solve this one?

Once we arrived home, I took a bath to wash off the icky morgue feeling. I'd hoped to nurse little naked Wendy again while I balanced her on my soft belly, halfway in the warm water.

Kai fed me French fries while I attempted to feed our baby and discussed the supernatural possibilities aloud. He took it in stride, ever the supportive husband. But I saw the raised brows.

"You don't believe me?" I asked.

After a shrug and a sigh, he stuffed a fry into his mouth. While munching, he considered this. "I didn't believe I'd survive watching you give birth, either. And look at me now, still kicking."

"Not the same," I groaned and tried to switch Wendy to the other side, but she fidgeted angrily.

"No, I'm serious. Parenthood has shattered everything I knew before. I never expected to be okay with poop on my hands or that I'd survive on a night of only two hours of sleep or that I could love someone so much that I regularly believe Wendy is some kind of angel or fairy or supernatural in her own right." He said everything I felt, but I refused to cry in the bath with French fry breath. "I'm positive now that there are things in this world I don't understand. This case of yours seems to be one of them."

Okay, screw it. I let the tears well up and spill over my cheeks.

"Aw, hun, I thought I only made my students cry. You know, when I announce essay questions on the test." He set the takeout plate down and wiped my wet face. He shifted to his knees and leaned over the bath to share a kiss with me.

If only I could have taken a snapshot of our family right then and there. I wanted to remember the moment forever, the moment when we both realized becoming parents made us both stronger and weaker at the same time. The moment where I decided this case and the murders growing closer to our house meant I needed to give it my all. Because now I had a family to protect, and this was no normal series of murders.

When Kai pulled away, he smiled, but I couldn't return it. Not with the faint sound of the howling coming from outside our building.

I filed away another mental note in yellow. *Go to the library first thing tomorrow. Then, visit the crime scenes.*

Nobody messes with Mama Bear, supernatural or not.

Chapter 12

A Historical Photo is Worth a Thousand Words

Someday, I'd return to the gym. Not because I gave in to those stupid 'get your pre-baby body back' lines, but because car-seats are heavy and Wendy would only get heavier. I needed stretch pants and sneakers just to get her strapped in the stroller.

After soaking through the pits in my cardigan, I finally got the car-seat to click into its special spot. But that was after dragging the million-pound contraption down two flights of stairs from the condo to the street. Wendy twitched her head to look up at the dangling fox. I flicked it to send the inside bell jingling, and she cooed on cue.

"I'll miss these days when you're so easily entertained," I said in a baby voice. But I'd eat those words later when Wendy wailed for two hours from gas bubbles. For now, she stayed quiet and happy with a belly half-full of formula and a soft blanket over her legs.

Though my arms almost snapped off after the stroller-car-seat workout, I pulled my hair into a ponytail and power-walked to the library. I wore my best resting-witch-face, so old ladies wouldn't insist I stop and let them ooh and awe over Wendy. The massive library immediately pulled me in with that book smell and the calm atmosphere. It was the potential to learn something new that fascinated me the most.

I pushed the stroller up to the front desk and whispered to the woman behind it. She shoved her glasses up and looked at me without blinking. Her tiny nose wrinkled at the mention of the Index.

"Index of Animal-Human Hybrids?" she repeated in a mousy voice. "I've never heard of it." Her nails tapped against a keyboard, and she squinted at the computer screen. "Nothing comes up when I search for it, either."

I sighed and leaned my hip against the stroller. It started rolling, and I stumbled.

"Sorry, Wendy! I'm so sorry," I babbled. The librarian shushed me with her finger and a sound louder than my apologies.

"That's a cute name," she said, as she straightened to peek into the stroller. "Like from *Peter Pan*. That was my favorite book as a child."

"Oh, yeah." I nodded. "I never thought of the connection."

The librarian's thin lips spread into a tight smile. "You know, we do have some books that are not documented in our system. Your index might be in that section." She pointed to the back corner of the library where the light over the center tables didn't reach. "Just past the horror section, there's a wall of books that never get touched. Odd histories and such." Her lips made a small smacking sound, and she returned to her filing.

I thanked her and spun the stroller around, almost colliding with a grumpy guy and his stack of thriller novels. I hurried away. I didn't have time to get on anyone's bad side. In approximately one hour, Wendy would scream like a banshee for milk that I didn't have, and we'd need to run home.

Rows of old books lined the dark corner. They were all so different it didn't appear organized, but I realized they were alphabetized by title rather than author. Many didn't claim a writer's name. I pulled one down that read *Unexplained Disappearances*. But I didn't flip through the pages because I didn't have an interest in the *Roswell* or *X-Files* conspiracies.

I ran my finger along the shelf, trying to make out the title of each book. The dark corner didn't help, so I pulled out my phone and used the flashlight to brighten the area, but Wendy fussed. Her eyes had closed, and the quiet corner had lulled her to sleep. A sleep which I ruined. I quickly flicked off the light and shoved my phone away.

"A-hah!" I whispered, as a thick green book caught my eye. *Index of Animal-Human Hybrids* sat right between *History of Reanimated Corpses* and *Fairy Tales You've Never Heard*. I sat back on my butt and folded my legs crisscross applesauce, ready to dive into the details of creatures with human heads and goat bodies. Reese knew something I didn't. And I needed to catch up before these unexplained murders got out of control.

I leaned over and pulled out my notebook and case of pens from the pocket at the bottom of the stroller. With the empty pages, I'd start an index of my own, marking species of creature in a different color. Then, I followed with a list where I tacked extra sticky notes to add my questions on top.

Wendy napped without so much as a grunt. I checked her breathing several times and returned to my warm spot on the carpet until the list satisfied me. I snapped the Index shut and stacked it on my notebook, then topped it off with my block of multicolored sticky notes.

Before I could unfold and stand, another book caught my eye. It didn't have the title on the spine, but a small rectangle etched in the cover resembled a door. I squatted and slid it out from the dusty shelf. The spine cracked as I opened it.

Doors to the Unknown. A scribbled drawing marked the page. Someone had drawn a door in ink and filled in the other side with clouds and stars. I flipped the page to find another drawing. My breath hitched, and my mouth hung open. This drawing showed a woman with squiggles of hair standing beside the door. The art style was crude and simplistic, but clear enough.

"Redhead?" I breathed, wishing the artist had used colored ink. I turned to the next page, and the drawings got gradually messier as if the artist was in a hurry. The doors depicted other places, one with the Eiffel Tower in the background, and another with the Egyptian pyramids. It appeared the woman used them to teleport between places.

My heart thumped at the note scribbled in the back. I whispered it aloud to process it. "The original *Doors to the Unknown,* written in

1723, mentions a woman traveling between death sites. They called her a Reaper, but she'd arrive before the deaths occurred. 1759, a woman was seen with a dark-haired girl in a glass coffin and seven stunted men."

My throat tightened as the creeping sense of the macabre grew closer. I'd felt this before when interviewing a serial killer. He'd tried to charm me with his sense of humor and explain his grotesque murders with love and affection.

I turned the last page over to see the writing continue. *She calls herself the Keeper. Also, referenced in* Before the Legends.

"*Before the Legends*," I repeated. "Is that a record?" I shook the book as if it would answer. The *Doors* book fell to the side as I hopped to my feet and ran my fingertip along the shelf again, mouthing the titles. "*Angelic to Demonic, Atoms and Other Things That Matter, Bait and Switch Stories, Black Plague Survivors, Before the Legends.*"

I doubled-backed, almost missing it since it was out of order. Someone hadn't returned it to the correct place, which meant someone else had looked at the book recently. My short stint working in a library told me that even *my* level of organization and color coding couldn't live up to that of true librarians. They'd never let something stay unalphabetized for long, even if it was in a dark corner of old books.

My fingers curled around the deep purple spine that reminded me of royals from long ago. I only slid it halfway off the shelf when a blasting bright light beamed over the corner. I jumped, shielding my eyes from the sudden sunshine coming from the shelf on my left. The book toppled to the floor, smashing my pinky toe. I squeaked and grabbed my foot, now both blinded and hopping on one leg. By the time I blinked and squinted enough to see anything, the light vanished, and the corner fell into darkness again.

The brush of smooth fabric whipped against my hand as something moved past me. Wendy gasped and wailed, a dry cry to announce that she was disturbed from her precious sleep. My eyes slowly adjusted to the quick changes in light. A hooded figure dashed down the corridor of shelves and past the stroller with a thick book in hand.

My vision caught up, discerning colors between the spots of black. I recognized the red hood, the purple book, and the orange curls tumbling down her shoulder before she disappeared around the corner.

"Hey!" I shouted. I glanced back in the direction from where the light had come, but only saw shelves. I tripped over my stack of books and notes as I grabbed the stroller and barreled down the corridor. The stroller didn't turn easily, and I didn't want to jar my already angry infant, so I slowed and gently angled it around the edge. Redhead's cloak fell off as she ran for the front of the library. Nobody stopped her, but a young man smirked at her bouncing you-know-what as she ran by. Hey, at least it confirmed Redhead wasn't a figment of my imagination.

"Hey. Stop!" I yelled again, drawing all eyes to me. I didn't let that stop me from zooming past the shelves and toward the front door. A movement caught the corner of my eye, and I came to a crashing halt when the librarian stepped out in front of me.

She folded her arms and lifted her chin. "Can you please not run or shout inside the library?"

"But she. . ." I stuttered and pointed to the clear doors, as they slid shut and the fiery hair vanished down the stone steps.

"I wasn't quick enough," the librarian said with a sigh, as she eyed the doors. "Usually, people try to steal the computer keyboards, though, not books." Her gaze flicked to Wendy, who continued her desperate screeches. "Did you have something you wanted to check out?" She looked at me over the rim of her glasses now, and I understood she wanted us to leave. I'd been asked the same question by employees in stores when Wendy cried. Sometimes it worked to my advantage when people in the grocery shop line pressured me to go before them just so that I'd get the screaming banshee out of the store faster. Nobody sympathized, not unless they had a stroller by their side too.

I nodded and retrieved my pile of books on the floor from the corner, carrying them under one arm while bouncing Wendy in the other. I pushed the stroller along with my hip until a young mom with a toddler wrapped around her leg offered to help me out the door.

I thanked her before she went back inside. "Excuse me," I said.

The mom stopped, but her child tugged on her arm and bounced back like her limb was a bungee rope.

"Did you see a bright light in the library just a few minutes ago?"

She nodded, and a flood of relief washed over me, not unlike when the prison gate opened and I left the serial killer behind after the interview. "Yeah, someone took a flash picture or something, I guess."

"I guess," I mumbled, processing this. She continued on her way, and the doors rolled shut on their automated track. I knelt and stacked the Index, the Door book, and my notes in the pocket at the bottom of the stroller that looked more like a hammock to me.

At home, it took me three hours to calm Wendy and two and a half failed attempts at nursing. It might be time to hang up the breastfeeding bra. I sighed and flopped onto the couch after Wendy started dozing in her Moses basket. Kai woke from his nap since he'd agreed to do all the midnight wake-ups with Wendy this weekend.

He rubbed his eye with his fist until he spotted the title of my book.

"*Doors to the Unknown*, huh?" He tilted his head and leaned on the kitchen counter to squint at the book.

I sat up, using my arms to propel myself forward. A sudden burst of energy rippled through me, and I dove into the explanation. He listened intently while he poured himself a cup of cold coffee that had been sitting in the jug all day.

"You know history, right?" I asked, as he sat down on the couch beside me. Of course, I already knew the answer, so I continued. "Have you ever heard of a cloaked woman? Or a reaper woman? Anything like that?"

Kai pursed his lips and leaned his head back on the cushion to stare up at the ceiling. "Hmm. I know if you go into the bathroom and say bloody Mary three times, a ghost will appear."

I socked him in the arm. He splashed a little coffee from his mug as he rubbed the spot I punched.

He gave me puppy dog eyes. "I'm serious. I mean, not about the ghost thing. But some form of that legend appears in other cultures too, and before Bloody Mary herself even existed, there was another witch-like woman that was said to have appeared when summoned by her name."

"What does this have to do with anything?" I asked, as my tired brain tried to knit it together.

"My point is stories repeat themselves. It's human nature to share experiences, and often, the very basic human stories are similar across time and cultures."

I stole the coffee mug and chugged. Kai opened his mouth, but I put my finger up, warning him not to judge me. "Wendy doesn't want my milk anyway." I shrugged after polishing off the cup. He knew my shrug was a weak attempt to cover the pain and disappointment I felt with my motherhood status. "I need some caffeine to fuel this research." I needed to change the subject back before we lost track of the clues.

I sat up and set the mug and book on the Coffee Table of Evidence. Kai rubbed my back in little circles as I stared at the words on the page. *Dark-haired girl and seven men. . .*

Ebenezer Scrooge!

"You say stories repeat themselves?" My words stumbled over one another as they fought to be the first out of my mouth.

"Yeah," he confirmed.

"So, you wouldn't think I'm crazy if I told you that the investigation I did on the poisoned girl at the Portland museum in the past was Snow White?"

The circles stopped. I twisted my torso to face him.

"Look at what it says here. Her body was hidden inside a glass coffin, and there were seven men, who worked at the museum. Exactly seven," I said, jamming my finger against the page. "And it was her mother-in-law who tried to kill her, then she hid her and claimed her body was a wax depiction of Margaret Tudor, Henry Tudor's sister."

"So, what are you saying?" he asked.

"I have no idea!" I nearly shouted. "Oops." I slapped my hand over my mouth as Wendy stirred and punched her arm out of the swaddle. She settled again and made a suckling motion with her lips. "Okay," I whispered. "I'm thinking these fairy tale writers just aren't original, right? History repeats itself. That's not uncommon with murders, either. People murder for the same basic reasons. It's the criminally insane ones that throw us off." I shuddered at the memory of the serial killer interview. "I don't know how sanity works in the supernatural world, but I imagine it's double the craziness. If I can find a pattern to these murders, maybe I can find this woman's connection to them. Since it says here that she arrives before the deaths, I might be able to track her and get to the scene before the next killing."

Kai nodded along but pulled out his phone and tapped at the screen. "Are you listening?"

"Yeah, yeah," he said. "I'm seeing these supernatural connections now." He sat up. "I looked up a reaper story in 1759, and the same thing came up on this Wiki site. There's a picture here of an ancient book with artwork of a girl in a glass coffin and look, one, two. . ." He counted seven men in the picture and one curly-haired woman.

"Ebenezer Scrooge, Kai." My jaw dropped. "That's her!"

His Adam's apple bobbed with a slow swallow. He raised his eyebrows and slid his finger up the screen to close the app and open another search page that he'd already pulled up.

"That isn't even the strangest thing. Well—" he blinked rapidly, then paused. "It is. But what's also interesting is that Snow White wasn't written until 1812, and this book with the reaper picture wasn't discovered until 1935, so the Brothers Grimm couldn't have plagiarized it. Plus, that murderous mother-in-law in your case last year even got close with the name Margaret. The Grimms based Snow White on a girl named Margaretha von Waldeck."

We both looked up from the phone and spoke at the same time. "History repeats itself."

And it has something to do with my stalker, AKA the Keeper.

Chapter 13

Bit off More Than I Could Chew

Armed with pepper spray, a switchblade, and my self-defense moves (though pregnancy may have stolen a few of my muscles since my Muay Thai classes), I snatched my red jacket and exited the condo before Wendy's little face could convince me to stay in for the night. Though prepared, I didn't expect too much excitement in my quick visit to the park, so I left my Sig at home. I hadn't been able to locate my holster since bassinets and baby wipes had taken over our house. But I loved all of Wendy's little things: little toes, little clothes, and her perfect not-so-little chubby face.

After the long second day back at work, I ached to be home with her more. But I'd secured the Index of Something Or Other That I Didn't Understand and gained a few scant clues that required a thorough analysis into the crime scenes. The chilly evening air cut into my nose and white puffs of breath obscured my vision.

I needed to stop by Bay Side Media's office and grab my notebook with the color-coded clues I'd discovered and other facts about the attacks. Kai always told me to use my laptop so that I could access my notes anywhere, even on my phone, but my brain worked better when I wrote the cases out by hand. Still, I regretted that the handwritten notes meant I didn't have copies and I'd need to take an extra trip to the office.

My keys jingled as I dug them out of my jeans pocket and stuck them into the door. When I twisted the doorknob and stepped into the dimly lit office, I flicked on another overhead light and made for my cubicle. After shuffling through papers and checking drawers, I let out a frustrated breath.

"Where is it?" I groaned. I'd spent half the afternoon studying the Index and categorizing the creatures. If I'd lost all that work, I'd kick myself.

A cough caused me to jump. I gasped and snapped my head up from my cubicle. Scruffy hair poked up from the other side of the makeshift white wall. Purposely gelled and messy hair that I'd recognize anywhere.

"Jameson?" I squeaked, still startled. He only grunted. "What are you doing here right now?"

His narrowed, sharp eyes glared at me from his hunched position in the ergonomic office chair. "My job," he snapped. "Which is more than I can say for you. Some of us don't get parental vacations to take time off whenever we feel like it."

"My maternity leave is over," I said, as I folded my arms. The leather-bound book in his hands caused a hiccup in my throat. "Is that my notebook?"

Jameson smirked and slapped it shut. He offered it to me with a wry look on his face, and I snatched it from his hand.

"I have hope I'll become the lead investigative journalist after all," he said.

I hugged the comforting feeling of notes and organization and leather to my chest. "What is that supposed to mean?"

The chair squeaked when he leaned back and kicked his feet up on his desk. "While you're chasing wild mythical theories, I'll be solving murders." He nodded toward the notebook and grinned wider.

"Good luck." I raised my brows and turned away from him to march for the door. Armed with the notebook, I felt safer than ever, but

I wanted to put distance between me and the guy who insisted on being my rival.

The chair squeaked again, and his stomping footsteps followed me to the door. I sensed him but refused to look back and give him any more attention than he'd already gotten. He pushed past me, his shoulder bumping into my back, and exited the office as soon as I opened the door.

"You're the one who needs luck," he said before shoving his hands into his coat pockets and skulking off down the street. I scoffed and shook my head, refusing to let his microaggressions get to me. He'd never been a nice person. I couldn't let it bother me.

Right now, I needed to focus. I redirected my thoughts during the walk back to Main Street, and the cold air helped to clear my head.

I hiked the uphill climb to Pioneer Park with hands in my pockets and fingers curled around my little weapon. Kai didn't love the idea of me going out again at night, but if he had joined, it meant Wendy would have to come too and neither of us liked that risk. Tala hadn't answered her door for a babysitting request, though she rarely left home. Maybe she'd joined a Tuesday-night knitting club after I'd begged her for more homemade baby blankets.

And Mom had returned my phone calls with a text that said, 'finishing that date with E tonight.'

At least the precinct had answered when I called, though they'd said Detective Wilhelm was out and asked if I wanted to leave a message. I declined. How could I say *hey, I spent my day at the library, out of your way at least. Call me back so I can tell you about these mythical creatures that our murderer is emulating.*

So, there I walked, alone, against all my mother's childhood warnings. But such was the life of a journalist. Investigations didn't happen between the nine to five on workdays, and I had no desire to buddy-system this case with Jameson.

Stupid? Maybe, but at least I planned to arrive prepared. I pulled out the planner full of sticky notes from my little book bag. I'd color-coded the pages of the Index book as well as rewritten the creatures into my planner.

I'd used green for the animal-human hybrids and created bullet points for pieces of each that could leave behind clues. I studied the notes but kept my ears pricked and aware of my surroundings as I walked. While reading, I still picked up the details around me, like a teenage couple who laughed and kissed at the entrance of the park, a man who jogged in shorts that showed more than I wanted to see. . . and a red-headed woman on a bench.

I snapped my head in that direction, but the bench was empty. I paused and looked around, then returned to the bullet points.

Angel- look for feathers left behind from wings.

~~Centaur~~- crossed out because hooves cannot create scratch marks.

~~Faun~~- also nixed because of hooves.

Selkie- find shed skin? Coming out of San Fran Bay?

Werewolf- makes the most sense + the howling and fang, but Index says they're only active on nights with a full moon. Does not line up with murders. But didn't the Keeper mention a wolf?

Sphinx- eagle talons match Paige's description.

Dryad- scratch marks could be from branches?

The walk cleared my head. It was time to take this supernatural bit seriously, but it still played tricks on my mind. This felt like an alternate world, yet I hiked only ten minutes from my house. Reese's words popped into my head.

"Underbelly of the unnatural," I whispered under my breath, as I arrived at the location of the first attack. I'd come across more than a few unsolved cases. Those stories, though frustrating to me, actually drew a lot of readers to my content. People liked to read about what they couldn't explain, yet they also needed that distance—an article online, rather than acknowledging the mysteries of the universe.

What existed out there that we humans ignored after the rubbernecking got to be too much? Too creepy? I used to dread talking with Reese because he always acted too excited about death, but now I understood. It wasn't death; it was uncovering the unknown, even if only a teeny bit.

I surveyed the concrete trail, but the crime scene was long cleaned. No blood, and nothing left behind, of course, because that'd be a biohazard. *Duh, Mari.* Still, the cleanup crew wouldn't have identified feathers or human-shaped branches as clues to the murder. I parted the branches on a bush off to the side but only found a discarded Sprite bottle that blended with the green leaves.

The park lamps offered little more than a dim glow, so I whipped out my phone and blasted the flashlight in and around the bush, over the sidewalk, and around a tree trunk. I wrinkled my nose, attempting to picture the face of a human inside the gnarled oak. If it was there, it wasn't obvious, so I squinted and tilted my head. A knot in the trunk almost matched a yawning mouth. I tilted further and further until my head was almost upside down. At the sound of footsteps, I snapped back up.

An old woman eyed me as she power-walked by with her handheld weights. I offered a smile, but something in the branches caught my eye. My heart jumped at the thought of the tree coming to life and waving its branched hand at me as it turned to its dryad form (I'd watched a YouTube video. In cartoon form, of course). The woman sped away from me and glanced over her shoulder as I slapped my palm to my chest and let out a little gasp.

After ignoring her obvious judgmental gaze, I fixed on the little thread dangling from a branch. The wind tossed it around, almost ripping the tuft of gray wrapped around the string. I tripped over a root but didn't fall. After repositioning the flashlight, I plucked it from the branch before the breeze swept the hair away.

On closer inspection, I noted the thread. It was yarn for knitting or crocheting. It had frayed, but I could make out that it was thick and forest green. The tuft of hair, or fur, tangled around it. If this thread came from a scarf or knitted sweater, its wearer must have had the hairiest arms or neck anyone's ever seen.

I bit the bottom of my phone to keep the flashlight shining on the clue as I knelt and balanced the tangled thread and tuft on my knee. With my hands free, I pulled out my notepad and scribbled in green *the thread* and in red *fur or hair*. Neither showed supernatural tendencies, but the fang hadn't, either. Not until Reese examined it, that is.

It wasn't much, but I still had a second location to scour. I stood and tucked the notebook under my arm. The little walk to the bridge left me breathless. I kept my eyes wide and ears pricked for anything unusual, but thankfully, I only passed a jogger with his earbuds cranked so loud it left Green Day lyrics stuck in my head.

I hummed the familiar tune as I scaled down the muddy bank toward the stream. The tiny trickle of water left me skeptical that a selkie would come here. From what I'd binge-read in the Index, they avoided heavily human areas because greedy, creepy men often forced them into relationships by stealing their seal skin. Sounded like something Jameson would do.

My foot slipped in the mud, and I landed smack on my butt. The fall continued as I slid down the bank, and my Nikes landed in the water. I groaned at the sure stain that the moist ground must have left in a precarious place between my jeans pockets. *Ick.*

I shifted my hands to one side to push up and out of the mud without moving my sore butt too quickly. My palm landed in the moist, cool mud, and I grimaced. You'd think I'd be used to getting dirty with this job, plus my clumsiness, but muddy hands meant muddy fingerprints on my notebook. Before I could push off the ground and wipe my hands on my pants, which already looked poop-stained, a paw print caused me to pause.

This was no mark from a city pooch. Holes dipped deep into the dirt, indicating massive claws or talons. The paw pads spread so wide that the print looked larger than my head. I pushed weeds out of the way and found another print. And another. I crawled up the bank, forgetting about my trashed pants and the new stains that now formed on my knees. The prints grew closer together and the paws smaller, the claw holes not as deep.

My heart raced as the next set of marks were elongated. The paw pad extended out the back, and the smaller pads shrank and added a fifth. The dirt away from the bank grew dryer too, more solidified in the marks. The colors in my brain's filing cabinet exploded.

Green for dog prints- did the detectives ignore this, assuming animal tracks?

Orange for strange, unidentifiable prints- was this an animal trans-formation?

Red for. . . human feet?

I came to a dead stop and stared at the trail of tracks that ended with bare feet, larger than mine, but not huge. My hand covered my mouth, and I chewed on the inside of my finger, absorbing the sight.

Ebenezer Scrooge. It's a werewolf.

"I'm not in Kansas anymore, but I sure wish you were as harmless as Toto," I spoke to the tracks as if the suspect could hear me through them.

Still, *werewolf* didn't match up with the murder times. Broad daylight? Multiple attacks in one month? I'd thought transformations happened on a cycle, like that crappy womanly time that breastfeeding had temporarily rescued me from.

I pulled out my phone and took a series of snapshots. The flash blinded me, and I rubbed at my eyes. The quiet of Pioneer Park rippled with an ear-splitting howl. My heart stopped, and my breath stuck in my throat. The rhythmic thump in my chest continued, and for a second, it was all I could hear.

My feet moved without my permission, and I turned toward the cry. Pounding footsteps raced toward me, thump-thumping against the dirt. My pulse throbbed in my neck, and my throat squeezed shut before I could scream.

A figure ran off the concrete path in the distance and vanished into the trees. It reappeared, close enough now for me to catch the sight of it bending forward. Another howl exploded, and a distant siren blared from the city. A city that now felt hundreds of miles away.

Run. No, watch. Film it! Wait, no, RUN! My brain skipped around, but my feet, my arms, and none of the outside parts of me dared to move. Except for my jaw. It hung slack as I watched the silhouette of the figure drop to its hands and knees. A series of popping sounds echoed, and the figure's back doubled in size, the spine expanding and protruding.

A cry escaped the creature's mouth. It sounded like a human cry, whimpering before it twisted into a snarl, and the shape of the face stretched into a snout.

Finally, and without my permission, my legs broke from their frozen state, and I stumbled back. My notebook dropped from my armpit and landed with a thud on the dirt. The creature snapped its neck toward me. Bright yellow eyes flashed and fixed on me, the pupils expanding like an abyss ready to swallow me whole.

Fingers gripped my wrist and yanked me sideways, nearly ripping my arm from its socket. I yelped, both from the pain and the shock of another figure beside me. I tore my arm from their grasp.

"Come. Now," a woman's voice whispered in demand.

A branch broke, and my head flicked back to the creature. It loped on all fours toward us at a speed no slower than Kai, driving me to the hospital while in labor. The woman grabbed my arm again and pulled me along.

"My notebook!" I squealed my misplaced priorities. But thoughts of color-coded clues vanished when we made it to the concrete trail and into the glow of the streetlamp. The woman's crushed velvet cloak rivaled her fiery curls.

"You," I said, breathless.

"You can't be here," she spoke in a hushed but clear voice. Then, it dipped into a mutter, something I likely wasn't supposed to hear. "I don't know which Fable is Red, I need more time." Her eyes darted around the ground in front of us but landed on nothing specific. Redhead snapped her chin over her shoulder at the sound of the creature's approach. "Run that way." She pointed down the trail and back toward the city. "There is a woman. When you see her, walk calmly and say nothing of this. This story isn't ready." Her hands quivered, and the blood drained from her face. "I've lost control."

I opened my mouth, but Redhead pulled the hood over her head. The cloak flew out behind her as she vanished back into the trees. The creature didn't change course to follow her, but it did pause when another series of pops echoed, and it whimpered.

I refused to make the same mistake twice, waiting and watching. I ran down the trail, not because Redhead instructed me to, but because it was the smart thing to do. And I'd warn the supposed woman.

But when I ended up back in the park, with the playground to my left, Redhead was already there, speaking to a young woman with a tiny dog in her purse.

Redhead's eyes flickered over me for a second. Then, she smiled at the woman.

"Run," I shouted, but it was too late.

The creature burst from the narrow trail with overhanging branches and dark shadows from the trees. Redhead spun around and used both hands to shove me out of the way as the massive beast sprung off its hind legs. My tailbone smacked against the ground for the second time that day, and pain shot up my back. The wolf creature smashed down on the innocent woman. Together, they rolled in a tangle, and she didn't have time to scream before its jaw clamped down over her face. The little dog tumbled out of the purse and skittered away, barking in a screech.

I screamed as the beast tore into the woman's flesh with claws and fangs. Redhead waved her arm at me violently, pointing and yelling for me to run. I scrambled to my feet and backed away. I dodged behind the playground, making for Main Street, but felt for my phone instead.

Call 911, my brain reasoned, but my body froze again in the shadow of the big slide. Sudden silence caught my attention, and I looked back at the carnage.

It wasn't the attack that shocked me the most.

The creature stopped chomping on the woman's neck and popping echoed again as its body shrank before my eyes. Breath escaped me, and my throat squeezed even tighter as I watched Redhead calmly approach the beast and its prey. She knelt and dipped one finger into the victim's blood. With her red-stained finger, she started writing something on the sidewalk.

Just when I thought it couldn't get any weirder, Redhead stood and backed up. A small round object appeared on the ground in front of her, and she crouched to pull on it. A door appeared on the concrete, and she jumped inside, but not without grabbing a handful of gray fur and yanking the creature in after her.

My phone slipped from my fingers and fell with a thud into the sand. I jumped at the sound but responded quicker now, my body finally obeying my brain's commands. After scooping it up, I tripped and stumbled toward the woman. Her arm twitched, and my mind raced with how I could help.

CPR. Tourniquet? 9.1.1. I collapsed on my hands and knees beside her, but she was gone before I could dial. Her body went completely still, but it didn't stop me from starting compressions.

Sirens screamed their chilling cries in the distance. They grew louder, shrill and piercing as they approached and blared down Main. It happened so fast. Paramedics and onlookers appeared and echoed something about hearing a disturbance.

One minute, I was alone, and the next, surrounded. Or so it felt. Like giving birth, watching death seemed to stop time. The concept of minutes and hours melted together and washed away.

"Mari?" Combat boots stomped up beside me on the sidewalk. I looked up from my kneeled position to see Detective Wilhelm fold his arms and raise his eyebrows.

Then, my gaze dropped to my red-covered hands and behind it, the words in blood.

Mari Fable.

Chapter 14

A Taste of My Own Medicine

The ache in my boobs served as enough torture without Detective Wilhelm's interrogation added on top. Like a cherry, the color red sat above me on the mirrored wall across the table. It reflected the hood that I'd pulled over my ears and head to avoid frostbite in this awful holding room.

The door flew open, and Detective Wilhelm's boot shoved through the threshold to stop the door from closing again. Through the crack, I saw him nod.

"She'll be out when I'm good and ready," he said to someone I couldn't see. "You're welcome to wait, but I'm going to warn you, it'll be a long night."

I blew out a sigh and dropped my head in my palms. He'd already asked me why I went to the park, how I knew the victim, and about my alibis for the other murders. We'd yet to arrive at the most pressing piece of the puzzle, my name written in blood.

My own questions swirled in my mind. The questions didn't stop to attach with any color to be filed away in my memory for later, tangible organization. It gave me a headache that throbbed between my eyes. I needed a cocktail of aspirin and acetaminophen ASAP. Then, I might nail down some answers.

What did Redhead want from me? Why frame me for the very murder she saved me from? Was it even a murder since the creature wasn't human? At least, not fully. The first thing I needed to do, once my answers satisfied Detective Wilhelm, was call both Elsie and Reese and apologize for my stupid vampire jokes.

When you know better, do better, I repeated Kai's phrase. He used it to help his high schoolers mature from their mistakes, like cheating on exams or their boyfriends and girlfriends, but I'd adopted it as my mantra. My job taught me to be wary of those I interviewed while also gentle and sensitive to their situation. I'd try to put myself in their shoes and consider how I'd act while being drilled for information after a loved one just died.

Now I didn't need to imagine the drilling part. Detective Wilhelm was determined he'd hit oil, but I had nothing to give him. I ran my hands over my arms, trying to warm up. The last time I felt this cold was the freak frost in San Francisco two Christmases ago. Someone had dreamed of a white Christmas, and Santa had granted their wish.

Was Santa real too? Elsie's Tooth Fairy comment came back with added tension in my temples. I rubbed the sides of my forehead with my fingers-turned-icicles.

Detective Wilhelm stomped inside and plopped down across from me, bringing with him the scent of bitter coffee. Lack of sleep and caffeine plus mom-brain might have me admitting something I didn't do just for a pillow and Wendy snuggles.

The detective removed his fedora, unbuttoned his trench coat to let his stomach out, then tugged to loosen his tie. The bags under his eyes sagged, and looking at them made me feel more tired. I yawned, sparking a scoff from Wilhelm.

"Making yourself right at home there, Ms. Fable?" He raised his thick caterpillar brows.

I sucked in a slow breath to temper my voice. "My last name is Rowan now. You know, the name you call me every time you see me?" It was always *Rowan* this and *Rowan* that when I questioned onlookers before him or found a piece of evidence he had missed. The precinct appreciated my work. It was basically free investigative work, and I got a story to write out of the deal.

The chair creaked as he sat up and leaned over the table. I'd used this trick before too: get into the suspect's face and break their personal bubble. They're more likely to be honest when their privacy was invaded.

"Then, why'd you sign your masterpiece with your maiden name?" he asked.

I flinched at the suggestion. Masterpiece? *Ebenezer Scrooge.* Did Detective Wilhelm really believe me capable of premeditated murder? And then expect me to be of a sane enough mind to sign my name in the victim's blood. And finally, stupid enough to stay at the scene with the sound of sirens? Each unsaid accusation hit differently and chipped away at my calm.

"I didn't write that!" I squealed. I clamped my jaw shut, then took a long inhale before bursting out that a crazy, portal-creating woman was the author. . . but also not the murderer. *Ugh.* I had nothing to tell him. Nothing that'd keep me out of a straitjacket, that is.

"You say you were at Pioneer Park to investigate the previous crime scenes?"

I nodded and opened my mouth to ask if anybody nearby heard howling or animal noises.

"The same crime scenes with the word Fable written all over them," he said with a sniff. "So, Mari, tell me. Who would write your name next to all the victims if not you?"

"Someone framing me," I said, and I resisted following it up with *obviously.* "I'm an investigator. Of course, I returned to the crime scenes to double-check for any missing clues. I want to solve this as much as you."

"You write stories—"

"Reports."

"Don't interrupt, Ms. Fable."

"Stop calling me that," I snapped. He gritted his teeth, as evident by his square jaw shifting back and forth. "Please?"

Satisfied with my riled emotional state, Detective Wilhelm got comfortable. He leaned the chair back and kicked his feet up to rest on the table, then folded his fingers together across his stomach. "I can sit here all night. But you look a little chilly."

"I have an alibi for the other attacks," I said. "The first murder happened the day I gave birth. I was too afraid to pee and sleep. Do you really think I could have killed someone?"

He only shrugged. "I've heard motherhood gives chicks extra strength. Lifting cars off their kids and such."

"Well, I'm not one of those women," I said. "But I do need to get back to my daughter so I can nurse her."

"Your hubby said he needed a microwave for the bottle," he said. "I've confirmed your first lie." Detective Wilhelm gestured a check-mark in the air. *Kai was here?* I needed to end this and get to my family before Redhead started stalking them or the werewolf creature got hungry again.

"Look, I found some clues when I went investigating." I straightened, my mind finally making sense of things. In green, I noted the animal attack. In orange, I recorded the framing. Maybe someone else saw Redhead? And speaking of red, I'd keep that color for the pieces of the attack, including the magical door and the werewolf. And I'd keep those to myself.

Detective Wilhelm looked vaguely interested but tried to cover it by suddenly picking up and inspecting his fedora for an imaginary stain. Still, I caught his eyes shifting to me as I both smoothed and raised my voice.

"I found paw prints near the second crime scene. I also heard growling."

"Yes, there's a common companion that many pedestrians enjoy keeping company with on their walks. Maybe you've heard of them?" When my face fell flat, and I didn't answer, he finished. "Dogs."

I took another big breath and released it in a controlled manner. "These were big prints, not from a domesticated animal. Pioneer Park is huge, and this wouldn't be the first time someone spotted a wild animal in a big city. Construction drives them to confusion. I've read a ton of articles on it." Detective Wilhelm's bored expression didn't change, but I continued anyway. "That would explain the huge scratches and bite marks." I glanced at my stubby fingernails, then held up my hands to show him. "Not something I could do."

"I suppose you're going to tell me Mountain Lions can become literate too?" He smirked.

This time, I took the initiative and leaned over the table, my eyes fixed on his. I wanted to hurry this along and get out of the cold, get some food in my belly, and some snuggles with my family.

"There was a woman at the park. I believe she framed me." I refused to let my voice waver despite the evidence against me. I did nothing wrong. Except that I stole something from a crime scene.

Goosebumps pricked the back of my neck, and I promised myself to buy a new, less worn zip-up, maybe in blue so I didn't match Redhead. I thanked my lucky stars that I didn't have the fang on me when Detective Wilhelm found me.

"A woman, huh? Like the one mauled to death?" he asked, as he pulled a small square of floss from his pocket and started pulling the thread through his teeth. "The same one whose blood was on your hands when I arrived?"

"No," I said firmly, practicing my stern mom voice for later when Wendy refused to do her chores or begged for extra screen time. I'd truly become a mother. Who else would sit in an interrogation room and think of their child while being accused of serial murder? "I've seen her before. I can give you a description."

"No need," he said while inspecting the blood on his floss and grimacing. He twined it around his finger and looked at me before starting the dental cleaning again. "I'm too busy with a suspect right now to go chasing after a mysterious woman." The thwack of the floss pulling from his teeth filled the silence between us. My shoulders fell, and I frowned at the rainbow of spittle flying across the room in an arc of clear and red.

"What about the handwriting?" I sat up from my slump. "Remember that case we solved—"

"I solved it," he corrected.

I resisted rolling my eyes as I continued. "The case with the letter that matched the fake doctor's prescription. The medicine killed the guy because he was on blood thinners."

He rolled the floss back up and stuck it inside the little green container, then smacked his lips together. "Your point?"

"Compare my handwriting to my name on the ground."

"Way ahead of you, cupcake," he said, as he dropped his feet from the table and leaned his elbows on the counter, mirroring my position. "Except I don't think you're going to like the result."

"I. Did. Not. Write. It."

"But. You. Did. Kill. Her." He copied my staccato way of speaking. "What is this? For a story? I know you journalist types can be a little unsteady, like that predecessor of yours a couple of years back. Murdered her boss. Didn't you write about that case? Anyway—" he shook his head before I could respond. "You're guilty of creating chaos, and for what? A prize? A promotion?" He leaned closer, eyes shifting back and forth to catch my every twitch and blink. "You killed her for fame, didn't you?"

"No!" My fingers curled into fists. The rhythmic thump in my chest skipped and started speeding up.

"Admit it," he spoke under his breath, another tactic to force me to quiet and listen carefully, focusing all my attention on him. I only used that when I was confident. My voice would get quiet when I was about to learn something crucial, usually a confession.

It was time to bring out the big guns. I chewed on my lip, and my leg bounced under the table. "Okay, this is going to sound insane, but I saw the attack."

This time, Detective Wilhelm only raised *one* bushy brow.

"There was a—"

A knock at the door cut my story short. Detective Wilhelm held up one finger to shush me, but I'd already paused, not wanting the whole precinct to hear my crazy tale. Not yet, not until I'd convinced the detective to speak with Reese or find Redhead. He stood and stomped to the door, where a woman whispered to him.

Good thing my hearing grew sharper after giving birth. I spent all my time around Wendy listening for cries. I'd try to decipher if the cry meant she was hungry, or if she wore a sock that was too tight, or if she just wanted snuggles. I wrapped my arms around my stomach, wishing I could hold her right now.

"Unusual." I caught the woman's whispers. "First three. . . on the way to visit their family. . . killed before arriving. . . "

I held my breath and tried to catch the bits of conversation.

"And?" Detective Wilhelm prodded in an impatient and loud demand.

"Mrs. Row. . . Estranged from. . . "

My father. *Ebenezer Scrooge.* Was he involved? My mother had assured me it wasn't possible. He was codependent, but not a cold-blooded killer. I shook my head. *Wait.* I knew the truth because I'd witnessed the whole thing. But could Redhead be some kind of messenger for Mr. Fable?

A shudder rippled through me. Cold air drifted in from the crack in the door, then blasted my face when Detective Wilhelm swung it open again. A baby's cry echoed in, and for once, my body made the magic baby drink on cue. My milk let down, leaving huge circled wet marks soiling my shirt and sweater in two precarious places.

The detective didn't seem to notice as he marched behind me and flicked his hand. The gesture was an unspoken pressure for me to stand. I did, ready and willing to leave this freezer room behind me. Instead, he gripped my wrists and slapped the cold, harsh metal of handcuffs against my skin.

There I stood, handcuffed and covered in breastmilk with supernatural answers to impossible questions.

"Mari Rowan, you're under arrest for the murder of Aliyah Thompson."

Chapter 15

Kill Two Cases with One Clue

The cold cell exacerbated my raging migraine. The buzzing fluorescent bulb hanging on the other side of the bars reminded me of home, at least. Well, the outside corridor of our condo's building. My arms ached for Wendy, and my heart cracked at the thought of a night without her.

If I couldn't survive this night without my family, how could I spend the rest of my life in prison for murder? Shivers rippled through me, and I tightened my arms around my stomach.

All the evidence was against me. My name at all the crime scenes, *myself* at the crime scene. Yikes. I pulled my legs onto the little cot and huddled in the corner. My dark cell reminded me of the back of the library where the weird books hid. Books with the Keeper in them.

I rested my head against the wall, exhausted emotionally, physically, and mentally. My eyelids drooped, and I took a slow breath. I closed my eyes and drifted into my first full night's sleep since Wendy was born. But a full night did not equal a pleasant night. I tossed and turned and woke the next day drenched in sweat after repeated nightmares of the beast chasing me.

I'd sunken down, and my neck ached with an awful crick.

"Good morning, sunshine." Detective Wilhelm tipped his hat at me like the perfect conniving gentleman.

With a groan, I pulled myself to the edge of the bed and rolled my neck.

"I still can't believe it, either." He shook his head, and I looked up at him. I had said nothing. He gazed at nothing on the floor, then sniffed. "A lady murderer. It just doesn't make sense."

What century did he live in?

"There are plenty of female murderers," I said. Why did I say it? Because apparently, my mouth wanted to commit treason against the rest of me.

"And that's what I came here for," he said, as he leaned an elbow on a horizontal bar and rolled his head toward me. "Who helped you?"

I palmed my forehead. A dull throb beat at my temples, threatening me with another day of head pain. My stomach grumbled as the scent of coffee drifted from the mug in his hand. He took a slurp as if to brag that he had what I couldn't.

"Out with it, Rowan," he barked. "I know you weren't working alone. The attack on Paige Brown couldn't have been you, so who was it?"

"The person framing me?" I answered with a question.

He laughed without joy and took another steaming sip. A wisp of hot air swirled around his five o'clock shadow. "Alright then, if you won't tell me that, how about telling me why Aliyah Thompson doesn't fit the M.O.?"

I stood and paced back and forth in the small area, if for nothing else than to keep warm. But I hoped it would power up the ol' engine in my skull too. Movement might do me good. Detective Wilhelm was a talented investigator, but he wanted this case shut quickly, which meant he had no other leads and his superiors were pressing down on him to make a call.

"What do you mean?" I asked.

"As you know," he began, "the other victims, Ms. Brown included, were attacked on their way to visit family. But according to Ms.

Thompson's boyfriend, she was just out to take her dog on a potty run. What made her different?"

I mulled over the question. The wheels in my brain finally started rolling, a little rusty after last night, but they quickly gained speed.

In green, I pictured a list of the detective's information that I knew. *Victims visiting family. All violent attacks. All near my house.*

In orange, I made a note of the connections to me. *My name. The fact that I'm estranged from my family.* Did he believe I hurt these women, women around my same age, same build, and living in the same town because I was jealous of their families?

I never made it to red where I intended to file away thoughts of the supernatural pieces that I knew, but the detective didn't. The bulb suddenly stopped blinking, and the cell brightened. I almost laughed at the cue.

"It's my fault!" I blurted.

"A confession?" Detective Wilhelm's arm slipped off the bar, and he almost smacked his forehead into the cell. He stood up and straightened his fedora.

"No, no." I shook my head and marched toward him. With my hands wrapped around the bars, I fixed my gaze on him. "I'm an investigator. I was at all the scenes to search for clues. But this time it was different. This time the, the—" I paused. *Creature? Werewolf?* Human. They were turning back into a human when Redhead squirreled them away into her portal door. "This time the killer meant to attack me, but Aliyah Thompson was in the wrong place at the wrong time, and they jumped her instead."

Detective Wilhelm's eyebrows disappeared behind his hat. "Pardon me but—"

"And Redhead shows up before the deaths." Redhead stood and watched while the beast bit Aliyah Thompson's face in half. The Keeper wasn't trying to save the victims, she was making sure they died. But why?

"She's off her rocker," the detective muttered to himself.

I squeezed the bars in my grip. The Keeper held the key to my escape from this holding cell and would save me from prison. She had answers, and I wouldn't stop until I found her, or convinced the detective to find her while I stayed trapped. Not only did she frame me by writing my name next to the body, but she also saved me and knowing she wasn't in the business of saving, that was what intrigued me the most.

"This murder was an outlier. Aliyah Thompson is a clue," I said, more to myself than Detective Wilhelm, but he perked up.

Another cop jogged up to the detective. "There's been another attack, two blocks down from the precinct." He glanced at me, then back to Detective Wilhelm while he caught his breath. "The victim is alive, for now. It's the same type of assault."

Detective Wilhelm arched a brow and smirked at me. "Looks like someone has plagiarized your work, Rowan. Or should I say, *Fable*?"

. They vanished from the holding cell hall, and a door clicked shut behind them before I could gather a response. The bulb started buzzing and blinking again. I snorted and slumped my back against the bars.

"Plagiarized. . . " Kai's words came back to me and mixed with Redhead's comments. *Or should I say, the Keeper?* If history, or a story, repeated itself, what was my story that the Keeper had referred to? She'd said she lost control. Of the beast? Of the story? How many times had an occurrence similar to *Snow White and the Seven Dwarves* played out?

In blue, I imagined another list. I knew of exactly three separate times the story came about. Once as depicted in the ancient book, once when the Brothers Grimm based their story off Margaretha von Waldeck, and once in Portland when a man's mother poisoned his fiancé. I figured mother-in-law was close enough to stepmother. Plus, poor Waldeck died for her romantic interest in a man from Spain, and the Portland murder followed that same storyline.

I shuffled back to the cot and took a seat. Did this mean I needed to identify a specific story for the *Howl Murders* since the Keeper kept showing up? And where did I come in? Did she target me because I write?

I returned to my note in orange, the connections to me. *Wasn't I the opposite of the victims?* I didn't know my family well. Nobody other than my mom, that is. And she'd told me only my father and his mother were still alive on that side. The pattern showed the victims violently attacked while on their way to visit with loved ones. And my Aunt Janie wasn't really my aunt, just a friend of my mom's from my childhood.

Thoughts of my loved ones muddled my process. Notes in orange and green and purple all mixed in my head as my vision blurred. Tears burned at the back of my eyes, and my mom-hormones, plus lack of sleep, multiplied by being accused of murder was an equation that resulted in a sudden and uncontrollable sob. My shoulders shuddered, and I dropped my face into my hands.

I longed to see Kai and Wendy. Did she grow out of her zero to three-month size clothes? Did I miss her first smile? Would Kai remember to check if she was breathing throughout the night and didn't break free from her swaddle and get tangled in the blanket? My whole body shook until I took a huge inhale and blew out from my circled lips.

It's been one night, get it together!

I scrubbed my tears away with the heel of my palm and straightened.

Did my mom hear about my arrest yet? Maybe she'd go to our house and help Kai so he wouldn't have to skip work. She'd love to babysit her granddaughter, and I wanted them to be close since I'd never gotten the chance to know my grandmother.

Being estranged from Dad meant being estranged from my grandma too.

The lump in my throat eased. Finally, the tightness of emotion released, and I breathed easily as my mind cleared. Only one color and one note remained, a record of a similar story. A story with grand-mothers and beasts with gray fur.

And red cloaks.

The Keeper is Little Red Riding Hood.

Chapter 16

Every Detective Has His Day

An entire day passed while I remained arrested for the murder of a girl I'd never met. A random woman at the park at the wrong time that I had hoped to save set this all into motion. But I couldn't blame her entirely. I *did* go to the park to investigate after dark. I *did* stand there like an idiot and watch a person transform into a furry beast and run straight at me before I got enough sense to run. Even then, I needed my stalker's help.

Still, I wanted someone to blame. In another three hours, I'd have gone an entire twenty-four hours without seeing my baby. What kind of mother does that? Other than my mom, of course, who abandoned me with my father when I was five and then returned to retrieve me, barring good ol' Pop from ever seeing us again.

Wendy needed me. A hole opened in the pit of my belly, and it wasn't because I'd skipped the dry ham and cheese sandwich offered to inmates. Once my holding time added up to forty-eight hours, law enforcement would process the paperwork and. . . I gulped, and a sickening thud slammed into my stomach. After only one more day, the system could transport me to prison, far away from my precious family.

"Okay," I said under my breath, as I unfolded from my crisscross position on the cot. "I have twenty-four hours to solve this with no internet, interviews, other research materials, or. . . " My shoulders slumped, but I didn't let myself sit back down and wallow. Not yet. I didn't have my notebook or color-coded pens, but I'd gotten darn good at organizing the evidence in my brain.

Only one color stuck with me. The red cloak, my name in blood, and the Keeper's hair all floated around in my brain, knocking into one another and blocking my mind's eye from seeing anything else.

"She specifically didn't want me to see that book. What was it?" I spoke aloud, but quietly. I didn't want to disturb the woman in the cell across from me that uniformed cops brought in last night smelling like whiskey and soda. She'd slept the day away, and her snores still echoed in the little hallway. But I preferred my privacy. Speaking my thoughts helped me arrange them into sections, each starting with a question.

"Legends something," I said. "*Before the Legends*!" I poked one finger into the air, and a shot of positivity brought energy. I shuffled across the cement floor in my socks. "Legends are mythologies, popular stories, definitely repeated like these fairy tale deaths. And she always arrives before the deaths occur as if she planned them."

So, she's a copycat killer. Some serial killers wanted notoriety, they wanted to be remembered. Were fairy tales the Keeper's inspiration? Was she using the werewolf to do her bidding? What other supernatural beings could she create to complete her stories? A sea witch? A beast in a castle?

A smirk snuck onto my face despite my chilly living conditions. Just the thought of Beauty's library sparked flutters of joy inside me. The research I could do with such an ancient collection of stories. . . I shook my head and returned to pacing. The metallic taste of the tap water swirled in my mouth, and I gnawed on my lip.

"If she's Little Red Riding Hood now, does that mean her persona will change with the other deaths?" I gasped and slapped my palm against my chest. "That's where I know her from!" I recalled her in the interview's background with the reporter on *The Ugly Duckling* case. Had she been involved with the girl they called 'Ugly Duckling?' The

Keeper wore the red cloak then too, and as far as I could remember, no hooded woman fit into that story. Of course, the duckling didn't die in the original tale, either.

"And why me?" I still couldn't pinpoint her reason to target me other than the story's angle. "Maybe that's it!" I almost shouted. The drunk woman stirred in her cot. Spittle dripped from her mouth and landed in a puddle on the floor beside the bed. I shushed myself. *Ebenezer Scrooge, Mari. One day in the slammer, and you're already losing your sanity.*

I waited for the Drunky to start sawing logs again before I allowed myself to keep working the case out loud. It took only a minute before her snores continued. Instead of returning to my marches, I threw in some yoga. I balanced in tree pose, then shifted to stretch in triangle pose with one hand on my ankle and the other extended above me.

"She wants me to report on this story. She wants fame, maybe she even wants the world to know about her supernatural abilities." I dipped into a lunge and went full Warrior pose. "And who better to deliver her story than an investigative journalist? But I haven't reported anything yet, so she'll keep killing until I do!" I leaped out of my lunge. After a quick celebration of jumping up and down with a quiet squeal, I glanced at the camera pointed at my cell. I returned to Warrior on the other leg, my arms stretched out on both sides of me before they caught me on camera looking like I needed a straitjacket.

Now, how could I connect her to the murders and convince Detective Wilhelm to release me? I squeezed my eyes shut. Picturing red triggered another migraine. The throbs spider-webbed across my temples, and I groaned, knowing the pain would slow my roll. Before the headache stole my thunder, I waved my arms in SOS fashion and mouthed 'help' toward the camera.

After several long minutes of painful impatience, an officer appeared in the hall. "Is there something the matter?" the woman droned.

"I need to speak with Detective Wilhelm," I said, then remembered my manners amongst my excitement. This could be my ticket to seeing my husband and baby again before the night ended. "Please."

"He's out of the office right now. Can I take a message?" She folded her arms across her chest. The officer did not appear amused with me. My smile didn't soften her demeanor.

I sucked in a deep breath and came out with it. "I think I know who committed the murder he's investigating right now."

The cop arched one perfectly manicured eyebrow. If I wasn't behind bars, I might ask for the name and number of her aesthetician.

"I'll notify him." She dropped her arms and sauntered for the door. Before exiting, she called out over her shoulder. "But I wouldn't hold my breath that he'll come running this way."

The door slammed shut behind her, and Drunky snuffled. The hungover woman blinked and then rolled to sit with her head lolling so much it made me uncomfortable to watch.

She smacked her lips and squinted at me. "What're you in for?"

I didn't want to cohort with a criminal, but the woman's voice soothed me. She spoke like a radio hostess, even in her post-drunken stupor. It worked like a charm on my migraine, so I took a seat on my cot, directly across from the bed in her cell, and readied for a conversation. Hey, maybe in her hangover, she wouldn't judge me for spouting supernatural nonsense that I knew now wasn't nonsense at all.

"Murder," I answered. "You?" Though, her crime was clear.

"Little too much champagne, you know?" She smirked, then hiccupped and patted her chest with her palm as if she could knock the hiccups out of her.

"Then, got in a car, huh?" I asked.

"Oh, no." She hiccupped again. "I'd never do that. Just got a little warm in my sweater dress. So, I took it off on my walk home. Apparently, using a trash can as a restroom isn't allowed, either."

I internally cringed but kept my face straight. Who was I to judge? I watched a wolf person eat a lady in the park and then my stalker opened a door on the ground. Not exactly a crime, but I'd wager my nuttiness extended beyond a little public nudity and urination.

"Right." I nodded. "You know, I got these adult diaper things from the hospital when I gave birth to my daughter. Maybe try those next time you go drinking," I joked, hoping to keep her talking. My headache was almost cured, but tears burned behind my eyes now.

My daughter. . . Okay, Mari. You've got this. I planned to share the information I'd pieced together to prove to Detective Wilhelm that I studied the murders, not committed them. Then, if my predictions came true, we might find the Keeper before she chomped her next victim. Well, before her canine beast did.

"Darn right you are," she agreed. "I ain't never going to walk alone at night again until they catch this zombie murderer." Her eyes bugged, and she swiped at her sweaty forehead. "That's what they're calling them. I saw it on Facebook. Zombie attacks all around San Francisco. Guys biting heads off and such."

"Zombies? Is that what the cops are saying too?" I asked, hoping to glean at least a few facts. Clues may have popped up during the twenty-four hours of my incarceration.

She squinted and stared at the buzzing bulb between us. "Hmm, no. The news said something about a woman in custody. They believe she's the suspect since all the victims have looked similar to her."

I arched an eyebrow, and my heart rate sped up. Detective Wilhelm already shared that information? I needed to get my butt in gear.

Natural light flooded into the hall between us, and Detective Wilhelm stomped up in his combat boots that still didn't, and never would match his noir-style clothing. "So, you're definitely not working alone." He smacked his lips and folded his arms as he stopped in front of my cell.

"The only thing I'm working on is this case, Detective," I said, a little snappier than I intended. Even my new criminal friend raised her eyebrows behind him, though I think she might have been admiring the detective's behind. "I think I can predict the next attack."

Detective Wilhelm's laugh echoed in the cement chamber. "Of course, you can predict them, you planned them!"

"Listen." I stayed calm. "I have hurt no one. But I can help you catch the person who did. I saw a redheaded woman at the park before the attack on Aliyah Thompson. She had—" I paused and considered how to explain it. "She had a dog with her. Trained to hunt or something."

The detective snorted, but he kept listening, and the slight tilt of his head showed me he believed my words. The dog made sense, more sense than my murdering people while locked up.

"You could try verifying this with Paige Brown and the other victims' family members to see if it is true. But I believe each of these girls was on her way to visit her grandmother." That sounded too specific, and nerves trickled up my belly and sternum. "Or grandparents. I think this killer wants fame and does this for the story. It's possible she's copying a popular children's tale."

"Okay." Detective Wilhelm dropped his arms and rolled his eyes. "I've had enough of your embellishments. I've got a job to do." His boots slammed against the concrete.

"We can set up a trap!" I called out after him, and the footsteps stopped. I could no longer see him from my cell but knew he considered this based on the silence.

"And how would the killer know they're going to Grammy's? Huh?" His voice came from the direction of the exit.

"Stalking? Following the victim's lives?" I suggested. "These are not uncommon serial killer tactics."

The footsteps grew louder, and his tall figure returned, casting a shadow across the floor in my room. *My* cell, *this is not your room, Mari!*

With his feet spread and arms crossed again, Detective Wilhelm looked ready to lecture me. But he didn't intimidate me. The wolf person? Or that the Keeper could skip out with a portal and possibly vanish into thin air, leaving me framed? Those made me want to pee my pants, but not the detective.

I walked up and held his gaze with nothing but the bars between us. He needed my clues, and one more push might convince him to listen to my plan. "I'm willing to bet my life you'll find the redheaded woman if you stage this. But it needs to be real."

A smirk twitched on his thin, cracked lips. I licked my own. It's the simple things you missed while in the slammer, like Chapstick and carpeted floors.

He pulled the keys from his trench coat and unlocked my cell door. With a hand, he waved me out.

"I hope you know where your grandma lives." His smirk spread into a knowing grin. "Since you're so sure about this, you're going to be the bait."

The hungover woman bent forward and wretched all over the floor. The stench of bile filled the closed-in area, and I almost followed suit with the contents of my stomach.

The flutters of excitement in my belly came to a sudden halt. I frowned, and my stomach continued twisting. After stepping out of the cell, I extended my hand to the detective. We shook on the deal, but a lump gathered in my throat.

Would he pull me out in time before the werewolf ate me?

Chapter 17

The Stakeout Before the Storm

Detective Wilhelm assigned a uniformed cop to follow me back home. And honestly, I appreciated the feeling of safety and protection, though I knew the detective didn't intend for that. Tears spilled over my cheeks as I ran up the outside steps. Even the buzzing bulb in the hallway seemed to welcome me home. I burst into the front door and dived into Kai's arms. He cradled a swaddled Wendy in one arm while returning the hug with his other. We kissed, and he wiped my tears away.

"Mmm, salty," he said before planting another big kiss on my lips. The cop stood on the threshold, but she turned to give us a bit of privacy. "We almost died without you," he joked. "I mean, there were not enough sticky notes in this house for my taste."

I laughed and swiped my cheeks dry with my sleeve. "I need to pump and call my mom."

He quirked his head, and I glanced at the cop before diving into an explanation. Kai hated the idea, but we had little choice. I needed to prove my innocence, but more than that, we both wanted to be free of my stalker. And pinning her down for serial murders would certainly put her away for a lifetime, saving both myself and many other young women in San Francisco while also bringing justice to the victim's families.

I hooked up the pumping contraption to my chest and settled into the section of the sofa that was worn in the shape of my rear end. The cop stood in the corner but awkwardly eyed my pump setup.

"You don't nurse?" she asked. My heart felt like it teetered on the edge of a cliff, and her loaded question flicked it right off, sending it tumbling down into the abyss. Instead of bursting into another round of tears, I sniffed and straightened.

"I did," I said. "But it didn't last."

She recognized my heartbreak as clear by her knowing nod. "I didn't, either," she said. "I couldn't produce."

That's when I realized her question wasn't judgment, it was a search for solidarity. We struggled together as mothers. And despite the chaos of my current life, I hoped she'd become my first mom friend.

For now, I needed to focus on the task at hand. I snuggled with Wendy while phoning my mother. She argued against the plan, telling me that nothing would warrant contacting my father. I didn't blame her. Mom worried that if Dad found her, he'd insist they reinstate their marriage, and she'd feel like a bird in a cage again. He wasn't violent or mean or anything, even Mom said so, but he was far too dependent. Suffocating, even.

"You're clever. I know you'll find another way to convince the cops," she said.

"What if I don't involve you at all? I can ask Johnson how to contact Dad's mom. I just need her address. It needs to appear that I'm traveling to visit her. This killer is smart. She follows the stories exactly."

"Does she?" Mom questioned. "I thought it was the grandmother who got eaten in *Little Red Riding Hood*."

"They both do," I said, confident in my research. "And a lumberjack cuts them out."

The cop flicked her head toward me. I shrugged and whispered. "It's a fairy tale."

"Shouldn't there be a target on the grandmothers too?" Mom asked.

Ebenezer Scrooge, she's right. . . Why didn't the Keeper keep to the correct storyline? My breath hitched. What if I couldn't predict her moves as easily as I thought?

"All I know is what I know right now," I answered. "And that's that the women are being hunted on their way to visit family."

Mom sighed. "Alright, Johnson should know the address."

"Thank you!" I squealed, ready to get this show on the road. But first, I needed to know how to contact Johnson. I carried Wendy across the hall with the cop at my heels, and Kai not far behind. It felt like I had an entourage just to go see Tala.

Tala agreed to share Johnson's phone number after her little date with him, which, I presumed, she only planned to make Mr. Geppetto, our other neighbor, jealous. Mr. Geppetto didn't step up to claim Tala as his official girlfriend, and that pissed her off.

Johnson didn't answer, so I left a voicemail. The waiting was the worst part.

And while I waited, so did Detective Wilhelm. He rang me several times to check in, and his patience grew thin. I felt the need to rush, the need for answers and safety, but I didn't mind the downtime with Kai and my new cop friend.

We shared stories of new parenthood over fried rice and broccoli beef. Officer Esmeralda laughed with me over my birth story.

"I'd prefer a fainting husband over a fake one," she said. Just like that, the laughs stopped. Kai and I glanced at one another. I set my chopsticks down and offered my new friend a sad smile.

"I'm sorry," Officer Esmeralda said. "It's not a big deal. We're married, but it's more of an arrangement than a marriage. I wanted a child. He wanted to please his dying mother and have her attend his wedding before it was too late. We're friends, best friends, but never in love."

I nodded, so fascinated by her story that I almost forgot the dangerous plan ahead of me. I jumped at the buzzing of my phone. All three of us stared at the little vibrating rectangle in the middle of the Coffee Table of Evidence.

I grabbed it and answered. "Hello?"

"I'm so glad you've come to your senses," Johnson said without a greeting. "It's time you recognize your bloodline, Ms. Fable."

"I just need an address," I said, still not trusting this friend of my father's. What did he mean by recognizing my bloodline? It still irked me he used my maiden name too. I didn't want to believe someone my father knew could be the murderer, but it almost made sense. I could lead him right to me. But Detective Wilhelm and other cops would be there, hiding in the bushes with snipers and sights, right?

I gulped. "Please."

"1700 Cygnus Island," he said.

I froze. *Cygnus Island?* A rumor went around a while back that when Alcatraz tours shut down decades ago, foreign invaders had claimed the island for their own. The viral rumor said that the invaders built a kingdom there and named the island Cygnus. This unknown monarchy infamously ruled, but other than that, the kingdom remained fairly private from the rest of the world. Plus, they kept the old buildings from being an expensive nuisance for the city to board up and fence off. The people who supposedly lived there bothered nobody and nobody bothered them, a neutral territory and self-sufficient. Though, many enjoyed the ferry rides out to their shores, where the beaches were open to visitors without passports or security checks. Despite my and many other reporters' attempts to investigate and get the truth, nobody knew what really happened to the island off the shores of California where Alcatraz once stood. They cut access off except for the beaches, and nobody ever made it past the walls built just a mile up from the sand.

An incoming call beeped in the silence between Johnson and me. I pulled my head away from the screen to see the detective's name.

"Thank you," I said before I clicked over to the other line.

"That's enough waiting, Rowan," Detective Wilhelm said. "We need to do this tonight before we've got another dead body on our hands."

I didn't have time to research Cygnus Island. I'd head out to the pier tonight, ready to board a ferry and hopefully draw the Keeper out of hiding with Wilhelm watching. Another time, I'd dive into my family history and see what Dad was up to in the mysterious place.

It pained me to hand over Wendy, which I only managed after about one hundred kisses on her little peach fuzzy head. Kai bit his lip and his brow knitted. I hugged him until Officer Esmeralda was forced to pressure me along. The law enforcement team had already posted up around the pier and the ferry headed for the kingdom in exactly forty-three minutes.

With 1700 Cygnus Island plugged into my phone (it actually worked) and a small backpack over my shoulders, I headed for the pier. I walked briskly and kept my eyes alert, though I didn't want to appear too obvious.

I forced myself to slow down. Officer Esmeralda followed several paces behind in undercover clothes with one eye on me and the other scanning our surroundings. I expected the Keeper, the *killer*, to attack before we reached the pier, where there would be an audience, AKA witnesses.

I kept my ears pricked for the howling. Now the absence of it rattled my nerves more than hearing it. I needed this attack. I needed answers. But I also feared that the supernatural being would be too strong and too fast for the officers' protection.

My heart pounded in time with my feet. My sneakers hit the concrete as I turned off Main and headed toward the smell of salty sea air. Another two blocks and the pier would be in my sight. Should I have done this closer to home? Would the Keeper break from that pattern? She did this with the previous target near the precinct. The victim came out with only several stitches and a concussion that left her with no memory of the attack.

Maybe now that the Keeper got my attention with my name, she didn't need to drag her victims toward my condo complex anymore.

Soup Cracker Street was a long downhill path that led to Pier 99 in a roundabout way. I took this slower, twistier route as agreed upon with Detective Wilhelm, hoping the secluded street would lure the killer out.

The abandoned buildings gave me the creeps. A wad of trash blew across the empty street and scratched the concrete as it tumbled. I pressed forward, knowing my new mom-friend wasn't far behind with a weapon in her holster and a stun gun in her pocket. I took a deep, shaking breath and wrapped my arms around me as a howl, finally a howl, split the night. Did Officer Esmeralda hear it?

The Keeper was close. The hair on my arms raised like the fur of an angry cat. I sensed the canine creature's presence. *It worked. She's here with her attack dog and all.* A leaf crunched from an alleyway between two old boarded-up houses. I hurried past, but the shadow of a hulking figure caught my eye.

Low growling brought me back to the hospital. Why had I thought I'd seen fangs on my OBGYN or heard the wolf sounds in the recovery suite? None of that connected with what I knew now, and I itched to record the differences in list form with my notebook and sticky notes.

I tensed and tried not to glance back at the officer. This needed to look natural. I noticed Detective Wilhelm posted up across the street. He looked ridiculous leaning against the wall of an old bar with a newspaper in his hands to cover his face. But I'd know that fedora anywhere.

The popping sounds echoed, and the detective peered over his paper. The transformation finished. And I was about to be dead meat.

My throat tightened, and my heart thudded against my ribcage. *Where are you, Redhead?* It took everything I had not to bolt across the street and run straight for the pier. The shadow lunged at me from the alley. I dodged to the side, but it was too late. The beast swiped a massive paw across my cheek, knocking me into the gutter along Soup Cracker Street.

The scratches burned, but I ignored the pain. The werewolf snarled and opened his jaws as his paws pinned my shoulders. I knew what came next, the feast on my face. But Officer Esmeralda excelled at her job.

A gunshot rang out, splitting the silence of the back street. The werewolf whimpered as he released his hold on me and licked at the wound on his side. But the bullet didn't hold him for long. He exploded into a deafening snarl and bared his fangs at me. The fangs that Reese confirmed grew in new each time the creature transformed.

I scrambled away, flipping over and crawling on my hands and knees. I glanced up to see Detective Wilhelm shell-shocked. His gun hung in the limp hand at his side, and he gaped at the creature.

The werewolf's claws landed on my back. I fell to the concrete, and the wind knocked from my lungs. Gasping for breath, I reached for the curb and ducked my head away from the heat of the animal's breath. Another gunshot fired, and the weight on my back lifted. When the claws released me, searing pain bit at my flesh where the salty air blew into the open wounds. I was vaguely aware of Officer Esmeralda approaching with her weapon balanced in both hands. She paused, focused, and pulled the trigger again.

Everything slowed as I watched the werewolf collapse. The bullet landed with a thud directly between the beast's eyes.

I tried to gather my thoughts. *What does this mean for my innocence? Is it over?*

Officer Esmeralda lowered her weapon, so I finally allowed myself a full breath of oxygen. The expansion of my chest hurt as my shirt's fabric rubbed against the torn skin.

The reprieve didn't last long. The werewolf would not be downed by the bullets, and the fantastical element of all this slapped me in the face. How could I have been so stupid to think regular cops could protect me against a supernatural creature?

The werewolf growled low, just loud enough for me to hear. I pulled my feet under me and balanced on shaking legs as I stood. I should have known Detective Wilhelm and his crew could not take down what they did not understand. Did we need silver bullets? Reese would know.

Officer Esmeralda approached the animal cautiously. I opened my mouth to tell her to stop, but nothing came out. I couldn't breathe or speak or think straight as the creature flipped from its side to all four legs and leaped at me in a blur of fur and bloody claws. *My* blood.

A blast of sudden wind rushed my back. One second, I was the target of a deadly beast, the next, I was falling to my side in the sand. *Sand. How? What happened to Soup Cracker Street and Officer Esmeralda and. . .*

The crash of waves replaced snarls and gunshots. My pulse pounded so fast I worried I'd have a heart attack before the wolf could even eat me. The wolf that I no longer saw or heard or sensed anywhere near me. The rush of blood in my ears didn't match the soothing, rhythmic lift and fall of the dark blue ocean before me. It reflected the deep black of the night sky, and I noticed, first, the absence of city lights.

"What in the wonderland?" I whispered, almost afraid of my voice.

A cry of frustration shocked me back into survival mode, and my heart skipped a beat. The silhouette of a figure on the beach kicked at the sand. Moonlight glowed bright enough behind them for me to see shapes but not details. As my eyes adjusted, I made out the ringlets in her curls, the curve of the velvety hood hanging over her shoulders.

"Ow!" the Keeper shouted, as she hopped on one leg, holding her other foot. She dropped to her knees, and her head fell into her hands. I almost expected her to arch back and scream heavenward again like Aragorn searching for the kidnapped Hobbits.

Wait, I'm the one kidnapped here. Should I run? Question her?

I needed answers. It hurt to move, but I straightened from my sideways position. Blood rushed to my head, leaving me with a flash of dizziness.

"Why?" the Keeper muttered. "Why is this happening? I'm trying so hard."

Trying to kill people? *Except I'm alive.* Trying to frame me? Anger built, and newfound energy surged through me. I struggled, but got to my feet and marched across the sand.

"It's not supposed to happen like this. The story is all wrong." She kept talking to herself, and I slowed my march, approaching quietly. "Why can't I identify which one Red is? I'm the Keeper of the Stories. Why can't I keep anything straight?"

The Keeper noticed my shoes and looked up.

"You owe me an explanation," I said, ready to use my interview tactics. She was just another suspect. Well, not *just.* She somehow portaled us away to a private beach and saved my life yet again from a werewolf.

She stood, undisturbed by my confident demand. The Keeper paced back and forth in small steps before me.

"What if I just ask?" Suddenly, she paused and looked me directly in the eye for the first time.

I opened my mouth to take control of the conversation, but she cut me off. "Have you survived a near-death experience?" Her voice turned up at the end in perfect question form.

"Excuse me, what?" I seethed as another breeze brought salt air into my wounds.

The Keeper threw up her arms in defeat. "I give up! It's all gone to pot anyway. What more damage could I possibly do?"

"What is going on?" I yelled, trying to wrangle her attention over the whipping winds. "Where are we? Who are you?" I'd lost control.

I was no longer the composed, organized investigative journalist that I needed to be. But who could blame me? I suffered werewolf wounds on my face and back and was teleported somewhere unknown. I was bound to be a little reckless. Letting go felt good. A rush of adrenaline prompted me to keep questioning.

"Why did you murder those women and frame me for it?"

The Keeper stopped her nonsensical rants and put her hands on her hips like a disappointed schoolteacher and I the child, though she couldn't be more than a year older than me. "I did nothing of the sort."

"I saw you write my name in Aliyah Thompson's blood," I growled, nearly ready to pounce on her as the beast in me bubbled to the surface.

The Keeper's wild hair tossed back as she threw her face to the sky and released a laugh that caught in the wind and danced around me, mocking me. Her face was flushed as she stopped and sighed. It wasn't until then I recognized the source of her disappointment wasn't me, but herself. Her shoulders slumped, and her head hung. She shook it slowly, and a weak apology came out of her.

"I'm sorry," she said. "I can see how that might have appeared, but I hoped my messages would lead the wolf to the right person." She looked up, and her striking brown eyes enveloped me. I needed to understand this woman, because like it or not, we were tangled together in a mess of stories and murder.

"I don't kill anyone. Not directly," she said. "Nor did I intend to frame you, as you call it. I just need to know one thing: have you ever almost died?"

Rage built up like vomit in my mouth, and I almost expected to purge all over the Keeper's feet like the drunk woman did on the jail floor. But the tide of anger came out in words only.

"Ebenezer Scrooge!" I screamed.

"Ah, yes," she said. "The grumpy man Dickens thought he'd created." She laughed. "Silly human."

I grabbed the front of her cloak, where it tied together in a perfect bow, and yanked her toward my face. Her jaw dropped in shock, and I felt I finally had her attention.

"What. In the ever-loving wonderland. Are you talking about?" I breathed.

"I wish. I could. Tell. You." She copied my staccato way of speaking, but it was off balance like she didn't understand how serious I was yet not in the mocking way that Detective Wilhelm did.

I closed my eyes. Frustration burned as tears now.

"The wolf is trying to find Red before I do. This has never happened before in the world's history," she explained. "Legends follow tradition every one hundred years, but not anymore. Stupid modern society, and its stupid imbalances." Her voice drifted to an angry muttering. "People nowadays have information so fast and can move around the world too quickly. I can't keep up. I'm failing as the hunter."

I opened my eyes and took in her words. It was almost like I could see them on the page of Wendy's little fairy tale book.

"The modern world has sent the classics awry," she continued. "Whatever you do, do not let your mother, yourself, or your daughter get eaten on their way to visit their grandmother without me there to end him." The Keeper plucked my hand from her cloak and straightened, smoothing away imaginary wrinkles in her impossibly soft cloak. She started muttering again to herself. "If I didn't have all these other stories to chase around, maybe I could just sit and wait for this serial killing wolf at grandma's but no." The Keeper waved her hands around in frustration.

"My daughter?" That threw me off. My arms hung at my sides, like Detective Wilhelm earlier.

"I'm afraid I've said too much." The Keeper backed away from me and offered a little wave. She turned and stepped on top of the water. The waves didn't splash at her feet but merely vanished beneath her.

A rectangle appeared before her, and she opened the door. I glimpsed metal drawers and steel tables. The morgue *and Reese.*

"You think you can stalk me?" I shouted into the wind before she shut the door. "I'm coming for the answers you have!" The bay breeze carried my voice away, and when the door shut, it disappeared altogether, leaving me alone on Unknown Beach.

Chapter 18

Fortune Favors the Bold

Alcatraz prison towered in the distance, though it looked more like a castle with its glittering walls. The heavy-cinderblock walls reminded me it once held violent criminals. I shivered and redirected my thoughts. I needed to call Kai and tell him I was okay, but my backpack had slipped from my shoulders when the wolf knocked me over. I had no phone, no map, and no idea where I'd landed.

A lighthouse sent a spinning glow out into the ocean, and another source of light cast a beam back in response. I turned to see the ferry approaching. The ferry with Pier 99 splashed on the side.

I'm on Cygnus Island. Did a real monarchy live inside that prison-looking building? I didn't have time to explore. The ferry docked and would set off again as soon as the handful of travelers piled out, ready to mill the open beach.

I was the only passenger on the return trip, and I relished the silence. I mulled over my thoughts as I leaned on the railing and watched the water trail out behind in foamy bubbles. The cool salty air cleared my mind, a blank page for me to keep notes.

In green, I pictured the words *The Keeper is not the killer. Nor is she in control of the killer.*

In yellow, I noted the portal, Reese's involvement, and that Detective Wilhelm would know I was not a suspect. Not after what he witnessed with the attack. At least I could breathe easy with one piece of the puzzle in place: I was free of suspicion. Instead, he'd know I was the target now.

I closed my eyes and imagined myself writing on a red Post-It. *Classic legends in history. Could they be real? Am I Little Red Riding Hood?*

Or was Wendy?

My eyes shot open. The ferry docked at Pier 99, and I asked the captain to call me an Uber. I moved in a daze toward my ride. The ferry's horn blew, but it sounded muted to me. The glittering lights of the city blurred as frustrated tears filled my eyes, and I plopped into the passenger seat.

"Are you sure you don't want to go to the hospital?" the Uber driver asked.

I shook my head. "To the morgue."

He chuckled. "You're beaten up, but you look alive to me." His joke landed on deaf ears. I thanked him for the ride and I gave him all the cash from my pocket.

The plain gray building cast a shadow over me, blocking the glow of the half-moon. I stormed into the office, unbothered by the icy chill of the room now. Reese didn't move. Instead of a dead body, he bent over a book splayed out on the table. His high-top chair had his knees smashed up against the table's underbelly.

"What do you know?" I stomped up and slammed my hands on the table. The cold steel felt good under my palms. Something solid, something real. Reese flinched. His frizzy, thinning hair hung flat in his eyes as he looked up at me.

"It's not my place," he said.

"Reese." I leaned on the table and got into his face. "You better tell me what you know about the Keeper and these stories, or I'll consider you an accomplice to these murders."

He cowered away from me, pushing off the table to scoot the chair back. The book had fallen from his hand with a thud. The delicate font on the cover caught my eye. My brows knitted together, and I flipped the book over.

The Hunchback of Notre Dame by Victor Hugo.

The spine cracked when I pulled it open. On the pages, Reese had scribbled in the margins. He used a color-coded system too, and my heart did a little leap at the organization buried in all the chaos of notes. His handwriting looked familiar, but I couldn't put my finger on where I'd seen it.

Not a church, a morgue. Not a dancer, a cop. He'd crossed out lines and added extra words above them. *Not a bellringer, a medical examiner.*

"You think you're the. . . the. . ." My jaw dropped. I raised my head to meet his gaze but smacked the back of my skull into the lamp that hung over the table. I seethed and rubbed the spot where a bump would soon form. Another injury to my list of wounds.

"Quasimodo," he finished for me. "And I don't *think*." Reese's chest expanded with a huge inhale. He sighed. "I know."

The oxygen felt sucked from my lungs. Cotton filled my mouth, and I licked my lips, trying to form words. As many questions as answers slammed into my brain at the same time, and the chaos drove me mad.

"H-how," I stuttered. I forced out a breath and cleared my throat to start again. "How do you know?"

Reese rolled the chair away and opened a cabinet beneath the countertop. A row of books lined the top shelf. He grabbed one, then hopped off the stool and sauntered over to me, plopping it down in front of me. The thick tome landed on the table with a thud beside Victor Hugo's novel.

Before the Legends.

"As an investigator," he said, "I'd expected you to come to these understandings sooner. But this will help clear up some of it. I'm not an expert, but I know the classics now are not just stories, they existed long before the authors recorded them into words, and they'll exist long after."

"This book has no writer," I said, as I picked it up. It was handwritten, a document of history frozen in time with words. The pages were thin and stiff, old.

"It was me," he said and followed it with a shrug. "Or someone like me anyway. The handwriting is a perfect match to mine, but this book must be two centuries old."

"Did you know about my daughter?" I asked, my face tense, my jaw aching from grinding my teeth. The chill of the morgue started settling over me, tickling the back of my neck as the ventilation system kicked on with an icy draft.

"What about her?" He wiped the hair in his eyes away, but it fell right back into place, stringy and flat.

"If these fairy tales are actually history," I tapped my fingernail against the legends' book, "and human experiences repeat themselves in similar stories, then my daughter could be. . . I don't know." I palmed my forehead. My temples throbbed with lightning pain as a migraine threatened. "The Keeper woman. That teleporting-water-walking-supernatural-something seems to believe my daughter, or my family, is connected with the *Little Red Riding Hood* story."

"I suspected as much." Reese nodded. "But, as I said, I'm learning this too. I'm not an expert."

"The Keeper came here, didn't she?" I asked. "She opened a door to the morgue. I saw you in the background." My finger jabbed toward his face, but I didn't mean for it to be accusatory. He knew more than me but appeared to be as much of a victim in the whole scenario.

Reese scratched at his eyebrow. A scar snaked through it, and it gave him a rugged look. He was odd, a loner, and he seemed to enjoy his job picking through dead bodies a little too much, but he had a stoic, knowledgeable quality to him. "The Keeper uses my morgue a lot to open portals. I have my theories why." He pursed his lips and scratched at his skull, baring pale skin beneath thinning hair. "She seems to only move between locations where there is fairy tale story evidence. She calls it the story aura. And here there is the aura since I'm—" he swallowed, "the hunchback. But I can never predict when she'll show up. She skips out not a minute before she arrives."

"To where?" I asked.

He sighed, toddled back to his stool, and took a seat. "I don't know, Mari. You should go home and clean up your wounds. Maybe see your family and get some rest. As far as I can tell, if you're part of these historic legends, your fate is sealed."

My heart dropped like a broken elevator and slammed into my stomach. *Wendy.*

Nothing else mattered other than protecting my child, my husband, and our happy little family. Reese's words haunted me on the way home. I'd forgotten about the attack except for the dull burn of my wounds. I'd forgotten Detective Wilhelm and my success in proving my innocence. I'd even forgotten the wolf because the future was what mattered now. What came next for the Fable women?

Fable's Story. Mari Fable. The Keeper's crime scene scribbles imprinted on my brain. She took notes just like me, except when she wrote in red, it was blood. My stomach twisted and turned, wrapping itself into an awful, ever-tightening knot.

I dragged myself to the top of the stairs at our building and limped down the dim hallway. Just before I reached our front door, the bulb winked out. It had finally burned its last light. I snorted. It wasn't funny because nothing would ever be funny again if Wendy was in danger. Darkness was all that lay ahead for us.

Kai leaped from the couch at the sight of me. He tiptoed past Wendy's Moses basket and threw his arms around me, but only for a second. He pulled off me, and his eyes widened in horror at the scratches.

"I need some Neosporin," I managed, as he led me over to the couch and ran for our first aid kit.

"I was so worried about you," he huffed. His hands shook so violently he couldn't peel the Band-Aid covers off. I eased into the sofa, laying on my side, careful not to lean on my back.

I rested my unharmed cheek against the couch cushions and smiled sadly at the swaddled bundle of Wendy in the basket on the floor. Her chest rose and fell in a rhythmic peace.

She can't be Little Red Riding Hood.

Tears welled in my eyes, half from the lightly dabbing of alcohol-soaked cotton balls on the scratches and half from the joy of being home with my family. I allowed myself a moment of celebration. I might have been out of the frying pan and headed for the fire, but for now, I got to leave jail behind.

I reached out and ran my finger over Wendy's pudgy little cheek. She'd gained some Cabbage Patch rolls after going full bottle. I didn't want to think of that failure, either. Surely, Elsie's wife would look at me with disdain for not giving my child one hundred percent breast-milk, just like Mom judged me for not staying home with Wendy.

Everything I did was wrong, at least according to others. But I would not leave my fate or my daughter's fate in someone else's hands. Tonight, I'd sleep and snuggle and sit in the warmth of our little condo together. Tomorrow, I'd research. I'd find the crazy woman in the cloak.

"The Keeper, huh?" I muttered to myself. "We'll see about that."

After Kai finished sticking Band-Aids over the scratches on my back and cheek, he helped me up. The butt imprint on my spot on the couch called to me, beckoning me with its comfy squishiness. I needed something to sink into.

Kai kneeled in front of the couch and used it to lay Wendy on. He wrapped a fluffy blanket with puppies all over it around her. The comfy swaddled position sparked a long yawn from Wendy. The contagion of the yawn spread to me, then to Kai. He transferred the burrito baby into my arms, and I settled into my spot with her in the crook of my arm and a book in my other hand.

Doors to the Unknown. Between jail and being a serial wolf killer's bait, plus getting pulled through a teleporting door and talking with Quasimodo, I never had time to explore the books I'd rented from the library. And I knew this one would help me understand the Keeper better.

Kai bustled around while I read. He took the trash out before Wendy's diapers stunk up the whole place, and I took notes. He started a load of laundry while I started to get a grasp on the doors.

They're portals, I wrote in blue.

Sigils are suggested for anti-creation. My handwriting looked awful since I couldn't hold the notebook still, and it dipped into the couch cushion as I pressed the heel of my hand against the paper to line the pen up with the page.

I set the pen down and read the scribbled notes. Speaking of handwriting. . . my heart sped a little faster. This was Reese's handwriting, the way he exaggerated capitalized words. I knew I'd recognized his style from the notes in Victor Hugo's novel.

My eyes scanned the page, absorbing past Reese's, Quasimodo's, notes. *Sigils placed around a physical door can prevent its correct usage as a traveling door. The traveler moves from the first door to the second but cannot create another door.*

Symbols lined the bottom of the page. Two of them resembled keys, and one matched a lock. The rest looked like letters in another language I didn't recognize. They followed a particular order, which repeated. I counted and smirked when the number added up to the same amount of letters in 'the Keeper.'

"Kai," I said, as he plopped down beside me, ready to create his lesson plan for next week. By this point in the semester, he'd taught the Industrial Revolution after completing classical civilizations.

"Hmm?"

"I think we can trap the Keeper," I said. "Do you want to hold Wendy while I draw these around our door, or do you want to do the drawing?" The pen in my hand worked like a pointing stick to the sigils on the page.

His eyebrows raised and wrinkled his forehead into a bunch of lines. But he listened to my explanation and balanced our bundle of joy in his lap while I took a block of Post It's and my pen bag toward the door.

I opened the door, knelt, and slapped sticky notes in a half-circle on the outside and in a half-circle on the inside. The sigils proved tough to copy directly. After crumpling half my pad of Post-Its, I'd recreated the symbols, one on each note. I rearranged the sticky notes until they followed the correct order and smiled.

There was no guarantee the Keeper would come here. But my family was involved in all of this, and if Reese was right and she could only create doors around us fairy tale characters, then I might catch her.

With the Keeper unable to teleport away, I was sure to get answers on how to keep Wendy and my family safe.

Chapter 19

It's Always Darkest Before the DoorDash

Was it luck or fate that I'd married a history teacher? Kai and I dove headfirst into every ancient text and old painting or photograph that mentioned a reaper, then cross-referenced it with famous fairy tales.

"Ebenezer Scrooge," I cursed in a whisper while rubbing my temples. Kai paced back and forth in front of the window facing the city street. Bubbles popped around Wendy's mouth as she cooed and enjoyed watching the movement of people on the street.

"Hey, didn't you say the Keeper mentioned something about Dickens?" he asked. Wendy made a grab for the transparent, white curtains, leaving a soiled spot of spit on the fabric. The couch's back cushion sunk as I leaned back and stared at the ceiling. With the soft part of my elbow over my eyes, it dimmed the sunny day and slightly relieved my headache.

"Yeah," I sighed. "Which means we need to be looking into more than fairy tales. Is anything that's considered a classic part of this? Shakespeare? What about Jane Austen?"

A squeal startled me, and I sat up. Kai lifted Wendy above his head like an airplane and spittle dropped onto his head. I stifled a laugh.

"I knew it!" He brought her back down and spun around with her.

"Vampires are part of it." He paused and quirked his head at my scrunched nose.

"You can't joke right now, our daughter is in danger."

"Two things," he said, as he came around the couch and shifted Wendy to my lap. He picked up his laptop to continue our research. "Dracula is a classic and a vampire, therefore, likely real. And second, I can *only* joke right now, or else I'll have a nervous breakdown." The frantic tapping on his keyboard drove his point home.

I offered a sad smile in response because I felt the same way, but couldn't admit it. A breakdown was just around the corner. The only things keeping me from falling apart were my family and the fact that I finally had access to my color-coded pens, Post-Its, and notebook.

Familiar articles popped up on Kai's computer screen, and I leaned over. My first big case as an investigative journalist involved a girl in a glass coffin. A girl with black hair whose mother-in-law poisoned her and hid her in plain sight so that she couldn't marry her son. Poor Sophia, the victim of the murder in the museum, must have been Snow White. One of those articles bore my name since I'd written the story of Sophia's death after investigating the situation.

"What's interesting," Kai said, as he typed, "is that I can find two other young women who were suspected of being killed by a mother figure. One died in 1914, according to this death certificate, and another died in 1837. Plus, the photograph of the girl with the seven men around her in 1759, shows that there could be one version of Snow White every century."

I bounced Wendy in my lap while she grabbed at my hair. Several locks ripped out of my head from the pull of her little fist. I seethed and pried the hair from her hands before she could shove it into her mouth. Then, I kissed her hand, so she'd know I wasn't being a mean mommy by taking her hairy toy away.

"What if we add the real Margaretha von Waldeck to that list?" I asked, hinting for him to look up the date she died. Kai nodded and typed the name into his search bar, though as a history buff he already knew.

"It must have been in the fifteen hundreds because Philip the Second of Spain wanted to marry her," he said, then pointed to the screen when it confirmed his guess. "I knew it again! I'm on a roll." His little victory dance shifted the couch cushions, and I rolled my eyes. It felt good to be silly for a moment, to celebrate a tiny breakthrough in our research.

"Don't forget to add Sophia to that list." I scribbled the notes in orange with the dates and the girls' names on a Post-It note I'd labeled 'Snow White.' "She must be the twenty-first century's version of the story." I popped the cap off of a blue pen and started another separate note. *Revisit the Museum of Classical History. Question the curator and other museum employees if they remember seeing a woman in a red cloak around the time of Sophia's death.*

The scent of coffee lured me away from the couch. I positioned Wendy on her stomach to have what some moms call 'tummy time' on the floor. The intent was to help the baby learn how to lift their head, but Wendy resorted to gnawing on the edge of the purple fleece blanket.

"Okay, so this leaves us with a missing Snow White," Kai said. "If this century hunch thing is true, then there should be another young woman poisoned by her mother or stepmom in the sixteen hundreds too."

The kitchen, warm, and full of delicious smells (well, one smell), welcomed me. My stomach grumbled. With my arrest and all the other excitement, neither of us had gone grocery shopping, much less cooked anything. The fridge presented nothing more than a blast of cold air and a couple of plastic containers with molding vegetables. I grimaced and sealed it shut again.

"I guess we're living on coffee," I said, as I poured us each a mug of the steaming, aromatic beverage. The drink burned my lip as I stupidly tried to walk and drink at the same time while balancing Kai's cup in my other hand. *Not clumsy, just not graceful*, Mom would always say. I was fairly sure my mother could perch on a string ten feet above the ground and look comfortable doing it while I couldn't even balance *on* the ground.

Kai stood and headed for the coat rack near the front door. "Make mine to-go?" he asked and nodded toward his cup in my hand.

"Where are you going?"

"Nothing is turning up online resembling a Snow White story in the seventeenth century," he explained. "I'm going to head to the school and grab some history textbooks. We have a bunch of old, old ones. I want to pick through them and find anything that might look like Snow White. Or Pinocchio. Or I don't know, but I'll stop and grab brunch for us on the way back. Do you want waffles or pancakes?"

I froze, my arms at a right angle with the coffee mugs out. "I want to order in."

"I don't think you can get delivery from Jack's Diner."

"No, no." I set the cups down and grabbed my phone. "We need to order food from DoorDash. You said Pinocchio, and it reminded me of something. There was this weird delivery driver talking about robots and he called his project Pinocchio."

The app appeared on my phone, and I scrolled through pictures of decadent cheesecakes, cheeseburgers, and mozzarella sticks. *Isn't there anything without cheese?* I tapped the link for Jack's Diner.

"And you think this guy could be part of everything? Like he's actually Pinocchio?" Kai asked.

I shrugged. With my thumbprint, I confirmed the order of waffles and eggs and biscuits and crepes and—I might have ordered too much. "Remember how I told you I saw the Keeper with him? There's no guarantee that he'll deliver again, but it's worth a try. Maybe she'll show up, and I can corner her for some answers. And if that fails, then it'll be time to lure her out with another trip to good ol' Grandma's."

Kai's frown showed he didn't like the idea of me being bait again. I didn't, either, but I couldn't be a sitting duck. Reese's pro-activeness, his study, and his research were something I admired and strived for now that I knew supernatural beings existed. And what should I call the doors the Keeper created? Portals? *Magic?*

"Hello in there?" Kai waved his hand in front of my face. "I think I should stay home if we're luring the Keeper here." His shoes sat abandoned by the door, and he peeled his coat off.

I snapped back to reality and leaned over the Coffee Table of Evidence to give him a kiss. Oh, how I wanted to do nothing more than snuggle with him and eat syrupy brunch together. But he'd taken sick days because of my arrest, and even though I wasn't in handcuffs anymore, I needed him home until I solved this fairy tale case and secured my stalker in jail. Someone was turning into a wolf and hunting my daughter, and I intended to put that someone behind bars. We were too busy from brunch on the couch.

"I'll be fine," I said. "Just hurry back with the books, and maybe we'll get an idea on another fairy tale to draw the Keeper out with. Maybe she'll at least tell us how to find this wolf."

He sighed and nodded, turning to head to the door, but didn't make it two steps before swiveling back and stepping around the coffee table. He cupped my chin, his fingers in my hair and behind my ear. The warmth of his hand and the taste of his lips melted me. We kissed, leaning into one another, my hand up the back of his shirt, his fingers in my hair until Wendy whined. We pulled off each other, and I caught my breath.

A baby, a job, and life in general already kept us apart too much. Not to mention tracking a supernatural serial killer. I missed time with Kai, date nights binging stupid shows, or the rare days I wanted to go out into the world. We'd do scavenger hunts on our phones in the city or walk the piers and people-watch.

Another angry squeal cut my thoughts short. Wendy had had enough tummy time. She split into a wail, and it physically ached to let go of my husband. But I filled my arms with our bundle of joy and nodded toward the door.

"Get the books," I said. Soothing Wendy with a little bouncing, I headed for the kitchen to make a bottle. The plastic tops needed a good scrubbing, so I grabbed a fresh bottle from the dishwasher.

As I used my free hand to towel it dry, I kept planning. *See? Multitasking for the win.*

"I'll try to get in touch with the delivery guy to see if he knows anything that Reese didn't. Also, I can make some calls to the museum where Sophia died. Maybe I can get in contact with someone from that old *Ugly Duckling* case too." I shuddered, remembering the poor girl who'd killed herself over cruel comments on social media. Keyboard bullies called her hideous, and the entire story turned heartbreaking. I mixed the powdered formula with warm, purified water after realizing nobody took the bagged breast milk out of the fridge to thaw.

If the Keeper's words made any sense about classical stories going awry, *The Ugly Duckling* case matched. Plus, I'd spotted her in the interview, which meant someone might have seen her and knew how to get in touch.

"Okay," Kai agreed. "I love you. Be safe."

I nodded and lifted Wendy's little hand to give him a wave as he closed the door.

Be safe. His words echoed in my head. Armed with a full bottle and a happily eating baby, I hurried to his laptop.

I knew nothing about hunting supernatural beings, but that's where stories came in. With a bit of Google and a lot of guessing, I created a color-coded list of weapons needed to fight various mythical creatures. Just in case. But of course, I didn't have silver bullets or a machete lying around my condo.

At the top, in red, I underlined the closest objects I could think of and the first things I'd gather as soon as Wendy finished her breakfast.

Silver knife. Salt. Iron hammer. My pistol. And a bottle for the baby.

Chapter 20

Once Bitten, Twice Shy

I couldn't find my holster, but the baby carrier came pretty close. The front hugged my chest and fit snuggly with the straps crossing over my shoulder blades. The straps created an X-like target on my back. Target or not, I didn't have a choice. I was both a mother and now an investigator of the supernatural. Though the knives, salt, and hammer on my kitchen counter made me feel more like a hunter than an investigator.

If the same delivery driver brought my food, and the Keeper showed too, I was ready for her with the sigils. Though, she seemed to create the portals without actual doors. I sighed.

The oven light glinted off the edge of the hammer as I picked it up. I didn't know how to wield it, or even if one wielded a hammer. I'd only ever used it to hang pictures on the wall. Guilt stabbed my chest when I remembered I never filled the frames with infant photography and Wendy was getting big, fast.

Did time move like this for all moms? Or did I already miss out on so much that I couldn't get back? The hammer clattered back on the tile countertop, and I released a long sigh.

"I'm sorry, Wendy," I said. Her arms stretched out, and I caught sight of her fists punching the air over the edge of her little Moses basket by the coffee table. Already a fighter, that one. Maybe she'd grow up ready to take down werewolves and ghosts and whatever else was out there. The baby carrier bunched and dug into my stomach as I leaned over the counter.

A small smile tugged at the corner of my mouth. No matter how much I failed as a mom, I persisted, trying harder each day. But I kept tripping up, both metaphorically and literally. *Not clumsy, just not graceful.*

I had a list compiled of my motherhood failures. My brain forever filed them from least to worst offensive with least in pale colors and worst in the painfully bright shades.

Green started with little things, like holding the bottle wrong when I fed her. That resulted in gas bubbles and an upset baby. Blue failures included not recognizing her among the other babies at the hospital. Yellow got a little worse, like losing her in the first place. Orange. . . A shudder tickled down my spine. My eyes shot toward the Moses basket and breath returned to my tightened lungs.

She's fine.

But could I really risk orange? Would we have to use Wendy as bait to draw the wolf out and find the Keeper? I couldn't let these murders continue in my name, but strapping my baby to my chest and hunting down a grizzly bear-sized man-wolf didn't seem like the best plan, either.

And red failures?

No. Wendy is not Red. And if she was, I'd use my iron hammer to bash that wolf's head in before he could get those jaws within ten feet of her.

My fingers slipped around the handle of the tool, and I squeezed. I lifted it and armed my other hand with the knife, feeling the weight of them both. Self-defense wasn't new to me. I'd kept up with classes over the years. Despite Detective Wilhelm's beliefs, I didn't have any trouble defending myself. It was only smart as an investigative journalist of violent crimes. But I couldn't claim I knew how to fight a wolf.

Self-defense taught me to aim for the groin, use my elbow, and jab at the eyes—on human targets. . .

Then, I'll just have to get to them before they turn into the wolf.

I dropped the hammer, heavy side down, into the baby carrier. The oddity of it made me laugh a little, and Wendy squealed back a response.

"We've got this, don't we, Wends?" I said. I could see her little fist dripping with drool now and knew she'd gnawed on her fingers. Speaking of gnawing, I realized I'd chewed my lip raw.

Do I got this?

My stomach rumbled in response. How could I be hungry at a time like this? I ran the ridges of my thumb along the edge of the knife, careful to not push into its sharpness. Not until a high-pitched sound pierced the quiet stillness of our condo, and I almost jumped out of my skin.

The blade caught the soft, squishy center of my thumb and sliced downward. I seethed and dropped the knife back onto the counter. Was that our doorbell? My stomach said it was, but my head knew otherwise.

Our ringer didn't sound like a scream. Goosebumps prickled up my bare arms. I checked on Wendy as I ran past, but she kept kicking and punching at nothing, unbothered by the sound. My heart pounded as I crept toward the door, ready to face whatever was out there. Did I catch the Keeper like a mouse in a trap? What was the cheese? Wendy?

No, she can't be Red. She's not. Reese's comment about sealed fate left a bitter taste in my mouth, and I no longer craved waffles and eggs.

I swallowed, shoving the knot in my throat down to slam into the bottom of my stomach as I curled my hand around the door handle.

The Keeper never hurt me. She saved me. But nerves still fluttered in my chest. I turned the knob and yanked it open.

Red. Red everywhere.

Nothing hit me, except the sight of it. But the wind knocked out of me all the same. A woman lay on the ground. A woman I knew.

The flesh on her neck lay torn like a rag, pulled from her bones. Blood stained the concrete of our outdoor corridor. A familiar popping sound echoed down the hall, bouncing off the walls, followed by an ear-splitting howl.

Tala's front door flew open, and she joined the noise with a scream of her own.

"That's Katarina!" she cried, and her knotted hands shook violently. Every sensation around me tripled, and my mind honed in on all the details, arthritis in Tala's fingers, the open, unseeing eyes on Katarina, the shadow of the wolf's tail vanishing down the staircase. The organized investigator side of me calmed as I scanned the crime scene. Should I run back to get my weapons and follow the wolf? I couldn't leave Wendy alone.

"She's Mr. Geppetto's daughter," Tala said, her voice shaking now too.

I nodded, vaguely aware of Tala's words but agreeing with them all the same. I'd met our other neighbor's daughter several times. She visited her father every week since he'd started in-home care for his own mother. Neither wanted to put the aging woman into a nursing home, so Katarina and Mr. Geppetto created a plan to share her full-time care.

And there it was. A door. A portal opened on the concrete at the top of the staircase. Hands appeared at the edge of the swirling mass as the Keeper pulled herself up and onto the ground of our complex's corridor. She'd used the wolf to teleport to. I finally understood all of this magic and supernatural stuff, and despite the tragedy before me, a flutter of hope danced in my chest. Or it was heartburn, but that had vanished after pregnancy, so I went with hope.

The Keeper grunted and gathered herself. Once standing, she huffed. Tala only glanced at her, but the shock of the gruesome body on the floor stole her attention away from the portal.

"How am I always late?" the Keeper shrieked in frustration, throwing her hands up. "I was never late before the twenty-first century." She turned toward the stairs. The cloak splayed out and dusted the concrete with the bottom of the velvet fabric.

"Hey! Wait!" I called out. This was my chance.

Tell me Wendy isn't Red. Tell me this is all a nightmare.

Her fiery curls bounced and tumbled over her shoulders as her head swiveled to look at me. A bright look flooded her face.

"Ah yes," she said, pointing one finger into the air. "Mari Fable, just the person I wanted to talk to."

I carefully stepped out from the frame of my front door, avoiding the sticky notes and steering clear of poor Katarina. My heart split in half for Mr. Geppetto. The pain of heartbreak and loss weighed on my chest, and it wasn't the fact that the iron hammer still hung in the baby carrier strapped to my torso. I hurt for him; I hurt for Katarina and the other victims. But I needed to focus so that I could get answers, deliver those answers to the public, and not only keep other women safe, but ensure protection for my daughter.

With me out of the way, I waved for the Keeper to enter. I even threw in an inviting smile for good measure and resisted the urge to glance down at the sigils and double-check that they were all still in place.

Tala's voice blurred into the background noise of the city. I registered her calling for emergency paramedics.

The Keeper paid her no notice, nor did she flinch at the bloody death before her. Resentment built in me like those painful gas bubbles during postpartum. I grimaced. How could she be so cold and callous about the attacked woman right here? How could she keep secrets about these story fates when people were dying?

The Keeper did, however, notice me and my odd behavior.

She paused across from me, my front door between us, the body between me and Tala, my emotions between frustration and desperation.

"Are you inviting me in for tea?" the Keeper asked with one eyebrow arched.

Tea? Did I look like a studious British woman ready to sip warm beverages over a book club discussion? I flexed and unflexed my fists, almost ready to punch the answers out of her.

"Sure," I managed. *Whatever will get you to step into that circle so you can't leave when I demand answers.* I must have glanced down, giving away my lead because her gaze dropped.

Before she could move, I lunged forward, gripping her forearms and spinning her into the circle. She gasped and shoved me off her.

"I don't know who you are," I said through gritted teeth, as I tried to stand tall and block her exit. "Or what you are. But I do know you can tell me more about these fairy tales and doors."

"Oh, I—"

"And what in the wonderland does my family have to do with any of it?" I cut her off before she could change the subject.

Her eyes rolled down to the sigils, and a smirk curved on her face. "Are you trying to trap me?"

"Answer the question." I stuck my finger up to her face in a feeble attempt to be demanding. All of my knowledge and investigative training flew out the window when it came to the safety of my family. I couldn't stay calm and remember my interviewing tactics.

"Clever, like Quasimodo." The Keeper tapped her foot. The sole of her Mary Jane shoes rhythmically hit the concrete. "Which one was that? The fifteenth century?" She shook her head. "I can't recall."

"Listen, you will answer the question or—"

"Or what? You'll use this nail tool thing on me?" She gestured toward the baby carrier.

She almost got me. She almost tricked me into backing down. Because who was I against a supernatural-portal-creating-being?

Almost. I straightened and puffed up my chest. Wendy wailed behind the Keeper and her cries emboldened me by reminding me why I stood here. I was an investigator and a writer to keep the city safe, but I was also a mother now, and nothing would stop me from putting an end to the danger that hunted my daughter.

The baby carrier pressed against the Keeper's torso as I stepped up to her. She stood a head taller than me, but I didn't care.

"It's called a hammer," I said. "And yes, I can be clever. At times."

Don't shortchange yourself, Mari. You lured out the wolf. You've solved murders and interviewed serial killers. Plus, you survived post-labor gas pains. I sniffed and folded my arms across my chest, taking a cue from Detective Wilhelm's arrogant gestures—though mine was feigned confidence.

"Did you know that I'm an investigator?" I asked. The Keeper's expression didn't waver from boredom. "I notice details." My brain rushed to organize my thoughts. In green, I recalled what she'd said on the beach. In yellow, I noted her frustrated arrival today. In red. . . It all came together. I knew this woman wasn't in control. She *used* to appear before the deaths in the ancient stories, but her behavior, questioning, and desperation all revealed that she'd lost control. Of what, the stories? The villains?

"I'm noticing a few details myself," the Keeper said, as she mirrored my stance and crossed her arms. "Like your baby crying, and those sirens coming. If you would be so kind as to—"

"That's why the books call you the Keeper." I cut her off again, but my resolve and anger melted away to awe as the blank notes in my brain filled in.

"You're quite rude, aren't you?" She huffed and blew a perfectly smooth ringlet of orange-red hair from her face. The gesture reminded me of a child, someone who didn't know how to behave like everyone else.

"You're the Keeper of the stories," I said. "You move between stories and the characters involved, don't you?" My mind raced a million miles a second. "What you said on the beach about every one hundred years. I- I corroborated that with my research. And the stories are real."

The Keeper nodded and waved me along with one hand as if she were impatient, bored. Or maybe she was waiting to run off and play more in her children's stories.

My awe shifted to focus, and I saw the words in red in my mind's eye. *She needs my help.* "You're the one leaving the bloody messages," I said, and she finally met my gaze. Did I detect a bit of a shock in her chocolate eyes? "I'm alive because you need me. You're messing up!" I poked my finger into her face and almost laughed. The Keeper's jaw dropped, and she looked me up and down. For the first time since Wendy's birth, I didn't feel totally insane or out of control. Not even my notebook and color-coded pens ever fully calmed me. I paced during long nights while trying to get Wendy to nurse, feeling watched, wondering about my stalker. But the tides finally turned because I knew her weakness.

"What a wild suggestion," she said and tossed her head back.

"Why not leave, then?" I dared. "Create your *doors to the unknown* that aren't so unknown to me anymore and run away to prove me wrong."

Her jaw quivered, and her head shook ever-so-slightly as if she were about to explode into steam like a cartoon character. I caught her split-second glance at the sigils beneath us. The freckles that dotted her nose and cheeks complemented the velvet red of her hood.

"It wasn't me!" She stomped her foot and dropped her arms to her sides. "The stories aren't keeping to tradition. There's an imbalance."

"Is my daughter Red Riding Hood?"

The Keeper flinched at the name. Her hand drifted toward the strings that kept her cloak tied around her neck. The crimson string tightened around her fingers as she played with it, twirling and twisting.

"The story aura has led me on a wild goose chase," she said. Her eyes shifted around, and she gnawed on her bottom lip.

I furrowed my brow and didn't drop my gaze. Finally, she met my eye again and sighed.

"Oh, what's the difference if you know." She said it more to herself than to me. "The story aura is all awry, and I couldn't identify which one of you is Red. It moves until the right person is ready to take on the role of the character. Their life and intentions must match with it. I thought Red was one of those babies. Then, I thought it was your mother."

Babies? The four in the office room at the hospital?

"Is Wendy Red Riding Hood or not?" I asked again, impatient, exhausted, tired of research for once in my life, and ready to confirm the answer so I could begin reversing whatever had made Wendy Red. *Or find a way to defy fate before it sealed.*

"Yes," she whispered, and a sparkle reflected in her deep brown eyes. Was that a hint of a smile on her face? The Keeper lifted her chin and eyed me before speaking louder. "Yes. I have figured it out. Wendy is Red." Her gaze shifted around the room, then landed back on me. That familiar look of determination flushed her face, but fear didn't join it this time.

Suddenly, the sounds of the world flooded in around me. Sirens grew closer with their piercing, rhythmic screams. Tala hyperventilated behind us. Footsteps rattled the staircase leading to our floor. The rush of it all threw me out of focus, but it was Wendy's cries that knocked me back to the situation at hand. I cursed under my breath for letting her scream for so long without me there to comfort her.

I shoved past the Keeper and into my home, where I scooped up a pinched, red-faced Wendy. My hand circled her back in a soothing motion, and I bounced, swaying my hips back and forth.

"But I know this," the Keeper said, turning to face me. "If the wolf lures Red out of her immortality and eats her when I'm not there to kill him at the height of his mortality, then the story will seal and the person who has become the wolf will live on, an invincible, blood-thirsty. . . " She snapped her finger and looked around the room. "Oh, what is the word?"

"Murderer?" I squeaked.

She frowned. "Yes."

"The wolf is just a person?" I clarified. Wendy's crying sputtered out, and her tense little body eased into mine. I held her close against my chest.

"An. Immortal. Person," she said in skipped beats. "And he'll be thrown back into the story cycle if I don't hunt him."

"Okay. . . "

"Isn't that how people speak when they're aggravated?" she asked.

I ignored her question. "He's immortal only until he hunts Red on her way to her grandmother's, right?"

The Keeper pursed her rosy lips. "Yes, it is story protection. They're part of the story too. The story finds those who belong to it. Just like it found your family. One of you wants to visit her grandmother," she said. The Keeper lifted her foot and stepped from the sigil circle. My breath hitched when I saw that I'd knocked a sticky note to the side in my rush for Wendy and broken the circle. She marched into our living room, bent over the Coffee Table of Evidence, and picked up a pen.

My brow scrunched, and I squinted to see what she was writing. Wendy burped and something wet soiled my shirt and shoulder. I patted her back, and she spit up a second time.

The Keeper straightened. Behind her, my door stood open and the rush of paramedics and cops filled the corridor, shouting orders and kneeling over Katarina's body.

"How do I stop the wolf?" I asked.

"You don't," she said. She turned and walked toward the front door, heels clicking. "I do. And I left a message for you about how you can help me. You can lure the wolf out of his immortality by taking Red to her grandmother's house." The Keeper nodded toward Wendy, and I hugged my baby tighter. A strange look came over her face, and the Keeper gave her head a slight shake. "Her grandmother's true home, that is."

"Excuse me?"

"The other Fable, your mother, is it? Her true home is with her husband on Cygnus Island." The Keeper's curls bounced with the movement of her head. "If you want to know who the wolf is, take her there," she smiled, "and you'll find out." Her voice sounded excited as she suggested I put my daughter in danger.

I grimaced and watched the Keeper swivel around. The cloak grazed the faux wood floor. Instead of daring to step near the sigils again, the Keeper moved to the side and pressed her hand on the wall.

The wall beside the coat rack lit up as she traced her finger in the shape of a door, using the blank space between the frame of my actual door and the empty picture frames.

"What about stopping the man behind the wolf?" I asked.

She stopped her portal creation and arched an eyebrow at me.

"How would I find him?" I recalled the fangs on my OBGYN, the howling at the hospital, and the yellow eyes I'd seen outside my house. Was that the story aura she mentioned? Was it shifting from person to person and trying to find a place to land?

My living room wall opened into the morgue. Reese's head shot up from where he sat on his stool at the counter. The Keeper stepped over the threshold and out of my living room.

She glanced over her shoulder, and the hood slipped off her head. "Who have you wronged? Who do you know that would want to hurt your family?"

With that, the door closed, sealed off, and vanished. Wendy's breaths came slowly and even now. Her wailing quieted, and it left us with only the sounds of the bustle outside. The empty pit of my stomach felt heavy and sick when I thought of her words.

Someone wanted to hurt us, outside this whole story thing. I didn't need to lure the Keeper out; I needed to lure the wolf out. Then, I'd wait for the beast to transform back into the person it once was and take them down. Just like every other killer I'd tracked and reported on.

I snuggled Wendy close, breathing in her sweet baby scent. She bundled the collar of my shirt in her tiny fist and gnawed half on her hand and half on the fabric. I carried her to the other side of the coffee table and plucked the sticky note from the block of paper. It shook in my quivering hand, but I read the message the Keeper left for me.

It is time to meet. Visit them. You must let the story be told.

Chapter 21

Actions Speak Louder Than Words

"Like heck I will!" My stomping caused our downstairs neighbor to bang on their roof with what I assumed was a broomstick. At another time, I might have grabbed my pens and made a note to research if witches exist, but the only supernatural or magical beings I cared about right now were the wolf and the Keeper. I continued pacing the living room, with lighter steps.

Kai sat on the couch in front of our uneaten piles of breakfast food that soured hours ago. My stomach growled at me to eat something before the day ended, but I was too riled, too focused, too thrown between both feelings. Should I sit down and research more before facing the wolf?

"If I visit my father's side of the family, it will be because I'm coming after the wolf. Not to help *the Keeper*." I gritted my teeth. I paused in front of the kitchen counter and gnawed on my fingernail while watching Wendy sleep on the baby monitor. The black and white video stream showed her twitching her head to the side. She'd wake soon, hungry and cranky since she'd slept most of the day away after the long cry that morning. Her crying sessions exhausted her almost as much as they exhausted me. I picked up the monitor and continued watching her as I paced.

"You really want to go after a serial killer knowing that they're supernatural?" Kai said. He kept his voice level to talk sense into me.

"I've done the research. The Keeper herself said that we can stop him when he's human." I ran my fingers through my hair. It tugged against my skull as I pulled it up into a ponytail shape, then let it fall again. I repeated the process while I paced. "I've tracked serial killers and exposed them to the public. This is no different."

"Except those serial killers didn't have fangs. . . " he offered with an apologetic frown. He wanted me to do more research, to be safer about this. I couldn't blame him. Coming from a history teacher, I expected nothing less. He needed to look at it from every angle and analyze it. I did the same, but my job required me to get to the answers quicker. If I didn't find the evidence and write the article, people in the city wouldn't know how to keep themselves safe from this unknown threat.

I pulled out my phone and dialed Detective Wilhelm for the eleventh time. It went straight to voicemail now. On my second call, he answered and told me to stay out of his way. By the fourth call, he relented and listened to me long enough to call me crazy and hung up. He reasoned away the wolf's attack by labeling it 'a wild animal,' 'a fluke,' and 'not related to the killer.' After another demand to leave his investigation alone, I heard the dial tone.

Textbooks and Styrofoam food containers buried the coffee table. Kai cleared a small space and scooted to the edge of his cushion. With everything pushed to the side, he cracked open *Before the Legends* where I'd marked it with a red tab. He rubbed his temples while he reread a mention of someone we believed to be the Keeper. Or someone like her.

"It says here that a legend existed, passed by word of mouth through several cultures around the world. A child known as the Little Cloak Girl wandered the woods after her parents died."

I paused. I'd read it already, but hearing Kai speak the words sparked different ideas. Could this really be the Keeper herself? She'd mentioned immortality. My serial killer, the person hunting me, would become permanently immortal themselves if I didn't do something. And apparently, I couldn't wait around for the Keeper, since she repeatedly showed up late. From *The Ugly Duckling* case to Katarina's murder outside our front door, the Keeper kept failing.

And what made me believe I'd do any better? I couldn't so much as succeed at pumping milk or swaddling my baby (Kai always had to do it when the velcro swaddles were in the wash). I shivered, though the room was quite toasty with the fireplace burning.

But I had to try. I had to try for Wendy.

"If I cross-reference these accounts—" Kai said, flipping between pages, holding one section in place with his thumb, "then the Little Cloak Girl is mentioned over a four hundred-year time span. People record seeing her wander forests while she sang a song her mother taught her. In this account, in the year 1401, the Little Cloak Girl said she was waiting for her mother and father to return and take her home. She told people about how a hunter in the woods recited a story about her parents searching for food before they'd come back for her."

"So, she's a ghost or a spirit." I tried to piece it together. My knuckles turned white from clutching the video monitor so tightly. Something ached deep inside my chest at the story of the Little Cloak Girl. I hurt both for her and her parents. They'd lost each other. I didn't want to think of losing Wendy. Never. Ever. *Again.*

The story aura. Wendy's birth must have sparked it, and that's why the Keeper came to the hospital.

"Not a spirit," Kai said, shattering my theory. "These paintings of her show that she aged."

"What?"

"After she told the story about her parents, she didn't stay a little girl," he explained while chewing on a pencil, "But she stopped aging again. All the other accounts mention a young woman."

"Does the version of her as a young woman talk to anyone in the records?" I paused my pacing and took a seat on the floor next to him. My back rested against the couch, but the pressure hurt my still-healing wounds from the wolf's claws. I leaned my head back and let my eyes shut for just a moment, still gripping the monitor. I'd hear her if anything happened.

But my eyes flew open again at a rustling sound on the video. Wendy had only squirmed in her sleep. One arm slipped from the swaddle, and she settled again. Her chest rose and fell in a soothing pattern.

Kai nodded. "Yep." He took the pencil from his mouth and used the pointy end to scratch his head. "She still told the people about waiting for her parents. It says here that the Little Cloak Girl believed so strongly in the story the hunter told her, that the story itself transcended time. And she still wears the same looking cloak." He picked up the book and held it in front of me.

The story itself. . .

I jumped to my feet and tucked the monitor under my arm.

"Where are you going?" My husband looked up at me, his eyes squinting with worry.

"I can't wait here, Kai." My voice cracked. A lump of emotion gathered in my throat. It was a mixture of fear for my family, sadness for the Little Cloak Girl, and determination. "I can't."

His brow furrowed, but I knew he knew what came next. I intended to lure the wolf out again. I'd make the jump on him before he had another chance to hurt anyone else.

"Women are dying because of me," I said. "I have the answers to this story, and I haven't shared them. I *can't* share them!" I threw my arms up. "Nobody would believe me, and I'd be under twenty-four-hour watch."

"Mari, you're not a supernatural hunter."

"Who is, Kai?"

"The Keeper?" He proposed with a crinkled expression, inquisitive but hopeful. Normally, I'd find it endearing, but I needed him to understand me right now.

"No." I rounded the coffee table and sat on the couch beside him. He put the book down, and I took his hands in mine. "The Keeper makes sure that the stories stay the way the stories should stay. The whole 'sealed fate' thing. She would let Wendy die."

He flinched. His gaze trailed to the monitor in my lap. Wrinkles lined the edges of his eyes and crinkled on his forehead as worry covered his face, so I squeezed his hands.

"How many times have I already almost lost you?" he whispered.

"I know."

"No, you don't know how hard it is being the one at home. Waiting." He shook his head and strands of his thick brown hair fell into his face. "I know you're a fighter, Mari. But this is a supernatural being. This is something we don't understand."

"Then, choose not to worry," I said and stood without letting go of his hands. "When Wendy wakes up, I'm taking her to my grandmother's house. I'm going to walk right into the place the wolf expects, but he won't know that I know he's coming. And when he turns back into a human, I'm going to have him arrested."

"Won't the Keeper help the wolf get to Wendy?" Kai's Adam's apple bobbed as he swallowed hard.

"She'll be late," I explained. "She's always late." I tugged to pull him up, and I traded my hands for the monitor.

The weapons still sat on the counter beside the baby carrier where I'd left it. The strapping contraption had gotten easier since I'd taken it off and put it back on several times this afternoon. I could do it with one hand now and that felt like the tiniest bit of accomplishment that I'd claim for the day.

"Mari," he begged. "Are you sure about this?"

"Not at all." I shook my head and marched over to the counter. The carrier slipped over my shoulders as easily as throwing on a T-shirt. I wrapped a towel around a kitchen knife and tucked it into my pocket. "But what I am sure of is that the next murder will not be outside our front door. There's nowhere left but inside our home. So, I'm going to find him before he can attack us. As Wendy's mom, I don't doubt that I'll be next. I don't have the story protection that she does."

"By yourself?"

I prepared a Ziploc baggie of salt and secured it in my other pocket just in case the Keeper turned out to be a spirit. Then, I marched across the room, armed and ready to carry a baby hands-free. I offered Kai the hammer.

He took it with a quizzical look.

"No," I said. "You're coming with me."

The smirk on his face confirmed his agreement, and it took me back to one of the first cases I worked on while interning as an investigative journalist. He'd worked as my background researcher while I dealt with Detective Wilhelm. Together, Kai and I figured out who murdered Sophia—Snow White—at the same time. He gripped the hammer's handle and looked at it with a gleam in his eye.

"I'm coming with you," he repeated, nodding.

"You're okay with this?"

Kai scrubbed his hand over his hair to move the brown locks out of his face and grinned, dimples and all. This was where we thrived when we worked together. He was the Richard Castle to my Kate Beckett, the Mary Margaret to my David, the Sam to my Dean. . . *Wait. Scratch that one, it doesn't make sense.*

But with the leather jacket he pulled on and the makeshift weapon, he reminded me of a supernatural hunter.

"Are you ready to make a few changes to Little Red Riding Hood's story?" I asked after returning from the bedroom. Wendy yawned and bundled my shirt into her fist to snuggle closer.

"I'm ready to make history." He winked, and I groaned from the cheese. He'd embraced his role as a dad, and it fit nicely with his geeky teacher status

Together, we secured Wendy into the carrier and I plugged Alcatraz into my phone. When that didn't come up, I resorted to 1700 Cygnus Island again. It still shook me that the address actually worked.

"Okay," I breathed. "Let's go for a walk."

Kai nodded and opened our front door. The cold, salty wind rushed in, and hope mingled with adrenaline inside me. It warmed me from the inside out, plus the baby on my chest kept me cozy.

I'd already made a lot of mistakes as a mom. But motherhood made me brave. And despite the situation, for the first time since Wendy was born, I knew we were making the right decision as her parents. We refused to sit around and wait for danger to come to her.

Screw. Sealed. Fate.

Wendy would make her own future if I had anything to do with it.

Chapter 22

It Is Always Darkest

Twenty-two acres of mystery lay before us. The ferry ride was quiet except for the splash of the water behind the boat. I tucked my phone in my pocket after some last-minute research about the island where Alcatraz was built. Aerial shots showed that if anyone lived on the island, they'd planted many trees and bushes for privacy. What was once an open, rocky land had grown over with green shrubs.

I leaned my back against the railing and cupped my hand around Wendy's face to block the cool wind. We'd given her a bottle right before leaving the house, but I worried tracking a serial killer would take more time than expected, and we didn't have any formula with us. Kai rested his elbows on the edge and observed the bubbling water below us.

"I was just thinking," he said in that curious tone he used when pointing out a historically inaccurate flaw on a TV show.

"What's that?" I asked. I looked past him and watched the shore of the island come into view. Only two other passengers rode the last ferry from Pier 99 of the night. A young couple, maybe just into college, cuddled in the seats in the middle of the boat. I wouldn't be surprised if they planned to sneak out to huddle under the rock outcroppings on the beach and steal some privacy.

"The wolf is following the story like the Keeper. Which also means he's following Wendy. Wouldn't he be on the boat with us if that were the case?" Kai reasoned.

"There's a lot we don't know about the stories and how they work yet," I said. I fully intended to uncover the truth behind the supernatural underworld, this strange fairy tale cycle, and everything connected to it after I secured Wendy's safety and put our stalker behind bars. *It's what I do.* "But we know the story. And the wolf is already at Grandma's when she goes to visit." I recalled the brightly colored pages in Wendy's board book. Did Tala know about the fairy tales? Was the baby book some kind of warning? She had given it to me the day Wendy was born.

Kai nodded and sighed. With his breath came a puff of white air. He slipped off his jacket, though his rosy nose revealed he needed it. He wrapped it around the outside of the baby carrier to keep both Wendy and me warm.

"Do you think that means the wolf knows we're coming?" he asked.

I took a deep breath. The sea air refreshed me and provided clarity. Instead of color-coded notes to file away in my brain, I thought of only one thing: the plan. *Find him. Detain him. Have him arrested.*

"Yeah." I turned to look at him, my brow furrowed in apology. "I wish we weren't in this mess."

He tightened his hold on the surrounding coat until we turned into a mass of jackets in our family hug. He held me from the side so our embrace wouldn't squish Wendy. I buried my face in his warm neck, and Wendy looked up at us with huge, curious eyes.

"The good news is," I said, "that he doesn't know that *we know* about the story and that he's really a man. Since we're letting the story play out, he's losing his immortality. Just like Wendy." My breath came in shudders now, short and quick. Nerves twisted my stomach, but taking control brought a sense of power with it. I was anxious, but not afraid. I refused to let innocent women continue to die while hiding away with my daughter. I refused to cower and let the wolf devour me, leaving Wendy without a mom and Kai without his wife.

"The element of surprise, plus a hammer." Kai chuckled without joy.

I appreciated his attempt at humor. The ferry docked, and we untangled from one another. But I didn't want to let go. As we shuffled off the boat, my hand wandered to my pocket, the holster at my side, and then landed in Kai's hand.

He wore the handle of the hammer tucked into the back of his pants and had hidden a knife of his own in his boots. We came prepared with the weapons ready to keep the wolf in place. The wooden planks creaked under our feet. The young couple ran down the dock, giggling and letting the blanket blow out behind them like a cape on a two-headed person.

I stepped from the dock and onto the rocky shore. The couple had turned and climbed down the rocks where the sand was close to the water. Several paces up off the shore was a line of trees, and behind that, the top of the tall concrete wall that was built when the national park of Alcatraz shut down. According to my guesstimates, the wall was only a short walk up from the shore. But the only break in the concrete that I'd found in my observation of the aerial photos was on the opposite side. We'd have to hike half a mile to the other end to get inside and find out if my father's mother really lived there.

And I expected we'd meet the wolf along the way.

I looked at Kai, and he nodded. The grim smile on his face let me know he was in this with me wholeheartedly.

The salty wind tossed my ponytail around. I tugged the hood of my sweater out from underneath the straps on the baby carrier and covered my head with it for extra warmth.

"This way." I pointed to the dark rocks and shrubs that dotted the shore. Kai followed. Each step demanded I take it carefully since the rocks were jagged and the wind unforgiving. I calculated every move to keep Wendy as safe as possible.

Who wants to hurt your family? The Keeper's words echoed in my head. I'd once thought Detective Wilhelm was out to get me. He hated that I solved so many of his cases and that the precinct would often invite me to come help with murders. That meant he had to put up with me whether or not he wanted to.

But his look of shock at the attack on Soup Cracker Street proved he wasn't involved. Plus, he couldn't have been the wolf, since the wolf was literally on top of me at the time.

Reese used to creep me out. He'd make weird jokes about death, but I'd since come to learn he accepted a sealed fate, the fate of his story, and I understood his obsessions. It definitely wasn't him.

Jameson was my rival and an all-around jerk, but I didn't think work drama was enough to send him over the edge.

And Pam enjoyed making my life miserable, but that was only for her own gain as the boss at Bay Side Media. I'd never suspect Tala or Elsie.

At least it made sense now why I saw fangs on Doctor Perrault and the intern. The story aura was searching for someone to take on the role of the wolf, and I'd upset both of them, so they were tempted to harm me to get to Wendy.

But all the howling and the yellow eyes outside my condo were the real wolf once the story finally settled on someone. But who?

My ankle twisted as my foot slipped on a rock. I yelped, and Kai spun around. He grabbed my elbow before I fell, and he steadied me while I straightened. As we moved away from the lighthouse and into the groves of trees, the darkness surrounded us like a quiet, heavy blanket.

Kai flicked on a flashlight, but I still had to squint and focus to see where I stepped. We moved slowly but didn't stop.

And what about my father? Had I offended him by keeping my family from him? I'd chosen Mom since I never really knew him. She always insisted he wasn't violent, that he was incapable of hurting a fly. It didn't sit right. My understanding of motives and killers didn't match up with my family's situation.

I only knew one other person who held a grudge against me. He hated me for getting the lead investigative journalist title at Bay Side Media.

But before I dove into another theory and considered who wanted to hurt us, a howl split the night.

A shiver trickled down my spine. Kai glanced back at me and nodded. He understood it was time to space out. He'd follow two steps behind, as out of sight as possible, to jump the wolf and smash its skull when it came for me. But we both knew that alone wouldn't bring down the supernatural creature.

That's why I had my Sig and the knife. They'd at least help detain the beast until it transformed back into a person. I shuddered, knowing I might have to take a few hits or scratches or even a bite to spark his transformation back to human.

I cursed the wind for covering the more minute sounds. Still, with my focus sharp, I identified the sound of a twig snapping. The breeze carried growling up toward us, and I silently pointed at the rocky outcropping below us so that Kai would be aware.

I have her. Come out.

My hand rested on the gun at my side, and I willed my pulse to slow. Tall shrubs and trees blocked my view around us. Kai had put the flashlight away, and we used only the glow of the moon to see.

Another branch snapped. This time, right beside me. I swiveled toward it, my stomach leaping into my throat. But the wolf's jaws didn't greet me. Instead, fiery curls framed a pale face. The Keeper's crimson lips matched the strings of her cloak fastened around her neck. She grinned and opened her mouth. Despite the rush of wind through the trees and crashing waves below us, I heard her whisper.

"You're mortal now."

Kai reacted as planned. He lunged forward with the hammer swinging.

"Kai, no!" I shouted.

It bashed full force into the Keeper's ribs. She gasped and shot him a glare, but did not so much as stumble despite the iron head of the hammer that hit her slight frame. She wasn't short, but Kai definitely towered over her and should have knocked her out completely.

In the distraction, I let my guard drop. Red-hot pain seared through my arm. I screamed and yanked my arm to my side. From the opposite side, two yellow eyes glared at me. The beast perched on a rock across from the Keeper, with Wendy and me in the middle. He opened his snout, and the moonlight gave just enough illumination for me to see the saliva dripping from his canines.

My heart pounded in my throat so hard I thought it might knock Wendy right out of the baby carrier. The wolf's massive front paws extended out as he took the leap. I stumbled backward, nearly crashing into Kai to avoid the attack.

Before the wolf landed, his claws swiped across the Keeper's pale, freckled cheeks. She gasped and slapped her hand over the torn flesh, then immediately went for her hood. The velvet fabric fell heavily on her thick hair.

In a rage, the wolf snapped at her hand. He was nearly seven times her size and at his full power now, with the story coming to its close. I pulled out my gun and flicked the safety off, ready to push back against the wolf's attack and help her. But it didn't matter. She didn't so much as flinch when his teeth sunk into her fingers. The Keeper pulled away. With one hand, she covered the wound on her face, and with the other, impossibly unharmed one, she tugged the string of the cloak tighter around her collarbone.

The Little Cloak Girl. She never aged with it on. And she didn't get hurt with the hood up, either.

I steadied the gun and flexed, ready for the slight kickback when it fired. I had to stay focused and calm when the wolf turned on me, but I kept my eye on the Keeper too. She hopped from the rock beside the wolf and disappeared into the darkness. The red of her hood caught my eye again, closer to me.

The wolf snarled, and Kai stepped from the side, continuing our defense as planned. He swung for the wolf's head, but the wolf was ready. He snapped at the air when Kai dodged. But the rocky island was unforgiving, and Kai lost his balance. He stumbled in the sudden movement and dipped again to avoid another bite aimed at him. The hammer fell from his hands and tumbled down the rocky cliff.

The wolf sliced at his thigh. His claws cut deep, and Kai went down, smacking his hip on a rock.

I fired.

The bullet landed with a thud on the wolf's flank. He growled and shot his yellow gaze at me.

You're mortal now.

She wasn't looking at Wendy when she said it, though my poor baby cried in a weak, but persistent wail. I cuddled her closer to me.

It's me. And the Keeper had spoken right before the wolf made a lunge for me. She'd set me up.

The wolf recovered from the gunshot wound. The bullet fell out of his side and landed with a clink against the rock, and the beast turned toward me. My pulse thudded in my ears, and I could hear nothing outside of my body. I swallowed and steadied myself, focusing on the most immediate threat.

Green. Yellow. Orange. Red.

Red. The color of her cloak caught my eye. The Keeper had positioned herself behind me. Was she going to push me into the wolf's mouth? When the supernaturally sized wolf opened his jaws, I knew I'd fit. All it would take was one push for the Keeper to feed both me and Wendy to the wolf. After releasing an ear-splitting howl, he licked his snout and snapped his jaws shut. The wolf put one paw in front of the other, stalking me. He knew I couldn't outrun him, and with Kai down and our element of surprise gone, we'd lost our advantage to wait out the transformation back to human. The beast stalked toward me.

Instead of firing another shot, as it appeared I would do, I dropped the gun, reached for the button at the bottom of the baby carrier, and pulled Wendy off me. After ripping the knife from my pocket, I spun around. I shoved Wendy into the Keeper's arms and used my blade to cut the strings of her cloak. With her hands now full, and in a moment of shock, the Keeper didn't stop me. I yanked the cloak from her neck.

In one last desperate act of hope that I understood the story, I wrapped the crimson cloak around me. With the hood secure on my head, I turned to face the wolf.

He'd already leaped into the air, ten times my size now. His massive mouth was an abyss of black past the gleaming white teeth. I dropped to a huddle, crouching and making sure the entire cloak covered me.

Darkness shadowed me, and warmth surrounded me. The wind ceased. I could no longer hear the crash of the waves. And Wendy's cries were muted and muffled. But she was safe. Not eaten, at least.

I held my breath as his jaw closed. Sharp teeth clamped down on me, but they couldn't penetrate the fabric. The cloak held firm, and I registered only a vague pressure from the pointed canines. The pressure of the wolf's swallow moved me into total blackness. A sticky, humid atmosphere settled over me.

I had landed inside his belly. The wolf must have opened his lips again because I heard Wendy's distant wailing clearer for a moment before he broke into a howl that vibrated from the inside out.

My heart cracked in half for my daughter. She was in a stranger's arms, in the cold, at night.

But not for long.

I wasn't a perfect parent, but I was a parent who refused to give up. And a woman who never stopped fighting for the safety of women, and everyone else.

With the handle of the knife still in my grasp, I angled it away from me. I protruded my hand from between the two sides of the cloak, peered out from under the hood, and sunk the blade into the wolf's belly.

Chapter 23

Before the Dawn

It required all of my strength to drag the knife upward where it stopped at the wolf's sternum. I struggled to breathe inside the beast. The muscles in my arms burned as I brought the blade down and used both hands to separate the two walls of the stomach I'd split.

My head spun, and I gasped for breath, but black dots spotted my vision. I pushed again until his belly finally split open. The flow of fresh air kept me from fainting, but I fell out onto the rock with the wolf's blood and entrails.

I sucked in the pure, cool air, letting oxygen fill my lungs while the taste of salt lingered on my tongue. On shaking legs, I pulled myself from my curled position and stood. The blood and goo sloughed off the crimson cloak like water over a duck's feathers.

All the blood and crying and exhaustion reminded me of giving birth. *And crying*, my brain repeated.

I tossed the hood off to see the Keeper standing in front of me, dumbfounded. Her lips were parted and eyes fixed on the dead wolf on the rocks. Wendy's pinched screaming face drew my eyes, and I tore her from the Keeper's hands after dropping the knife. The baby carrier had fallen from Wendy's legs, and the Keeper had clutched her out away from her body in both hands like she had a dirty diaper.

Wendy bubbled and sputtered out as I enveloped her in my arms and held her against my chest. Warmth and comfort flooded me as I wrapped her in my hold.

The Keeper gingerly touched her face with her fingertips. Her mouth hung open, and her eyes stared at nothing.

"Y-you," she stuttered, "you sealed the story." Her gaze dropped to the wolf behind me. I turned, finally able to move without my head spinning. I didn't want to drop Wendy, so I moved slowly, carefully, though I wanted to run to Kai.

The sight on the ground froze me in my tracks.

"This is the wrong ending," the Keeper's voice shook. All her arrogance had vanished, and she stepped beside me to stare at the body on the rocks.

The wolf was gone. In its place lay a man with a face I knew all too well. A face I'd seen around the office, at the crime scenes. A face that belonged to a man who waved me away when Wendy cried and dug under my skin at any opportunity he could. He'd complained to Pam about my work performance and tried to get me fired many times. He'd tried to steal my job while I went on maternity leave, but failed. I suspected his microaggressions and sexual harassment had turned into full-blown thoughts of murder. And so, the wolf landed on him.

"Jameson," I whispered, still in shock. I snuggled Wendy tighter into me and grimaced at his open, unseeing eyes.

A groan interrupted my paralyzed state. I snapped my head up to see my husband lying on the rocks. The wind tossed his overgrown hair into his face while he clutched his leg. Blood spilled out from the deep gashes that had torn through his jeans and flesh. My stomach turned at the sight of the white bone beneath.

"This is the wrong ending." The Keeper raised her voice this time. She dropped to her knees with her head in her hands. Her curls spilled over the sides of her face. "It isn't just the wolf's death. It-it's. . . it's the death of a fairy tale!"

I didn't stop to comfort her. The strings of the cloak tugged and unraveled as the bottom of the fabric caught on a jagged rock and fell from my shoulders. I shifted to balance Wendy with one arm while I knelt beside my husband.

Pain paled his face. I brushed his hair back and cupped the back of his head so that he could lie back and relax without the sharp rocks digging into his skull.

"You're alive." Tears spilled from his eyes. "I thought I'd lost you, and that woman holding our baby. . . " He couldn't finish as emotion and shock and pain overwhelmed him.

"I'm okay," I breathed. "I'm fine, actually. This isn't even close to as bad as giving birth."

Kai sputtered from sobbing to a sudden bout of laughter.

"And I'm not fainting," I teased, to keep him alert and distract him from the pain. He managed a half-smile. With my help, we eased him from the rock to a softer bit of earth where it was only dirt and weeds. He laid back, and I pulled my hand from behind his head to reach for my phone.

I tapped in the three digits for emergency paramedics and explained that we'd been attacked on the island. Kai needed medical attention and Jameson. . . it was time to get the detectives involved. I knew Detective Wilhelm would try to make this difficult for me, but the case was clear. I'd acted in self-defense, and all the old unfinished clues would lead to Jameson as my stalker. I sat on my feet, my legs folded under me, with Wendy balanced in my lap and one of my hands keeping her upright, though she'd be sitting on her own soon.

A shadow extended behind us, and I followed Kai's gaze. The Keeper stood before us, the cloak in her hand. It hung limp, ready to slip from her grasp at another blast of wind up from the shore.

I didn't know what to expect, but what she did was the last thing I could have imagined. The Keeper extended her arm until the cloak was in my face.

"You took the cloak," she said. Her voice had changed, quiet and desperate. "And you sealed the story with the wrong ending."

I furrowed my brow and exchanged a glance with Kai. My confusion didn't deter the Keeper as she continued.

"This is yours now." She stepped closer, pressuring me to take the cloak.

"I don't understand." I shook my head and looked from the crimson velvet back to her freckled, youthful face that now creased with concern. "You framed me. You tried to feed me to that wolf." Fury built within me. "And you lied to me. You told me Wendy was Red and let me live in fear."

Fiery curls danced around her face as she nodded. The movement was jerky, like a child attempting to calm down from a meltdown.

"I had to," she said. "The story is supposed to go how the story goes. How are you not understanding this? I'll admit that my methods of completing the stories have become illegitimate. How do you think I feel that all this technology and modern disturbances to the stories have forced me to resort to lying and cheating just to do my job?" She took a long, shaking breath, and her eyes widened. Her voice dropped from frustrated desperation to a quiet acceptance. "Even the air feels different against my skin." With her free hand, she touched her cheek again and hissed when she remembered the scratches.

I looked at Kai, and he nodded for me to ask. He knew it frustrated me when the Keeper spoke in cryptic responses. Even in his pain, he encouraged me.

I stood with Wendy in one hand and searched the woman's eyes. She pulled her fingers away from her wound and examined the blood on her hands. The expansion of her eyes told me she was unfamiliar with her own blood.

"I'd understand if you explained it to me," I said, finally ready to get the answers I'd been digging for from her for the past several weeks.

The Keeper's full brown eyes met mine, and she swallowed. A look of fear flashed across her face and vanished all in an instant. "All you need to know is that the stories are real. Any story, anything that can be imagined and told and passed down for generations, will come alive and spill over into our world if I do not help the stories we already know complete each cycle." The wind tossed ringlets of hair in her face, but she remained stoic and serious. "Or I used to," she mumbled, her gaze drifting from me and trailing the rocks. "I'd made mistakes before, and more stories slipped in. Most are old, ancient even because I was just a child then." Tears filled her eyes. She lifted her arm and used the back of her hand to wipe snot away as a little kid might. "The human imagination is not to be trifled with. The world cannot handle more monsters. Have you seen what people can create with their minds? Zombies and extraterrestrials. And that. . . " Her eyes got huge, and tears still swam in them. "That lizard beast in the movies. Godzilla." She shuddered.

"When did you know I was Red?"

The Keeper lifted her chin and gained her composure after the monster tangent. The tears had dried before they could spill from her eyes. "As I told you before, the story aura went awry. I couldn't figure out where Red landed, but I saw the aura at the hospital, near your family. Then, I thought I saw it near the babies. Once I tracked it to your family, I left notes for myself at the attacks. I knew this was Fable's story, but I could not tell who. You all seemed to have the story aura glowing around you and—" she looked away abruptly and caught her breath. Her chest rose and fell.

It was weird to see her without the cloak. She wore a simple plain corset that didn't look like anything you could buy on Amazon. Upon further observation, I realized it was attached to the black skirt that hung around her worn, tied boots.

"I was confused," she finally finished her thought. "So, I made my notes wherever he attacked because I was too late to see him change, and he'd fight me off and run while transforming back. I may have been immortal, but I wasn't stronger than the wolf. When I stepped into your home, I knew you were Red. I still saw the aura in Wendy, which I can't explain, but yours was much stronger, and the glow was. . . " She shrugged, her bony shoulders lifting and falling. It looked awkward on her as if she didn't know how to behave like a normal human. "It was red."

Behind the Keeper, I caught sight of a light in the distance. It glowed bright yellow and floated toward us in a slow, steady motion. I hoped it was the ferry bringing paramedics for Kai.

"Now what?" I asked, unsure of what I really wanted to know. *Where do I go from this? Do I investigate the supernatural underworld? I can't ignore it. Do I become a scholar of the classics?* And what about the Keeper?

"Is he lying down?" The Keeper peered past me to observe Kai. "I have seen that he collapses when there is shocking news."

The comment was so sudden that I had to stifle my laughter. I glanced back. "I think she's referring to when you fainted."

"Hey, that was one time! You'd faint too if you watched a screaming human come out of your wife," he said in defense. But the joke did him good. His twisted face temporarily relaxed.

"You sealed this *Little Red Riding Hood* with the story cloak," she said, pushing it into my arms. "That means the stories are your responsibility now. The cloak's protection has passed to you."

"That is killer," Kai said. He meant it as a compliment, but his choice of word earned a raised eyebrow from me as I glanced back at him. "Or, I mean, *awesome.*"

A brief laugh escaped my lips. *What. In. The. Wonderland?*

Wendy fidgeted in my arms. I took the cloak because I could think of nothing else to do in my surprise. Wendy gathered a clump of the fabric in her fist and gnawed on it. She let out a little squeal of happiness as her head bobbed.

I looked down to see my daughter's first smile.

Chapter 24

Well Begun Is Half Done

The light from the boat cast a glow over the side of the island. A gust of wind blew up from the shore. Kai shivered, his teeth chattering. I knelt and laid the cloak over him to help abate the cold.

The Keeper made an odd sound with her mouth, something between squelching lips and a high-pitched hum.

We both quirked our heads at her. She'd given me the cloak and a lot to think about, but right now, I needed to get medical attention for my husband and a bottle for my daughter.

The ferry's horn blasted in a long moaning echo as it docked halfway on the other side of the island. Our party of four would soon balloon into a crowd of cops and paramedics. Could the Keeper still portal away without her cloak? I knew I needed to prepare myself for a long night of questioning with Detective Wilhelm and plenty of research of my own into the entire story.

The Keeper bit her lip and shook her head. She kicked at a few loose rocks and made the humming sound again.

"Okay," I said. "What is it?"

"Oh, nothing." She shrugged and did a little 'I'm about to say something' dance with her head.

I stood and walked past her to pick up the baby carrier. My path gave Jameson's body a wide berth, and I angled Wendy away from the sight of him.

"I'm going to hike around the corner and help the first responders find us," I said.

Kai nodded. As he laid his head back, he winced, but he looked warm with the cloak over him, at least.

"You're already doing everything wrong," the Keeper spewed. "And the longer you don't wear the cloak, the more possibility there is for story creatures to come alive." She rushed in her explanation, tripping over her words. After she finished, she took a gasping, exaggerated breath and offered me a small, apologetic smile.

"Say what now?" My eyes flickered to the cloak that I'd used as a blanket for my husband, then back to the Keeper.

"Just, well. . . " She pursed her lips and twirled one of her ringlets around her finger. "You're already doing everything wrong, and you've only been the Keeper for. . . " she glanced at the moon, "not that long."

"You're telling me I have to wear the cloak all the time?"

Curls bounced as she nodded vigorously. "It's clean. It never gets dirty. If that helps. . . Plus, I know you're a reporter, but you can't tell anyone about the story cycle."

"How am I supposed to keep people safe?" I asked.

The Keeper chewed on her lip. "You're clever with words. You'll find a way. But can you imagine what people would do if they knew they could take on the role of a character and become immortal by tampering with the cycle? They'd be clamoring to act like Mother Gothel or the Evil Queen."

I sighed through circled lips and raised my brows. It was a lot to take in, but I'd seen what the story monsters could do. I saw it push Jameson over the edge. And the fear I had to live in while dealing with it was nothing to sneeze at. If I could help relieve that stress for anybody else by something as simple as wearing a cloak, I would.

Plus, Cygnus Island was freezing. But the fabric felt nearly nonexistent over my shoulders.

The first responders found us faster than I expected. Dozens of footsteps turned our intimate gathering into a crowd. Kai received what he needed, and he didn't have to shiver on the ground any longer. Speaking of shivering, I didn't feel any warmer in the cloak. The fabric molded around me and seemed to fit my body perfectly.

I watched as they lifted my husband onto a stretcher. Two strong paramedics had to carry him over the rocks and back down to the dock.

Detective Wilhelm and the other cops tied off the scene around Jameson's body and set to work on the investigation. I gave my statement where I admitted to cutting Jameson's stomach as he attacked me.

Detective Wilhelm confiscated my gun, and I watched as he found the bullet on the ground and no gunshot wounds on any of our bodies. His caterpillar brows furrowed into one long bush over his eyes. It was time I onboarded the detective to the understanding of the supernatural story world. Once I digested it myself, of course.

I tried to explain the cloak, but the officer in front of me only gave me a weird look.

"Do you mean your sweatshirt?"

With my free hand, I tugged at the strings to show him. He only shook his head and repeated the comment about it being my sweatshirt. I glanced around for the Keeper, hoping for an explanation, but she had vanished.

I suspected she slipped out in the chaos and didn't want to be seen by the cops, which meant I'd have to track her down later. She didn't really expect *me* to be the Keeper. . . right?

The official conclusion satisfied the detective, but not me. It wasn't the *truth*. But both the cop taking my statement and Detective Wilhelm brushed off my other comments. They didn't want to hear about an animal that they believed didn't relate to the case. They ignored my mention of another woman's presence at the time of the attack, and Detective Wilhelm interrupted me when I tried to explain that we'd come here hoping to find the killer and then detain him. The detective simply refused to believe that I'd come up with the plan. And apparently, he chalked up the supernatural bits and pieces of my story to a 'lady's overactive imagination.' I spied a peek at the statement after

Detective Wilhelm stomped up and took the notes from the other officer. He scribbled more.

Kai Rowan acted in self-defense to protect his wife, Mari Rowan, and their infant child, against serial murderer Jameson Crewd.

I rolled my eyes. Of course the detective gave my husband the benefit of the doubt and assumed that *he'd* been the one to stab Jameson.

Still, I couldn't totally write off Detective Wilhelm's work. He'd revealed to me, rather arrogantly, that he'd tracked the murders to Jameson just hours before. Paige Brown finally 'came to her senses,' according to him, and had given a sketch artist the description of a man who had followed her into the park. The sketch matched Jameson's photo, which was already in the system because of his past. A past that included sexual assault charges, breaking and entering, and more that I didn't care to think about. Then, a piece of forensic evidence at Aliyah Thompson's murder, a tooth, matched Jameson's DNA.

"Was it sharp and unusually large?" I asked.

"How did you know that?" Detective Wilhelm frowned at me. He knew I couldn't be to blame for any of this, except in self-defense. He'd never liked it when I figured out clues at the same time or before he did.

"I'm an investigator too," I said for the one-hundredth time to him since my career had begun.

And for the one-thousandth time, he scoffed and shook his head at something I'd said. A puff of white air escaped his mouth, and I wrinkled my nose at the smell of garlic on his breath. But before Detective Wilhelm walked away, he paused and glanced at Wendy.

"She looks cold," he said. "You might want to hurry before the ferry takes off with your husband. There won't be another one back until we're done cleaning up here."

I took this as an extended olive branch of kindness. Detective Wilhelm rarely showed himself in this way, but when he did, it was always at the height of a discovery. He'd solved the case of the young women killed on their way to visit family, he'd clinched the door shut on who my stalker was, and everything wrapped in a neat little bow that proved my husband a hero and myself another mediocre journalist in the detective's eyes.

When I cinched the cloak's strings tighter over my collarbone, I wondered if it offered protection to Wendy too. She kicked her legs at the bottom of the carrier, which threw off my balance as I climbed back over the rocks and made my way down to the dock. I didn't mind that I needed to step more carefully because her kicking showed me she was happy.

Someday, she'd talk too, and she'd tell me what she liked so much about the crazy red cloak.

I hurried to join the paramedics on the ferry before the horn blasted again. My legs felt like jelly when the boat started moving. I used the railing to keep myself upright and watched a paramedic bandage Kai's leg. He'd need a skin graft, but my husband stayed in good spirits.

And spirits were what he joked about. "Just throw a splash of whiskey on there, and I'll be good," he said. He laughed, but a wince quickly followed. I laid my hand on his shoulder and gave him a squeeze. I resisted adding a joke about rushing to the hospital and how I wouldn't pass out while he received medical attention. He deserved all my respect right now since he never gave up. He never questioned me or looked at me like I was crazy when I brought supernatural concerns home.

Instead, he'd researched alongside me and dove into the historical aspect of it all. We made a good team. But I still couldn't help wondering about the rest of our family.

Cygnus Island shrank in the distance. I sighed and watched the oval get smaller and smaller until we docked back on San Francisco's shores at Pier 99. The wolf's appearance there proved that my grandmother lived somewhere on that island. And his mortality solidified it.

But how? The national park and Alcatraz tours had shut down decades ago, and the island was blocked off, all except the rocky beach area. And why did my phone's map app show it was really called Cygnus Island? Did my grandmother live there with my dad and the rest of that side of my family? Why would they choose an abandoned island and live behind huge concrete walls?

Johnson's comments all those weeks ago came back to me. What did my father have to give Wendy? And why try to contact us after all this time? Mom wanted nothing more than for him to leave her and the rest of us alone.

What are you up to, Dad?

Wendy's cries shook me from my thoughts. I followed as the paramedics wheeled Kai from the boat to an ambulance. Wendy continued to wail. I ached to give my baby what she needed right now, but I didn't blame myself for moving past my attempts at breastfeeding. It only frustrated us both, and she never came away full. A bottle would do as soon as I could get some formula and pure water to mix. I didn't let myself wallow or dwell on it any longer.

After tonight, I finally felt like I'd figured out this whole mom gig. I understood what her distinct cries meant, and I'd kept her safe in the face of fear, chaos, and a supernatural monster. And maybe those aren't factors for the Mother of the Year award, but I felt pretty good.

WENDY SLEPT through the night that night, but Kai didn't. He woke up complaining of pain in his leg, and I dragged myself from the bedroom to the kitchen to retrieve his next dose of medication. While in the kitchen, I flicked on the coffeemaker and geared myself up for a day of writing.

Pam had called me while I was stuck in the waiting room at the hospital last night. She insisted I could get the article written and sent to our editor at Bay Side Media by the next night. Whether I could wasn't the problem, it was that I wanted a day to rest. I longed to do nothing more than lounge on the couch with Kai while he recovered. We planned to binge-watch a new fantasy TV show from beginning to end and eat nothing but the food we ordered on mobile delivery.

I'd stuff myself with cheesecake, and he'd already made a menu on one of my sticky notes of what he planned to eat for breakfast, lunch, and dinner.

But at 5:34 the next morning, I brought Kai his pill and a cup of water. When I laid down, sleep evaded me, and it was a good thing too because I'd already flicked on the coffeemaker and an entire pot would have gone to waste. So, I pulled myself back up and shuffled through the kitchen and into the living room wearing my robe and the cloak. The fact that it felt like I wore nothing still weirded me out, and it didn't even get wet in the shower.

I plopped down in front of the Coffee Table of Evidence that I'd soon transform into my writing space. From under my arm, I pulled the baby monitor and set it on the table beside a steaming cup of coffee.

The laptop heated my lap, and the cloak covered my shoulders but still offered no extra warmth. I tugged a blanket from its folded place on the back of the couch and draped it over my torso and legs, then set the computer back down. The *Little Red Riding Hood* board book on the shelf under the TV caught my eye. I opened a blank document, ready to type my article's title.

Just when I'd snuggled into the worn butt print on the cushion, a knock rapped at the door. The clock on my computer screen read 5:46 in the morning.

Who in the wonderland?

I hoped it wasn't my mother; she had far too much energy for me to deal with this early. And if it was Johnson, I'd need to slap myself awake and get a few answers out of him about Dad. Perhaps Tala needed some comfort after the disturbing murder of our neighbor's daughter.

But none of them stood at my door.

In my robe and fuzzy bunny slippers, I opened the door to see a poised young woman. Her fiery red hair frizzed a little from the salty air, and she looked older than I'd once suspected, tired even. But I'd know the Keeper's face anywhere, and she still wore the same white corset-like top and attached black skirt. Though she appeared to have aged slightly since removing the cloak, she still looked to be in her mid-twenties, though I knew she'd existed for centuries.

"Can I come in?" the Keeper asked. Did I still need to call her that? She had a name, once. Little Cloak Girl? But she no longer wore the cloak. I did.

A strange sense of relief washed over me when I heard her voice. I'd become familiar with it, and now that she'd shown up on my doormat, without sticky note sigils, I didn't need to spend my time and energy tracking her down. She could come inside, sit on my couch, and help me understand the cycle of stories.

I moved from the threshold and opened my arm. She nodded and stepped inside, then knelt to unbutton the strap on her Mary Jane shoes.

It was still too early to talk, so I let her follow me into the living room without a verbal invitation. I flopped on the couch while she perched on the edge of the sitting chair.

"I don't know how to be mortal," she said. "Especially not in this century." She nodded toward the baby monitor and the laptop on the coffee table.

"Did you come to take the cloak back?" I asked, but she shook her head before I'd even finished.

"Impossible. I can't. But I was hoping. . . " her hands fidgeted in her lap. "Maybe you could teach me how to be mortal."

My night owl's brain didn't like the crack of dawn, and it took a moment for my mind to catch up. I'd thought she said 'normal' rather than mortal, to which I planned to respond: *what is normal? I don't know normal.*

"I don't know if I've forgiven you yet," I admitted. I leaned forward and cupped the coffee mug. With my hands wrapped around it to suck in the warmth, I lifted it from the table and took a sip.

"I understand." She nodded. "But I know you're clever enough to understand that it was nothing personal. You're an investigator. I was investigating, of a sort, too. I tracked the stories, found where the characters landed, and helped seal the endings before the monsters could ravage the city in their immortality. I had to take the role of the hunter in Red Riding Hood's story because he never showed up. Not in any of the cycles. And if the story doesn't play out correctly, the wolf—a villain—is thrown back into the cycle where he can repeatedly kill and eat innocent people."

I breathed in, letting the coffee warm me from the inside out. The fact that she'd called me an investigator after my night of dealing with Detective Wilhelm's dismissals made me smile.

"And now you want my help?" I asked, though I already knew my answer. Of course, I'd help her. I'd help any young woman or any person who needed me. It was why I got into investigative journalism.

"I suppose I'll need a job. And to eat," she said, glancing around the room. "Could I stay here?"

A brief laugh escaped me, and the coffee splashed from the mug. It didn't stain the cloak. Instead, it trickled down in a bead of liquid until it landed with a wet spot between my crisscrossed legs on the couch.

"Is that a refusal?" she asked.

"You can sleep on the couch until you get your feet under you," I said.

She scrunched her face, but the confusion only lasted a moment before she moved on. A brightness came over her face that matched well with her dotted freckles and brilliant red hair. "Maybe we can start with a name," she beamed with an innocent, excited grin.

"Wait, you don't have a name?"

The Keeper–not the Keeper shook her head. "I don't remember it. Can I steal yours?"

"That's my name. . . "

"I suppose it is." Her shoulders slumped. "But I do like how it sounds. Maybe Ahri? Without the 'mmm' sound?"

I couldn't help but laugh again since it was too early to argue. "Ahri, it is."

Ahri clapped and smiled widely. A little squeal escaped her mouth, and she wiggled into the chair, getting comfortable. She'd have her own butt print on the cushion if she kept on bouncing in her seat like that.

"Mari and Ahri." I shook my head and took another sip.

"Perhaps I'll change it tomorrow," she said. "I like Scarlet too."

"That's not how names work. You pick one and stick with it."

"Maybe not for you since your names are locked," Scarlet said.

"Yeah, Rowan and Fable." I shrugged. "And don't you dare call me Red."

"That is not what I meant." A mischievous smile snuck onto her face. She glanced at the cloak, then back to my face, and I could have sworn I saw a bit of relief in her eyes.

What did I get myself into?

Scarlet finished her thought without my prompting, and I didn't hate how it sounded.

"You have two names. You're Mari and the Keeper of Stories."

Epilogue

Bay Side Media
Author: Mari Rowan
Title: A Dangerous Trip to Grandmother's:
The Story of the Serial Murders near Soup Cracker Street

*Alcatraz tours ended twenty years ago, but Jameson Crewd's string of
serial murders ended on the same island just last night. In this article,
I will cover the facts as closely as possible and outline ways you can
protect yourself and your family from future threats.*

1. *Study the classics.*
2. *Take self-defense classes.*
3. *Always expect the unexpected.*

UP NEXT, MARI WILL JOURNEY INTO THE NEXT STAGE OF MOTHERHOOD
AS THE KEEPER OF STORIES, WHERE SHE'LL FACE FRANKENSTEIN'S
MONSTER, HER FAMILY'S PAST, AND WITNESS HER DAUGHTER'S FIRST
STEPS, ALL WHILE SOLVING A MURDER!

Emily Fluke

Acknowledgments

I first have to thank my husband who re-watched Supernatural, Once Upon a Time, and Castle with me and bought us all The Dresden Files on audiobook. You've encouraged my love for urban fantasy and kick-butt characters. Though we're the opposite of Mari and Kai, you're the introvert to my extroversion, Death of a Fairy Tale wouldn't have been possible without you.

And where would I be without Hallie? You have continually supported, inspired, and uplifted me along the dark and twisty path of writing. I appreciate you always being honest, taking the time to read my dumpy first drafts, and championing my ideas.

I want to extend a big thank you to M. Todd Gallowglas who has taught me so much about the craft of fiction and storytelling. Because of you, I never want to stop learning and improving my writing and understanding of fiction.

Last but not least, I have to thank those who got me into this beautiful mess in the first place. To the Tuesday Fantasy Writer's group that I created on a crazy whim, I appreciate everyone's encouragement and perspectives. Thank you to Emily H, Jes, Danielle, Jordan, Kate, and Samantha. And a special shout-out to those of you who pushed me to publish until I finally pushed 'publish'.

About the Author

Congenital Heart Defect survivor, Emily Fluke, finds joy and peace through the expression of writing. She is a strong believer that all stories need a little magic and a lot of excitement. Emily and her husband spend their free time wrangling two children and playing video games in their busy California lifestyle. Otherwise, you'll find Emily solving an escape room, running, or writing Magic the Gathering-based poetry.

To stay up to date on new releases and connect with me, visit my website at Emilyfluke.com or follow me on social media under Author Emily Fluke, or @emilyflukefairytales